SOMETHING DRASTIC

SOMETHING DRASTIC

A Novel

LUKE INGLIS

CANADA

Library and Archives Canada Cataloguing in Publication

Title: Something drastic : a novel / Luke Inglis.

Names: Inglis, Luke, 1982– author.

Identifiers: Canadiana 20200256106 | ISBN 9781989689080 (softcover)

Classification: LCC PS8617.N525 S66 2020 | DDC C813/.6—dc23

Printed and bound in Canada on 100% recycled paper.

Now Or Never Publishing
901, 163 Street
Surrey, British Columbia
Canada V4A 9T8

nonpublishing.com
Fighting Words.

We gratefully acknowledge the support of the Canada Council for the Arts
and the British Columbia Arts Council for our publishing program.

For Floyd

TERMINATIONS IN SPACE

DAYS OF SOBRIETY: 0

A stomach, nestled in darkness, boiled and blasted volcanic brew. Earl watched yellow bile erupt into the wicker basket under his desk, soaking papers into oatmeal pulp, and infusing the air with noxious fume. Fluorescent light cast shadows on the spidery folds of his clothing, and illuminated the polar-white fescues scattered throughout his grizzly-brown hair. Earl belched acrid heat and slurped antacids, but this did little to assuage his inner turmoil. He rubbed his chest and felt sludge meander through his bunched intestines. He imagined the damage it had wrought. His stomach-lining must be a patchwork of membrane, ragged as Earth's diaphanous veil at the edge of space, where blue skies filtered into the blackness of his mind. Earl's thoughts scampered in darkness, wounded by paroxysms. His memories sluiced for survival through constellations of neurons. They thrashed in heavy juice and died as casualties of a fleshly civil war, waged over dominion to slaughter or salvage strategic organs.

Earl tried to still his eyes and focus his vision, but the poison in his nerves wouldn't allow it. The right angles of his desk became bulbous. His peripherals crackled with sheet lightning. The dust-grey walls of his cubicle flickered to life, broadcasting hallucinations of jabbering skulls, raging infernos, a fall from the sky. The room inflated like the diaphragm of a great whale, straining the drywall and plaster until the pressure became too great. The office building exploded and sent Earl cartwheeling into space. His body burst into a trillion specks that scattered about the universe, travelling in eternal solitude. He wondered if matter could break apart then transmigrate into something relevant. Or is it doomed to stagnate, whatever its reincarnation?

He stood and peered over the cubicle wall. Festive ornaments scattered the room. Santa Claus and his reindeer looked content, even jolly, to be nailed to the shock-white wall. Woollen elves, stuffed with turtle beans, sat atop dust-grey office dividers that cooped employees in their respective cubes. Mrs. Claus appeared in a felt costume, carrying a tray of cookies.

"Hello, Franc," she said to a wispy man in a grubby tweed blazer, shuffling about the photocopy machine. "Have you been naughty or nice this year?"

"Very naughty, Margaret—oh, uh, I mean Mrs. Claus. So naughty in fact, I'm going to steal your cookies. Hohoho. Mmmhmhmhmm, chocolate chip. You're a sorceress of the sweets. How about drinks at my place tonight?"

"You *are* naughty, Franc."

"Your husband will never find out. He's preoccupied."

"What about you, Cindy?" asked Mrs. Claus, turning her attention. "Have you been naughty or nice?"

"Nice, of course," said Cindy. "Are they gluten free?"

"Yes."

"Where was the cocoa grown?"

"I don't know, Cindy."

"Was it South America? Their farming practices are savage. And it's even worse in Africa."

Earl noticed the dust that swarmed around Cindy's head. It was caught in a ray of light that angled through a grimed window. He watched these pallid molecules float like pollen through barren air, as he struggled to sensitize his body to the world. He was a speck in limbo within an incomprehensibly fiery existence that terrified him to no end. He closed his eyes and flew through forces that bend the energy of the universe, crunch matter into eons of fire, and blast stars billions of light years through space. Chaos pulverised galaxies into shattered leviathans and sent them floating in darkness at the speed of light. He focussed on moments of heaviness. The gravity that persuades every small point in the cosmos to create seasons, freezing and thawing, lightness and darkness, life and death. Earl wished his mind could remain beyond the stratosphere and leave his body to wander the Earth insentient. But how might his mind manifest? As a meaty globule? Or a translucent soul impervious to anti-gravity, fluttering feathered wings to spawn hurricanes in the South Pacific? It could marvel at Mother Earth: the mirage in the desert, the liquid bridge to nowhere, the orb orbiting an orb. It could follow the contours of the continents and watch them turn dark at the whim of the sun's purpose. It could witness the discharge of energy plumes through tornadic spouts, volcanic eruptions, and earthquakes as the planet rationed its apocalyptic might over eons of destruction. And what judgment would his mind bestow upon the fleshly vessel it had left behind?

Earl saw himself as if through a satellite lens, grovelling through the city streets, bruised and bloodied by the gravity-laden atmosphere. He thought about his co-workers who despised him, his wife who loathed him, his father who had disowned him, and his few friends who had lost patience. He concluded that his mind should remain with him, for he required an ally in this big, airy world where survival hinged upon a nebulous atmospheric chemistry, and the fleeting control he held over oxygen. That benevolent gas. A gift from the great forests of the world. He took a deep breath and let it vanish into his circulatory labyrinth. It wiped away the grime that lined his veins. It watered his bowels and purged his liver. It fueled his pounding heart. He felt it swirl through his vertebrae like a gentle breeze, and twirl up his spine to caress and infiltrate the soft tissue of his brain—feeding it, influencing it, unveiling memories from the night before.

These memories came back to him slowly at first, like reflections on a dream. But soon the details became too clear, the features too lively. The haze of his subconscious gave way to the consequence of reality. Earl tried to shut the memories out, banish them, but couldn't. They overcame his will.

He had passed out on the living room couch with a bottle of rye on his chest. His dog Sigmund was curled on the floor beside him. He awoke to the sound of the door opening. Footsteps crossed the floor.

"Is that you, Samantha?" he asked through a mouthful of gristly saliva. Blinding pain knifed through his skull as the kitchen light flicked on.

"You're disgusting," Samantha said. She turned on the faucet.

Earl remembered vomiting into the kitchen sink. "What time is it?" he mumbled.

"Are you trying to say something? If so, please enunciate. Or is your tongue too saturated?" Samantha put leftovers in the microwave and poured herself a glass of Rioja.

Earl watched her expression reflected in the microwave door as it transformed from a deep, appreciating sadness to that of someone harbouring tremendous joy. The frowning creases that framed her mouth migrated to find refuge as smiling crinkles beside her vermillion eyes. Her small face and long red hair lit up with the little oven light. She grabbed the hot bowl of food by the edges and blew on the steam. Vapour wisps danced around her head.

"Earl, I want you out of the house," she said. "I won't live with you anymore."

Her joyful tone jolted Earl.

"Did you hear me? Or can you absorb nothing but alcohol?"

"Did Murphy put you up to this?" Earl asked.

"This is my decision. You can stay with your father."

"He never wants to see me again."

"I don't care where you go, Earl. I want you and your fuck-ing dog out."

Sigmund took his teddy bear to the corner of the room.

"You would do this to me now?" Earl sat up. His head was an anvil. "It's Christmas time."

"Since when has Christmas meant anything to you?"

"Since always."

"Really? What did you give me for Christmas last year?"

"I don't remember. That's not fair."

"Of course it's not fair. You don't remember *yesterday* let alone . . ." Samantha shook her head. "The answer is nothing by the way. You gave me nothing."

"That's what you're concerned about? Materialistic garbage?"

"Fuck you."

Earl unscrewed the lid of his bottle of rye and took a gulp.

"You think you're the only victim of your drinking," Samantha said.

"I'm not a victim."

"But you *are* my husband. You're supposed to love me. But you don't even like me."

"Of course I . . ." Earl tried to get up off the couch but fell back down. He took another drink.

"Are you even capable of love anymore? Have you ever been?"

"I'm still the man you married, Samantha."

"But you're poisoned. You're too far gone."

"I'm trying to get better."

"By drinking more?"

"It's the only way I can cope."

"It's the only way you know how to cope. You need help."

"No, I don't." Earl managed to stand. "Why should *I* leave? I pay the rent. And you're the adulteress. The home wrecker. Murphy has kids you know. And a wife, poor bastard."

"I can't take this anymore."

"What?" Earl took a step forward, swilling his rye. "You can't take what anymore?"

"Earl, please."

"Am I too real for you?" He took another step. "Do I remind you that everything isn't supposed to be bloody perfect? I'm real life, dammit." .

Earl's palm tingled. Sigmund barked. Samantha cried: "Get out."

. "So much for in sickness and in health." Earl stumbled into his blue winter coat and squeezed the half-empty rye bottle into the inside pocket. "I'm going outside for a smoke. But don't think I'm not coming back."

But he didn't go back. Instead, he stumbled around in frigid darkness, wandering through fractions of sprawling urban mess. He turned south and walked below construction cranes that rose from the glacial pavement like dragon silhouettes. They were poised in hang fire, awaiting the first vector of daylight to inflate demolition dust-bombs and elucidate the wounds of a city run down by human erosion. Police lights lit up fellow drunks across the street in slow-motion strobe. The officer hollered out his car window, ordering them to head for winter shelters. The drunks waved him off and burrowed deeply into their charcoal blankets. The car spun around at Earl, blinding him with its headlights, then raced up Bay Street. Its siren began to wail, cracking the night, and reminding everyone within its cacophonous sphere to fear the murderer, the rapist, the thief. The immigrant, the Muslim, the terrorist. Protect yourself and protect what's yours: your family, your wealth, your civilization. For others want to deprive you. Like a plague they will spread their desperation, poverty, fear. Trust your paranoia and listen to the rage pounding in your ears.

Earl spat. He drank his rye and walked until he reached the waterfront. He listened to the wind blow upon the surface of Lake Ontario, where it picked up momentum and ice before firing north through the streets of Canada's economic core, accelerating misery through pickets of skyscrapers. He drained his bottle as the low winter sun sliced his eyes above Toronto's skyline.

Earl's stomach churned again and threatened something ghastly. He reached for the wicker basket under his desk when someone behind him bull-snorted and spoke: "Earl, do you have the turkey file ready yet?"

Earl swallowed hard as the question deliquesced in his ears like a bird chirp in a dense forest. He pined for fresh air but could only taste ancient dust that crackled in spiderwebbed static bolts. He cursed the thermostat for pumping falsehoods in degrees Celsius and darkening the world with electrostatic smog.

"Well do you?" Murphy repeated.

Earl winced and swivelled his chair around. His stomach growled enmity. "Must I enjoy the pain I inflict upon myself to be masochistic?"

"What?" Murphy asked.

"Must masochism involve a sexual element?"

"Earl, I . . ."

"But I know I'm a sadist, considering the line of work I'm in. That goes for you too, Murphy."

Murphy would be easier to hate if his eyes weren't so blatantly clear, his jowls so sleek, his shoulders so expansive, his curls so lustrous and golden above his tailored suit, silk tie, and faux-leather shoes that squeaked a musky trail of virility. Earl knew Murphy had a large penis from frequent urinal peripherals. He hoped it was the type that struggled to lift its sleepy head from its scrotal pillow, rather than lurch like a king cobra to spread its hood and inject copious amounts of venom.

"Merry Christmas, Earl. Merry Christmas, Murphy. You smell wonderful as always," said a blushing Mrs. Claus, who emerged through the dust-grey cubicle dividers like a ripe cherry. "Have you two been naughty or nice this year?"

Earl kept his eyes on Murphy and said: "I was so drunk last night that I could be mistaken, but I'm almost certain that my wife was out balling another man. Do you know anything about that, Murphy?"

Mrs. Claus scuttled away and Murphy ignored the question. "Earl, I said I needed the turkey file. It's the Christmas push."

"Turkeys would rather spend Christmas with their families," Earl said.

"I needed it by noon. It's now noon."

"It's lunchtime then," Earl said, his voice lilting.

"You're not going for lunch until you have that file on my desk." Murphy's fierce hawk eyes glared and his nostrils flared. "Do I smell vomit?"

"That turkey file wasn't on the top of my list this morning."

"Oh really? What's above it on your little priority list?"

"Lots of things. Important files and memos and spreadsheets." Earl shuffled pages around his desk. "Power Points." He hit his keyboard to awaken the computer screen. The desktop background displayed livestock frolicking in a flowery meadow.

Fire blood flushed Murphy's cheeks. "You've been jerking off all morning."

"Well, I haven't had any help in that department recently, so what do you expect?"

"You pathetic . . ." Murphy paused a beat. "If you were any kind of man, your wife wouldn't despise you the way she does. She wouldn't need me to satisfy her needs."

"By that reasoning your wife isn't woman enough to satisfy yours."

"You don't talk about my wife," Murphy hissed.

"She's a beautiful woman, Murphy. I have to admit that when I first met her all I could hear were her torrid screams tearing through my mind. I couldn't help but imagine what she would look like spread-eagled on my bed, tied to the headboard, bleeding."

"Shut your mouth."

"I should pay her a visit," Earl continued. "Maybe ask her out. She and I have much in common. It wouldn't be one of those awkward first dates with forced topics of conversation."

"If you go near her I'll kill you." Murphy's voice broke over the din of the office. Earl watched heads with desperate eyes pop up like warts over the meandering maze of dust-grey office dividers. These people were hungry for conflict and gossip fodder—a hunger chocolate chip cookies could never satiate.

Earl observed Murphy's expression as that of a terrible predator with dripping fangs and snapping, sinewy tendons. He flicked venom at Earl and puffed his chest, before disappearing into the vile incubator of Bossman's office.

No one likes a tattletale, Earl thought as he rubbed his temples and quietly celebrated the death of the morning.

Earl pulled on his blue winter coat and crept down the building's staircase. Outside, in the cold, gravity-laden atmosphere, he lit a cigarette. Tobacco smoke billowed in the frigid air and melded with sewer steam and engine exhaust. He inhaled and retched. Fervent wind blew snow, ice and garbage in his face. A flying newspaper turned his vision to black, before it rifled over his head and switch-backed up frosted glass. It vanished in the skyscraper vapour pouring into the sky to choke hard winter birds. Above, dispersing streams of aeroplane contrail deflected strips of solar heat back into space.

With fangs in his eyes, Earl kicked his way through dirty snow and past an old Victorian church. He looked at it through horizontal snowfall and fleeting winter light. The church sat weathered and neglected, eroded by one hundred and fifty years of spiritual tenancy and desperate prayer. But its brick structure stood resolute as a relic in defiance of the modern cityscape. A shivering line of homeless people queued outside for a bowl of soup and an escape to the nineteenth century. Earl studied their sadness as he passed. Downcast eyes were devoid of confidence. Deep sighs were audible above the rush of traffic. The steam of their breath was thin and smoky. But there was the stubborn determination of life in them too—an inherent spirit destined to perpetuate forward. Their vitality would help forge the future of the planet.

Amongst them was a street prophet draped in charcoal rags. Her Medusa hair snapped in the wind as she screamed of the apocalypse, the end of days, judgement, rapture, damnation. She threw dusty pamphlets that pollinated passersby with perverted scripture, before catching in up drafts and soaring towards the heavens. "I'm not a God," she screamed. "I am not your God." Mirth was blasted on her face.

Earl passed by and found refuge in a temperate liquor store. He glanced around at his palace of myopic relief, drenched in a panoply of alcoholic beverages, refulgent under phosphorescent sparkle. He weighed a twelve ouncer of rye in his palm. It felt unsubstantial, like a politician. He replaced it with a twenty-six ouncer. The artful moose on the glass bottle's label was etched white on black and, with a wink, promised reprieve from all anguish.

"Good choice," said a familiar face with lively eyes and yellowing skin. "But I prefer vodka. Tundra Glass Vodka to be specific. It isn't detectable on the breath."

Earl nodded. He had seen the man before. He was another lunch-hour regular.

"I suggest you try it. It could keep you out of trouble."

"I'll stick with rye," Earl said. He turned away.

The man limped after him. "Why is it that we see each other every day but neither of us has had the decency to say hello?"

"I'm not a social drinker," Earl said. "I have to go."

"I know you do. You have to find your private nook to drown your misery."

Earl waved him off.

"I'm going to do the same thing," the man said, limping behind. It seemed that one leg was more shrivelled than the other. "Perhaps we could do it together."

"I don't think so," Earl said, making his way to the check-out line. The yellowing man queued behind him as the clerk eyed Earl with familiar judgment. Earl answered a question she never asked: "Yes, I bought one of these yesterday. And the day before, and the day before that, too." The clerk smiled at Earl and they recited together: "What about it?"

The man behind him snickered.

The clerk rang Earl through to the screams of the street prophet, whose lambast was muffled through the iced window.

"Have a nice day, Earl," the clerk said.

He nodded and left her to deal with the yellowing man, who jingled loose change in his pockets.

Earl stuffed the bottle into the inside pocket of his blue winter coat and walked outside. He accepted the pamphlet that the street prophet forced upon him, and heard the yellowing man shuffle in the snow behind him. His limping gait sounded like that of a wounded animal, beaten by the elements and ripe for slaughter.

"Looks like we're heading the same direction," the yellowing man panted.

Earl kept walking. His head was down against the wind and his clenched hands shook inside his pockets, but not from the cold. He crossed the street and entered his office building.

"How 'bout that," said the yellowing man, entering behind and shaking the snow off his clothes like a schnauzer. "We work in the same building. Elevator?"

Earl went to the stairwell and descended a flight. The man followed, saying: "I'm heading down to the basement car-park. I have a cozy van with tinted windows." He opened his bottle of Tundra Glass and took a slug. "We could keep each other warm in there." He offered his bottle to Earl.

Earl walked to the door labelled Food Court.

"You won't find much privacy in there."

"I'd like to be left alone now."

"Enjoy your lunch." The man smiled. His teeth were as yellow as his skin. "But can I ask one thing before you go?"

Earl nodded, wondering if it was wise to encourage this cretin.

"Do you dream?"

"My nights are dark nothingness."

"I mean daydream. Fantasize."

"Doesn't everybody?"

"Not if you're satisfied with your lot in life. What do you daydream about?"

"I don't know," Earl shrugged.

"Sure you do. Sports cars? Vaginas?"

"Outer space, I guess."

"About being in space? Like, flying around in space?"

"Sure."

"So, you fantasize about escape." The man took another slug of vodka. "Me too. I'd like to shed my shackles and fly away." He shook the bottle and wobbled his gimp leg. "But I'm stuck in this life." He pointed to the bulge in Earl's blue winter coat. "Have you ever daydreamed about where you might be if alcohol didn't control you? I would've been Prime Minister. You would've been an astronaut. But instead, we're hooked under the ribs and pinned on our knees."

"You don't know me."

"But I know what drives you: a despotic power that has lulled you into dependence, and eroded your will to meekness.

It has replaced your past and present and has doomed your future. The liquid in your brain has dowsed the fire in your heart." The yellowing man took another drink. "Damned alcohol. At least it allows me to pass out every night, oblivious to the fact that I may never wake up again."

Earl turned his back.

"Are you sure you won't come down and have your lunch with me? Tinted windows, remember?"

Earl swung open the door to the teeming food court. As it closed behind him he heard the yellowing man ask: "Are you meaningfully attached to life?" Earl looked around at a fence of sneeze-spattered food troughs and flares of greenery that looked like Jurassic skunk cabbage. Their cartoonish grandeur inspired thoughts of warmer days; a time before T-Rex battlegrounds broke down into cityscapes. Fat, heavy flies had settled in this humid bio-dome to gorge, procreate and die. Their black husks discarded in the planter soil. Offspring buzzed from plate to plate, french fry to pork rib, chicken nugget to spring roll. Others waited in the greenery, biding their time and waiting for the peace of night, when giant rats emerged from inky corners to nimbly sample gastro treasures.

Earl walked towards the bathrooms in the back corner of the expansive room. He watched people inject themselves with sweet and sour sauce, and bury their heads in mountains of fried flesh—piled high upon fecal-rimmed cafeteria trays. Harsh florescent lights shot ultraviolet sheets into glistening, feigned-food that squelched inside salty, sugary fat buckets. Earl's stomach churned at the noises made by this groaning human horde, that suckled bacteria and synthetic flavours. Their wet sounds echoed off greasy walls, enticing visions of well lubricated carnal extravaganzas. Saliva built in Earl's mouth as he trudged his way through the cafeteria confusion.

He reached the bathroom and entered the first stall. He sat on the toilet, dribbled canary-yellow urine, and cracked open the bottle of rye. He drank deeply. His esophagus writhed. His skeleton rattled. He shook and gasped. He clenched his anus and teeth until his body relaxed and began to luxuriate.

Succouring warmth in his stomach smouldered steadily. It spread cell by cell, reaching for his tightening scalp and oozing all the way down his lean body towards his grubbing toes. Anxiety, pain and fear vanished. His brain and limbs calmed. His blood thinned. Reality dissipated. *Maybe I should stop now and save the rest for later,* mewled a faint thought. Earl raised the bottle back to his lips. His slit eyes reflected in the glass, absorbing the rye's auburn glow that flowed backwards through his body, feeling through pitch-black crevices until it found his soul, where it coiled and constricted.

He pulled the snow-blotched pamphlet from his pocket, drank from his bottle, and read about the Rapture.

> Matthew 24:29 *The sun will become dark, and the moon will no longer shine. The stars will fall, and the powers in the sky will be shaken.*

He flipped a page to a crude watercolour that depicted the righteous floating in the sky towards Jesus, who lounged benevolently upon a cloud. Below, the unworthy were on fire.

"Hey, you ok in there?" It was the janitor.

"Diarrhoea again," Earl said, while purging a bilious deluge.

"Clockwork diarrhoea." The janitor's velveteen voice greased the door hinges of Earl's clean cube.

Earl drank in haste and wobbled to his feet. He unlatched the stall door and swung it open.

The janitor leaned on his mop handle and leered at him. "Shall I discard your lunch box?"

Earl handed over the empty bottle. "And take this too," he said.

The janitor accepted the pamphlet and turned it over in his hand. "Afraid of the Rapture?"

"Should I be?"

"Probably."

"I have to go," Earl said. "Murphy needs the turkey file." He gesticulated as he described for the janitor how doomed animals meet grim ends in slaughterhouse execution queues. How

human monstrosities in blood-spattered aprons swing bolt
stunners, exploding brains one by one. "The animals hit the
blood-soaked floor, flopping and writhing. The shock of agony
can only kill their hearts slowly, you see? It's still beating when
limbs are hacked off." Earl felt the alcohol bore deeper into his
nervous system.

The janitor shifted his mop handle from one calloused hand
to the other. His precise goatee twitched under a twisted nose
and had bolts of ivory-white. The sideburns beside his cavernous
ears grew evenly in glistening oils. His thick, round-rimmed
spectacles, magnified the squiggly capillaries in his eyes that flat-
lined between each powerful heart beat. His bald scalp reflected
light and housed a contemplative mind that—judging by his
furled brow—was vexed over the man before him. "Have you
ever stopped to consider your situation?" he asked. "Do you
understand what has become of you?"

Earl did not respond. He was preoccupied by the comforting
weight he felt inside his body, and the way the gleaming tiled
floor looked like ice.

"You live in a cage like those animals," the janitor said.
"And you're on your way to the slaughterhouse just the same."

Alcohol fumes billowed from Earl's slack mouth that jawed
like a suffocating fish. He tried to step past, but the large man
gently put his hand on Earl's chest and said: "You're stuck in a
wicked cycle and you look worse every time you come in here.
You gotta let life flatten out, man." The janitor's eyes darted
around Earl's face. "I've been where you are. But I'm ten years
sober. If I kept going the way I was I would have been dead long
ago. But I chose life. Do you understand the weight of what I'm
saying to you?"

Earl's voice slurred through swarming alcohol atoms as he
said: "I'm sick of you preaching at me everyday."

The janitor patted Earl's chest.

"Touch me again and I'll put your head through the wall."

The janitor backed off and let Earl pass. He called after him:
"Seek clarity. Escape to the wilderness. Save your soul."

—

"Earl, my office please." It was Bossman flexing a come-hither sausage-finger.

Earl sat across from Bossman, swaying in his seat. He peered down at his knees with eyes that were the colours of Christmas. Why was there neon green vomit all over his beige Dockers? He looked up through the fluorescent light reflecting off Bossman's massive, sweaty face. It was like a carnival mirror in which he watched sheet lightning crackle through his own frontal lobe, as his medulla oblongata swallowed his threshold of control.

"You're drunk," Bossman said.

"I had a nip with a friend at lunch."

"You smell like malt."

"A hint of malt, maybe."

As Bossman took a deep breath and sighed, Earl could sense a great haze of carbon dioxide becloud the room. The area around him jilted and tilted. Light through the window brightened then dimmed, distorting longitudes and latitudes like continental drift. A sparrow hit the glass. It fell lifeless stories and left a reverberating blood mark. The pavement on which the sparrow landed, disappeared a thousand miles away, as Earl lost hold of the heavy gravity securing him to the surface of the Earth. He was in a tower that tickled the belly of the moon. From the window, he watched Earth's great glaciers crumble into the sea, freeing prehistoric bones as jetsam, which would one day wash upon Madagascan shores, to be clutched by the last leaping lemurs.

"Earl, I've been very patient with you. I've been decent," Bossman said.

Earl guffawed. "You're a demon who tortures animals for profit. A capitalist who thinks exploitation and greed is the natural order of things."

Bossman sighed again and rubbed his cheek with a pillowy palm. He leaned back in his chair, causing the folds in his neck to quadruple.

"You're a stooge," Earl said. "A cog in corporate hell."

"I'm not going to fire you," Bossman said. "But I am going to lay you off. This way you can collect employment insurance for a while. You can spend some time finding the help you need."

"I don't need help, you, you, you . . ." The information Earl was receiving filtered through a tough membrane. ". . . you . . . incompetent, evil . . . Who fires someone right before Christmas?" He struggled to his feet and swiped at Bossman's Rudolph mug, spilling coffee about the desk and ruining papers.

Bossman cursed and hurried to contain the spreading blackness as Earl walked crookedly out of the room. He stopped at Murphy's desk and said: "Hey Murphy, I got your turkey file." Earl unzipped his pants and squirted canary-yellow urine in Murphy's face. He grabbed his blue winter coat and stumbled sideways towards the exit. Heads popped up like boils over the meandering maze of dust-grey office dividers to the sound of Murphy's vitriolic howl.

Earl entered his one-bedroom apartment and moved to the kitchen. Sigmund came to greet him with a bark, a wagging tail, and a pirouette that Earl once taught him using potato chip rewards. "Hi Sigmund," Earl said, patting his dog's broad, one-eared head. He stroked the short hairs on his muscular shoulders and scarred flanks, trailing his fingers along a hundred and ten pounds of mutt love. Earl opened a cupboard and, to his delight, found a full bottle of rye.

He took a long guzzle as Sigmund looked up at him with wet-eyed expectation. Earl poured kibble into his aluminum dish and mixed in a splash of warm water. Sigmund attacked his food. He was starving. Earl felt sickening guilt over his neglected dependent. If only Samantha would share in this responsibility. But she loathed Sigmund for reasons Earl couldn't comprehend. She seemed to regard him as a burden, and didn't appreciate his unconditional love and affection, his emotions, or his great beating heart.

Earl slumped on the living room couch and sipped rye. A pile of papers on the coffee table caught his eye. There was a yellow sticky-note attached.

Earl,
Sign these separation papers and get out. You're pathetic
and I never want to see you again. Be gone before I get
home. Don't forget your fucking dog.
Samantha

Earl wondered how an ecumenically consummated union
sanctioned by God could be extinguished so unceremoniously.
He watched his pen strokes scribble away the only life he knew.
He looked around the apartment that sat hunkered in an anony-
mous urban nook and remained static throughout the seasons.
It was a place to wallow, like any other place that lacked the
power of transformation. He often thought that he should build
a fountain in the middle of the living room and dye the water
all the colours of the rainbow. He yearned for a home soaked
in vibrancy. But all he saw was a space forever void of purpose.
Magazines levelled lopsided furniture. Birkenstocks lay soggy
and deflated on the shoe rack. His once cherished art hung
crooked, acrylic-cracked and wine spattered. His books lacked
symmetry on the shelf and had lost their curiosity. Wedding
gifts, fastened appliances, dusty dumbbells, meaninglessness.
They were possessions that would inflict a horrid kind of nos-
talgia if he came across them years later. He would leave them
for Samantha to burn.

He did not expect this termination of a life, but as he rubbed
Sigmund's neck, he was not surprised that it had come to pass.
He couldn't remember the last time he was in Samantha's pres-
ence when he wasn't drunk or hung over. He was not a partner.
He was a parasitic monomaniac.

He remembered the Christmas staff party a year ago, where
Murphy introduced himself to Samantha. He wandered over
from across the room and planted himself between Earl and his
wife, flirting incessantly as if Earl didn't exist. Earl didn't rage or
wallow in misery until the first night she didn't come home, and
the first morning that he awoke in an empty bed. What bothered
him most was that she didn't attempt to hide it from him. She
thought he was too numb to feel emotional pain. But he could

feel it, especially when he was alone at night, in the darkness with his bottle of rye.

He had met Samantha on their first day of high school. They sat side by side in their home room, sharing a silent terror of their surroundings. Earl recalled the years before, when he was pre-pubescent, and the outside world was accommodating and conducive to happiness. He was comfortable, oblivious to fear, a class clown, a social juggernaut. But then his pubic hair sprouted and the testosterone that surged from his testicles gave him an early taste of masculine sorrow. Suddenly, the judgement of others mattered deeply. The world turned ominous, chaotic and uncontrollable. He became aware of his frailty and mortality. It was Samantha's friendship that quelled his panic, and hand in hand, they navigated the dark forests of young adulthood. He remembered the trampoline under which they first kissed, the cramped back seat of his Toyota where they made love, the rain clouds on their wedding day, camping trips, endless topics of conversation, nights spent reading silently together. They had a natural love that had grown organically, fertilized by gratitude and empathetic support, until it ploddingly evolved into complacent interdependence. But their love was buried now, and to Samantha it was dead; wasted like napalm that re-manifested as hatred, resentment, scorched wasteland. She didn't understand the metempsychosis of love like Earl did. To her, it was a chemical brain function—tangible, materialistic and individualized—that could breathe and flourish then burn off and disappear. Earl believed that his love had an immortal soul that could be spread thick or thin. Or it could lay dormant and protected, waiting for a remarkable moment to coax and kindle it to the surface. He felt the warmth of it flutter in his heart as he took a long drink of rye and signed the final paper.

But those vermillion eyes of hers. Did they bear a smoldering love? A love belied by misery, biding its time until it found a new outlet: Murphy.

Earl pulled his phone from his pocket. He flipped it around in his palm then whirled through his contacts, dialled, and left a voice massage. "Murphy, I know you said something to

Bossman. You got me fired and I'm coming for you. I'm going to skin you alive and rip out your throat with my teeth. I'm going to chop your corpse into bloody bits and scatter you all over the office. It will add to the festive cheer and give all those soulless slaves something to chat about around the water cooler." Earl took a swig in contemplation as the voicemail beeped off. Content, he vomited into the kitchen sink.

He went to the bedroom and rummaged through his drawers. He stuffed an assortment of clothing into a backpack and zipped it shut.

"Is there anything else we need?" he asked Sigmund.

Sigmund barked at his teddy bear.

Earl stuffed the half empty bottle of rye into the inside pocket of his blue winter coat, then rubbed his dog's head and clipped on his leash. He looked around the apartment one last time, scanning for any important scraps that he couldn't be without. He walked into the kitchen and drained Samantha's bottle of Rioja. He licked his lips where the red wine left its indelible mark and saw the yellow sticky-note-pad on the counter. He wrote on it, tore off the top sheet and stuck it to the empty bottle. It read: I'M SORRY.

Sigmund sniffed every inch of pavement and purged his system of twenty-four hours worth of excretion abstemiousness. Earl flicked a glowing cigarette butt into the street, not out of contempt for the Earth, but out of contempt for the city's rapacious inhabitants: Hummer drivers, pesticide sprayers, overnight gadget campers. The cigarette sizzled in the snow as he lit another. The filter gave between his purple lips as he pulled through tobacco leaf. Chemical smoke filled his mouth and disappeared into his vacuum bag lungs. He exhaled a cloud of smog that intertwined with the oxygen plumes puffed by the city's vegetation.

They walked down the street with no particular destination in mind. The wind had died, leaving calm, cold city avenues, lit by street lamps. He drained the bottle of rye and smashed it on the sidewalk. He ducked underground into the ratty depths of Ossington subway station.

On an eastbound train that smelled of groundsels and cat spray, Earl watched darkness fly by the windows, broken occasionally by the screeching careens of trains trundling westward. The opposing train's passengers flashed by like ghouls with faces blurred by speed. A woman sat across from him, holding an infant child. She smiled at Sigmund who sat quietly between Earl's legs, before she closed her eyes and breathed the child's small breath. The baby's translucent, blue-veined head poked through a cozy scarlet blanket that the woman held closely to her breast. Their warm, infectious love spread about them as Earl, in a voice loud enough to fill the train cabin asked: "Did that ugly creature mangle your vagina?" He was hunkered and smeared on his seat.

The woman bundled the child tightly in her arms and moved down the train as sympathetic strangers murmured to her and glared at Earl, who carried on after the woman. "Why is society so uptight? What happened to our sense of humour? We should all take deep collective breaths and be mindful of oxygen."

The train's ground brakes screamed and shot hot sparks. The doors chimed open and people filtered out, led by the woman who held tightly to her child. They were replaced by replica passengers who did nothing for Earl but pollute his consciousness and steal his air. They were faceless and interchangeable drones, consuming and defecating, travelling life's currents like oil slicks on water, their souls trapped like argon in the biosphere.

Earl stood and offered his seat to an elderly woman who plumed a glandular perfume. Her crunchy white hair dazzled in the hard green light from overhead signs that panelled the length of the train, advertising Tundra Glass Vodka, Spitfire Sexual Lubricant, and the Prophet Muhammad. The elderly woman patted Sigmund's head. She smiled at Earl and accepted the seat with a grateful nod. Earl smiled back and asked how she managed to survive for as long as she had. And was it worth the effort? She turned her attention to the zipper on her purse.

Earl looked down the length of the train and saw Murphy slip inside as the doors pinched shut. The train rumbled back up to speed with the sound of brooding drones and murderous screams. Murphy stood a full head taller than the passengers around him. He had his phone to his ear and a scowl on his face. He was probably checking his voicemail.

At street level, Earl gave Sigmund's leash a gentle tug to keep him focussed on the task at hand. They kept their distance so not to be detected by Murphy. Earl stumbled along the sidewalk a neighbourhood block behind, until Murphy reached his destination. He hopped up some steps onto the front porch of a semi-detached townhouse. He opened the door and entered. Earl was close enough to hear the door lock behind him.

The blinds were open and Earl could see inside. His view was partially blocked by a large twinkling Christmas tree but behind it he could see Murphy's wife setting the dinner table. She stopped to greet Murphy. They kissed as two kids, a boy and a girl, ran into view and joined the family embrace. They took their seats around bowls of steaming food.

Earl cringed at the wholesomeness of the middle-class aspiration unfurled before his eyes. He wondered if this was the kind of life Samantha had envisioned for herself. The nice house in the nice neighbourhood with the nice family that kept their blinds open so they could be examined in their natural habitat. But all the while, behind the rosy cheeks and Christmas bells, lay a deceit so treacherous it would rock this ideal to its rebar.

Earl watched Murphy stir at the table and pull his phone from his pocket. A shadow of rage descended upon his features, but only for a second. He put it back in his pocket and smiled at his wife. But then he pulled it out again and said something before rising from the table and walking towards the front door.

Earl yanked Sigmund's leash and charged across the front lawn. He rammed his back into the corner where the porch met the house. He pushed Sigmund's rear down on the ground and held onto his snout. Murphy came outside and paced across his porch directly above them.

"Are you out of your mind calling me now? I'm having dinner with my family. For Christ's sake . . . I'm juggling too much . . . These overnight business trips aren't holding water anymore . . . I mean my wife is asking questions . . . What? I'm glad he signed the papers . . . Yes, he's out of your life now . . . Yes, I do know how good it feels because he's out of my life too. Did you know he got fired today? And he peed in my face. He actually peed in my face . . . Yes it stung my eyes . . . Samantha, we can't move forward right now. You have to be patient . . . No it's not my family. They will cope. They'll move on . . . Yes of course that's what I'm talking about. I'm close now. My agents are in place. We're ready to execute. I can't have any distractions . . . When this is all over we can begin our new life. The entire world will start again . . . We'll talk later ok? . . . Calm down . . . You're getting crazy again. I'll call you . . . Bye, Samantha."

Murphy shuffled around the porch. Earl could hear him taking deep breaths. He opened the door and went back inside. The door lock did not turn behind him. Earl placed his backpack behind his head to use as a pillow. He counted down some time.

Earl told Sigmund to "wait here," as they stood on Murphy's front porch. He had watched the family turn out the lights and go upstairs thirty minutes ago. His thirst was itching and his impatience had outgrown his caution, which was now only a vague impression, sloshing around in the slurry of his skull. He tried the door. It swung open and Earl entered.

He felt around the darkness until he found a reading light on an end table. He put it on the lowest setting and slunk around the living room and kitchen until he found liquor. He cracked the seal of a rye bottle and took a long drink. He opened the fridge to pick at leftovers. Perfectly cooked asparagus and a bean salad with avocado and lime. Murphy was a good vegan. Earl took the food and slumped in a rocking chair by the Christmas tree. He nibbled and drank.

He heard footsteps coming down the stairwell. Murphy yawned and entered the kitchen, wearing only his boxer shorts. He went to the sink and poured himself a glass of water. He downed it and poured another.

"Are you still orchestrating a global economic meltdown?" Earl asked. "I thought you would've been over that by now."

Murphy sputtered and almost choked.

"The door was unlocked," Earl said. "You should be more careful. There are plenty of crazies lurking about."

"You think you can invade my home and get away with it?" Murphy grabbed a chef's knife off the counter.

"I could ask you the same thing," Earl said, rocking slowly in the chair.

Reverberations of a Blackout

Days of Sobriety: 0

"Holy . . . Why are . . . How did . . . Are you friendly?" It was the janitor.

Earl considered spontaneous combustion as he sat on the toilet, listening through the stall door to the ingratiating swoosh of Sigmund's tail. Mothball blood rolled around his tongue, and cold clung to his marrow after spending the night on ice-blasted pavement.

He had awoken to the street sounds of early workday bustle. Light, hewn from gold and white heat, reflected off snow and split his ice crusted eyelids as the old bones of the city rattled to life. An urban kaleidoscope spun around him. Skyscrapers twisted into the sky. Grotesque pedestrian faces fluttered in and out of view. The homeless slumbered under piles of charcoal rags. Rumbling streetcars, balanced on brittle steel rails, accelerated the flow of the proletariat endowment.

Would anyone care if I erupted into flames? Earl wondered as he adjusted himself over the toilet bowl. *Would the sun burn a little less brightly at least?* He took a gulp of rye. Agony staggered cognition as alcohol dripped from an open wound slashed across his jowl. His eyes billowed black smoke in anti-septic shock as he surveyed the vomit, blood and road salts that sullied his blue winter coat. He was too sick to whimper and too thirsty to croak. He was a refugee of normalcy. He was a booze-soaked miscreant crawling through the peripheral darkness, smearing the streets with rancid fluids and death-dealing blights. The indifference of time would soon strip him naked and devour his flesh like a cloud of blow flies.

"You ok in there?" The janitor asked.

"No."

"You're a little early today."

"I got fired."

"That's a rough thing to lay on a guy with a thunderous hangover."

"Apparently I got fired yesterday. It wasn't a pretty scene when I showed up this morning. Bossman called the cops."

"Is this your dog?"

"I thought it was bring your pet to work day. I should've shown up with a herd of mad cows to settle some scores." Earl cackled.

"Come out of there. I got something for you."

"I'm kind of busy."

"Yeah, you sound pretty nasty. When's the last time you had a solid bowel movement?"

Earl squirted hot, sputtering liquid.

"It feels euphoric," the janitor said. "It's one of the millions of things you will appreciate with a sober mind and body. Imagine delicious food in a hungry stomach. Or cold, crisp early mornings in the open air with lungs full of vitality."

Earl hacked up battleship-grey phlegm. He spat and said: "I don't want to hear your wisdom today."

"But I have something for you."

"I don't care."

"All right. I'm going. I hope you find everything you're looking for in there."

Earl heard the bathroom door open and close. He took another gulp of rye and grimaced at the pain in his face. He stuffed the half empty bottle into the inside pocket of his blue winter coat and exited the stall after one last tumultuous rectal explosion.

The janitor was leaning against the row of sparkling sinks and feeding Sigmund a ham sandwich. He recoiled at Earl. "What the hell happened to your face, man?"

Earl spat blood into a sink and looked at himself in the mirror. He could see his teeth through his cheek. "Maybe I got hit by a streetcar." He imagined the rush of stepping in front of a speeding locomotive. He saw the instant of panic on the conductor's face, his own head exploding like a cantaloupe and his body splayed about the street in gory ribbons. "I thought you left."

"That's a knife wound."

"You should see the other guy," Earl said. He smiled like a putrefied crypt troglodyte.

"What *did* happen to the other guy?" The janitor gaped at Earl. "Oh Jesus. You killed a man. His name was, uh, Mickey. Murray? No, Murphy."

"Murphy?" Earl asked.

"It was on the news this morning. A woman found her husband on the front porch of their home with a knife in his heart and animal bites all over his body." The janitor looked at Sigmund. "There's grainy CCTV footage of the suspect recorded outside a gas station nearby. Caucasian, intoxicated, 6-foot, mid-thirties, slim build, medium length brown hair, scruffy beard, beige pants, blue winter coat. And he had a dog and a gash in his face. Does that remind you of anyone?"

Earl stared at himself in the mirror. "I need to go to the hospital."

"You need to keep your head down. There will be cops all over the place looking for you."

Earl unscrewed the lid of his bottle of rye.

"For Christ's sake, man. You need to skip town."

"What are you trying to tell me?"

"You're a wanted man."

"I'm going to the hospital."

"No, you're not."

The janitor led Earl to a neatly organized supply closet and pulled a first-aid kit off the shelf. Arranging sutures, he said: "I'm glad you're hammered. Otherwise this would really hurt." He threaded the needle and poked it into Earl's face. Sigmund slumped onto the floor and closed his eyes.

"Do you know what you're doing?" Earl asked.

The janitor shook his head. "This won't be pretty, but it'll at least make you less desirable in jail." He splashed iodine and hydrogen peroxide as Earl managed a grin. The needle pressed

Earl's flesh and slid through to the inside of his mouth. The janitor's vinegary fingers rubbed Earl's tongue as they looped the needle back around.

The janitor leaned back and admired his handy work. "Not bad," he said, and applied a gauze bandage. "Remember I said I have something for you?" The janitor pulled a brochure from his pocket and handed it to Earl. "You need to dry out. You need to travel far away from here."

"Rapture?" Earl asked.

"Read it."

"You trying to sell me something?" Earl flipped through the pages, looking at pictures of forested, snowy landscapes. He looked at the cover which read:

WANDERLAND ADVENTURES
—

EXPERIENCE MAJESTIC WILDERNESS
FIND TRUE CLARITY

Beneath this stood a man with wispy, dreaded hair and a vengeful beard that was the colour of thunderstorms. The creases beside his eyes were deep. His grin was ecstatic.

"What's this?" Earl asked.

"You need to go to this place and meet this man."

Earl swayed, looking dumbly at the pages. "You want me to head into the wilderness?"

"Take the trip," the janitor said. "Everything has been arranged. All you need to do is get there."

Earl looked at the geographic coordinates printed on the back of the brochure. "You're ridiculous," he said.

"Give me your bloody coat," the janitor said. "You'll be nabbed in seconds out there. Take mine. It's goosedown and coyote-lined."

Earl pictured a gaggle of plucked geese and a pack of naked coyotes. He would surely get an activist paint splashing—hopefully not blood-red. He accepted the gift and tried it on. It was too big but luxuriously comfortable. He raised the hood that swallowed his head. He checked the inside pocket. It was ample.

"Be careful out there," the janitor said. "The cops are probably swarming this place. They know what you look like and they know your face got slashed."

Earl nodded. He waved the brochure and folded it into his pocket. He led Sigmund through the food-court, up the stairwell, and into the lobby. He heard the elevator door grind open.

"Hey," said the yellowing man. He was dressed in a suit and tie. "You're famous. I saw you on the morning news."

"You look fancy," Earl said.

"I just quit my job." The man limped after Earl towards the exit. "It's the first day of my new life. I thought I would dress for the occasion."

Earl pushed the door open but let it swing back shut when the yellowing man grabbed him by the arm and said: "It's the first day of your new life too."

Earl shook him off.

"It's your chance to start again. Even if you go to jail, at least it'll be a clean sheet. Sometimes it takes something drastic to re-set the course." The yellowing man removed his freshly polished shoes. "You might get to be an astronaut after all."

"And you? Will you be the next Prime Minister?"

"Afraid not. Terminal cancer of the liver," the yellowing man said. He took off his jacket and pants.

"What the hell?"

The yellowing man pointed out the glass door at a congregation of cops as he continued to disrobe. "Make a run for it." He unfurled a bottle of Tundra Glass and took a slug. He winked at Earl, then pulled off his underwear and swung open the door. "Hey coppers. Does this impress you?" He limped into the street.

Earl watched the cops tackle the pale, splotchy body. The yellowing man hit the pavement with a sickening thud. He didn't scream. He didn't even whimper. It was a lifeless body that was peeled from the snow slush.

Earl secured the hood around his head and yanked Sigmund's leash. He opened the door and walked in the opposite direction of the commotion. There was a freshness in the air and a lightness in his feet. He felt an unshackling—from employment, from marriage, from societal expectation. He was an animal in the environment. Freedom, he thought. Freedom at all cost. If what the janitor and yellowing man told him held credence, he should sober up. Clarity of mind would help him achieve lasting emancipation. A police siren began to wail behind him. He quickened his stride and ducked into the side streets. "We can't get caught," he told Sigmund. "We won't be prisoners." He felt his heart pound against the bottle in the inside pocket of the janitor's coat. The beating quickened and strengthened. It was his life blood, his life force, and it was propelling him forward.

After a brief reprieve of afternoon sunshine, wind and snow had resumed in early winter darkness. Earl watched the elements pound against the great doors of the old Victorian church and wondered which would succumb to the other. There was a bulletin board mounted to the church wall. He read about Christians raising money for HIV treatment at home and abroad, supplying contraceptives to sex workers, and preventing the vulnerable masses from perishing upon frozen streets. He gazed up at the holy spire that stood as a grim reminder of heaven, a gothic monolith in the cold sky. It scowled down upon the city in which it was trapped, surrounded by a moat of decay that it had watched spawn and spread throughout the centuries. It had witnessed billions of tonnes of pollution fill the skies, the division of class, the emergence of status, the iniquity of opulence, the profitability of desperation. Earl looked to the south and saw the financial district's plagues of skyscrapers dwarf the non-secular. He had always believed that religion was the root of the world's conflict and misery, but from this perspective, it was clear that money was to blame. *But money is religion*, he thought. Neo-faux-spirituality, the green deity, the ethnosphere's big bang; and the global economy was the new planetary ecosystem—delicate, interconnected, capable of destroying civilization, and just as make believe as any God that would smite the world asunder.

With trepidation, Earl pushed open the heavy door. He entered with Sigmund and oozed like condensation down the stairwell and into the basement. He reached the door he was looking for and glanced around. He took a drink of rye. Then another. And one more, for courage.

The room was full and it took Earl a minute to find a seat. When he did, Sigmund settled quietly between his legs. Earl looked around at a sample of the world's human population that identified as alcoholic. There were men and women of all ages, of all versions, seated in rows that faced a microphone at the front of the room.

The meeting was already in progress. The session chair guided the proceedings within the dank and crumbly church basement that had witnessed meetings like this countless times before. Raconteurs had come and gone but the substance had remained the same, rooted in the teachings of the messianic alcoholic.

The session chair gesticulated, flashing crystallized wisdom. He was reclined, loquacious, and seemingly confident in the information he espoused. He scanned the room, absorbing all the faces. "Sobriety . . ." he said. The old brown shoe at the end of his crossed leg bumped up and down in rhythm with his heart. "God willing . . ." His plaid shirt was buttoned up to his chin. "Will deliver us from evil." He wore a camouflage-patterned fishnet hat. "Sobriety . . ." he said, and continued to scan the room, "is our absolution." His eyes settled on Earl. "Are there any newcomers today?"

Earl cringed. He wanted to be invisible—an apparition that people felt but did not want to admit they saw. But the session chair's dial did not falter. He waited patiently until Earl finally put up his hand and all heads turned towards him.

"Welcome," said the chair. "Would you like to introduce yourself?"

"My name is Earl." A long pause ensued and no one spoke. One hundred and thirteen eyes did not waver from him.

The session chair mercifully broke the silence. "Welcome, Earl. Why is it that you are here?"

Earl could hear his heart beat against the rye bottle.

The man seated beside Earl leaned over and said in his ear: "There's no shame in this room. This is your first step."

Earl tried again. "Hello, everyone. My name is Earl. And I'm an alcoholic."

"HI, EARL! WELCOME, EARL!" said the entire room, and the meeting continued under the guidance of the session chair, who now swung a coffee mug as he spoke.

Earl waited for his admission's consequent epiphany, but it didn't come. He sighed and said under his breath: "I'm an alcoholic."

The man beside him squeezed his shoulder and said: "You're on your way." Then he patted Sigmund, who appeared to be enjoying himself immensely.

"Our good friend Randolph has the floor," said the session chair. "Randolph, whenever you're ready."

Randolph winked at Earl, gave Sigmund one more pat, then stood and made his way to the front of the room. He closed his eyes, seemingly in prayer, before he addressed his cohorts. He took a deep breath, exhaled into the microphone and said: "My name is Randolph and I'm an alcoholic and addict."

"HI, RANDOLPH!"

Randolph appeared to be in his mid-fifties. He had chiseled features and a muscled frame. His hair was full and silvery, pulled back in a short jutting ponytail. He did not stand very tall, but compensated with steely eyes that dispensed an infectious air of righteous invincibility. He billowed in a green silk blouse that he had unbuttoned halfway down his chest, revealing a chain from which hung a modest gold cross, cozy in wispy silver curls.

"It's a true pleasure to be here today," Randolph began. "I'm very grateful to stand and share with my fellow warriors. I've learned from the twelve steps that it's good to be open and honest. So that's what I intend to do as we commune indoors on this blustery winter's day.

"Ever since I sobered up, I've had choices. My first choice was to put all the money I would have spent on booze and drugs into pilot training, and eventually my very own Cherokee 180 propeller aeroplane. As a child I dreamed of becoming a pilot. I would play with my little toy planes and run around with my arms extended like wings, fantasizing for hours on end about exploring the skies and imagining the freedom it would afford. But for decades, alcohol had disallowed this dream to come to fruition. During my drinking and drugging career there was no dreaming, no aspiring, there were no choices. I had to drink and drug myself into sickness. I had to lie in bed for days until my supplies ran out and I was forced to muster enough courage to face the world again.

"But now I can choose how to spend my days. Today, I chose to go out for breakfast. I went to the diner down the street from my home and ate eggs over easy with toast and bacon. Afterwards I chose to go for a walk on the waterfront. I chose to wander around the museum to gawk at the dinosaur skeletons. I chose to catch a matinee film. And of course, I chose to come here. Sobriety has unearthed an energy within me that had once lain dormant and immobilized by poison. This energy is a powerful vitality that blesses me with rays of sunshine that sparkle through my bedroom window each morning. It nurtures optimism and the strength to choose direction.

"Last summer, I chose to take a trip to the west coast to drain my body of anti-depressants, anti-psychotics, and anti-anxieties. I had quit drinking, but to quell the insanity of my detoxification I sought the help of psychiatrists who put me on pharmaceutical slurries. For years I believed that I needed these pills to stay sane and sober. But eventually I realized that this was a chemical lie. So, I burned my prescription notes and figured a cross country meditation tour could salvage my sanity. I packed some clothes, readied my aeroplane, grabbed my pet ferret Doug, and followed the sun westward.

"The journey above the prairies was fraught with fear. Detox was severe. Headaches, nausea, nightmares. The Zoloft withdrawal sent electricity through my body and disallowed masturbation. The Lorazepam withdrawal turned my eyes yellow. And the Quetiapine withdrawal solidified my stool until I reached the eastern base of the Rocky Mountains, where I gassed up my plane and purged my bowels in the thorny brush.

"When my Cherokee 180 climbed the Rockies, my mind began to flatten out. It was at the summit of the continent that I began to feel grounded. It was amidst endless creation, and rows of snow covered imaginations, that I finally calmed down. And I thought about how blessed I was. I had everything I needed. Which made me ponder wants and needs.

"I'm a judgemental sort and what I judge most in people is their wants and desires. Our society is based on the liquidity of desire and blurring the lines between what we want and what we need. As a result, people are all mixed up. They say that they need a big house and big boobs. They need their cubed meat in cleaner packaging. They need floral air fresheners in every room. This is what people scream at their televisions about. But on the day that they need the grace of God upon them, their cries will go unanswered and they will be lost in a sewerage of desire. This will break them.

"I once had a great need. I couldn't control my alcoholism and I yearned for death. I was on the precipice and the noose hung ready. It swayed from my ceiling and waited patiently for me to take the plunge. But one day I closed my eyes, and for the first time in my life, I prayed. I prayed and I prayed. I prayed to God so hard I felt the Earth tremble. And in my time of great need, as I surrendered my will, my prayer was answered. Seismic events have led me to the grace of God and I have not had a drink in years. The noose still hangs empty as a daily reminder of the hell I can never go back to."

Randolph cleared his throat into the microphone and continued:

"At the break of dawn, past the great sierra I felt the light of God rise in the east and power my aeroplane through the sky above every possible shade of boreal green. I hit the west coast where the salt air covered my skin and all fear dissolved away. I felt it melt from my body to be lost as a pitiful spec in the mighty Pacific Ocean. I would sit at night and contemplate the sea, the billions of tonnes of power—enough energy to cleanse the entire world. I watched the memory of stars sparkle across the ocean's black eternity. Rolling waves unfolded on the shore to disperse the planet's might before returning to the sea. Ghostly wind hissed in the high, slow-swaying trees, painted in moonlight. Driftwood plunked upon shallow pebbles, in time with the long clock of existence.

"It was on the beach I realized that I could exist with a sober mind forevermore. And as the sun rose the next morning, it was as if the world had started again. I sat for hours watching the waves, reflecting upon my lifelong pilgrimage that had brought me to this point. It had seemed but a dream.

"My ferret Doug loved the ocean even more than I did. He saw it as his natural habitat. And I figured he was right. I threw his tether away and allowed him to roam free. He would swim and frolic with reckless abandon. He climbed boulders and went clamming. He travelled inland and came back covered in burrs. He ate starfish and garter snakes. Then he would come back to me after dusk, and we would go to sleep in the aeroplane. At least I would sleep, and he would busy himself, for he's an insomniac you see. He spent the nights building a nest in the back corner of the plane cabin. Whenever I was missing something, that's where I would find it. My toothbrush, my antacids, my pilot's licence. He also stole the photo of Mother that dangled at the front of the cockpit. But this he hid somewhere else for it wasn't in his nest. I screamed and raged at him but he would not disclose its whereabouts.

"Every morning I walked along the beach with Doug. I couldn't believe the freshness of the air and the extreme of the ocean's expanse. I yearn to go back because I can't imagine any human choosing not to live by the sea. On one particular morning, a sea otter came to visit. It flopped on the shore, showing its underbelly, and Doug ran out to cavort in the surf. The otter slipped back into the sea and disappeared like ink. Then its head popped up again, sparkling in the sunshine, and it grinned back at us. Doug hopped. The otter splashed water. It dove and cajoled with the waves. It emerged with a salmon in its jaws and tore out its skull. Doug and I watched as this otter did what it was put on this Earth to do: thrive. And to thrive sober. Well, I'm assuming the otter was sober."

"HAHAHA!"

"Like the otter, we have the right to be sober. We have the right to thrive. On that beautiful day the otter saved me. It's a small thing the otter did for me, but I use small things everyday to help me along my way. If I add all the small things up their sum becomes powerful. I now choose the small things and alcohol is no longer my higher power.

"Doug also experienced the power of the otter. He swam out only to get overwhelmed by the waves. The otter brought him safely back to shore where they wrestled in the surf, and the three of us dined on very fresh fish.

"One morning Doug was gone. I understood that he had found his soul mate, but it was hard to admit that it wasn't me. And it was truly devastating to think that I would never see him again.

"But one night I heard him as I slept fitfully in the Cherokee. I awoke to a rustling noise but didn't see anything. 'Doug?' I asked an empty space. In the morning I found the photo of Mother back where it belonged, dangling at the front of the cockpit.

"This was Doug's way of saying goodbye, and showing me that he had chosen a different life. I meditated upon Doug. He had left me, his guardian and family. His decision reminded me of my childhood, when I wasn't given the luxury of choice. I was forced to watch as Mother was torn from my life.

"I've been an addict since I can remember. When I was a youngling, I drank breast milk like a rabid shrew, and my tenacity for it grew into my teenage years. My first vivid memory is screaming in the living room of my childhood home. Mother ran in from the kitchen, unbuttoning her blouse. This relationship carried on until I was fifteen. Mother and I were so habituated that it had become a natural part of our life together. It was a closeness that we shared. I was an only child with no father or friends, so Mother was my world. Every morning I would wake up and scamper from my bedroom as fast as I could to find her waiting for me, mammal juice dripping. After school, I would run home for my afternoon feeding. Mother would be waiting for me on the living room couch, lying on her back. I would pounce on top of her and plug my face until I felt the full satisfaction of her intoxicating warmth melt inside me. Her breasts could hardly tolerate me by the time I was in my teens, with my strong jaws and hard teeth, not to mention the exuberance with which I pursued the activity. Her left nipple had been nipped off, but her right one had tolerated my hunger. All my suckling had stretched and swelled it, creating a long, calloused super-nipple.

"She would also give me a feeding at night. I would wait patiently on top of my bedsheets for Mother to tuck me in. It was during one of these feedings that my aunt entered our home and came up to my bedroom looking for us. She watched through the darkened doorway as I suckled her little sister. My aunt divulged our secret, which forced Mother and I apart.

"When I asked why we could no longer be together, Mother told me that our relationship was inappropriate and detrimental to my mental health. She said that I had been raised carelessly, and that the province would better guide my development into manhood. I went to live with foster parents. But they refused to love me the way Mother did. I bounced around from home to home until my wretched aunt was forced to take me in. I sent letters to Mother every day. I would tell her how much I missed her and how badly I yearned for the closeness we shared. I told her it was an obsession that tormented me. It was months before she replied. I tore open the envelope and her words have been burned into memory ever since. It read: 'Randolph, you're the only person I have ever loved. But this world wants to keep us apart and destroy the purity of what we have. Never forget me, Randolph, and do something special with your life. I will always love you and cherish you. Love Mother.' I immediately began writing a reply when my aunt informed me that Mother had taken her own life by overdosing on Olanzapine. I left my aunt's home that evening to become a street urchin and a beggar. It was at this time that I found a suitable alternative to Mother's milk that had left such an

indelible void in my soul. It was called alcohol and I dedicated
my life to it.

"Mother, watching down from heaven, would have been
appalled and deeply saddened to see what I had become. It was
only some years ago that I realized that my dedication to alcohol
was misguided. The epiphany occurred one spring morning
when I awoke in a rehabilitation centre. The tall red-brick structure, in which I came to, was only the nucleus of the place.
Surrounding it were tall trees, swan ponds and acres of green
fields. I rustled inside my bedsheets with stiff bones. I looked
around the room and to my delight and horror saw Mother doz-
ing in a chair at my bedside. She was as young and beautiful as
the day I last saw her. Her soft snores nicely accompanied the
bird song twittering through the open window.

"I had no recollection of how I had gotten there. I scanned
my mind for clues until my final memories unveiled themselves.
I had been preparing dinner for two. It would have been
Mother's seventy-ninth birthday so I was cooking her favourite:
lamb chops, cooked medium-rare and drowning in sweet Thai
chilli sauce and thwacks of ginger. I also prepared a crunchy side
salad of halved radishes and artichoke hearts, splayed over a bed
of arugula, drizzled with lemon dill vinaigrette, and fear. The
lamb was in the oven. The soft flesh tenderised in low, slow heat
while I drank from champagne bottles and snorted lines of
cocaine. I got started on dessert. I rummaged through the kitchen
and found flour, eggs, vanilla extract, butter, baking powder,
milk, but no sugar. Where was the sugar? Mother would never
forgive me for a sugarless white cake. I thought about my neigh-
bours. Surely someone would give me one cup of sugar.

"My neighbourhood sits concaved in a cul-de-sac and veiled
from Toronto's urban aggression by thin trees that line an
embankment and gulley that hurries brown water along. The
lamp posts are yellow and bulbous and when lit up, look like
rows of moons. The Smiths' house sits to the left. They screamed
at me every time I was within a hundred meters of their children.
The Browns never returned my hellos. The Whites had called
the police on me numerous times, and the Watsons once caught

me selling their tween daughters crystal meth. So, my options were limited. I chose the house kitty-corner to my own, where I had never before seen anyone enter or exit. The house stood silent and resolute in all seasons, the lawn always cut, the snow always blown, the windows always clean, and the eavestrough never clogged with anything but rain water. But no one performed this maintenance. It was achieved as if by sorcery.

"I walked up to the door that was oak and medieval. It was a towering semi-oval, six inches thick with iron reinforcements and a brass, life-sized lion-head door knocker, with fangs bared. I lifted it with all my might and let it drop onto the solid wood that did not buckle, but forced a thunderous boom which echoed about the cul-de-sac, setting off car alarms and animal panic. I waited a full minute but did not dare knock again. I took a blue pill and swallowed it down with single malt Speyside from my hip flask. I drained it as the great door inched open with stiff and ancient reluctance.

"'Hello. Welcome. Please come inside.' The voice was soft, almost a whisper, but commanded a strength that beckoned me hither. I entered the house and the door boomed shut behind. The room was dark and it took time for my eyes to adjust. It smelled of candle spermaceti, ash and mange. I felt movement behind me and heard the latch of the great hermetic door lock. 'Please come and sit down.' I followed the voice that had flowed into an adjoining and equally dark room. I felt around to find a seat as the fireplace erupted into flames and the place was flooded with light. My pupils constricted to pinpoints as the fire illuminated a tall, slim woman whose hair was raven black and eyes flame blue. Her beauty was enchanting and it swirled about the high-backed leather chair that ensconced her black clad body. I was bewitched.

"'You are a suffering man,' she said, 'but you will suffer no more.' Her voice had turned taut and soothsaying. 'My thaumaturgy was alluring to you?'

"'I came to ask for a cup of sugar,' I told her.

"'You've been conjured,' she said.

"The woman stood with billowing hair and screamed at the fire, causing it to slink into its embers before roaring back to life in the wake of her rune: 'What diabolism has brought you to your knees? You are poisoned. I invoke the necromancy of hell-fire upon this place to dispel the blackness of your soul. Grim augury must be vanquished by the druids of perdition to douse this devilry with divination.' The room calmed and hushed and the woman sat down and smiled at me.

"I was terrified. I rushed to the door, which was locked. I pulled and pushed on it. I rammed it with my shoulder.

"I turned to see the woman appear behind me fingering a large, gold dungeon-esque key with nimble fingers. It glimmered and disappeared, glimmered and disappeared. 'Please, I must go now. I only came for a cup of sugar.'

"'And sugar you shall have,' the woman said, then swallowed the key. I watched it bulge in her throat before it disappeared into her stomach.

"I was trembling.

"'Come to me, and fall to your knees, fall to your knees.' I remotely obeyed her incantation. She removed her black gown which fell to her feet. She stood naked before me. My eyes were wide with fear as an artful dagger appeared in her long, slim fingers. It vanished then appeared, vanished then appeared. She brought it to my throat then laughed while she reversed its position and placed the tip of the long blade in her belly button. 'Push it in,' she told me.

"I watched as she guided my hands to the dagger's haft and applied pressure, pushing the blade inside her, up to its quillion. I let go and watched as blood formed and began to pour into her pubis. She pulled the blade from herself and dropped it to the floor. She grabbed my head in her hands and forced my mouth upon the dilating wound. 'Suck,' she demanded. 'Suck my elixir.'

"I obeyed. My belly filled with blood and my mouth overflowed with it. I sucked and sucked until the blood flow slowed then stopped, and the gold key emerged from her belly. She crumpled to the floor.

"The next thing I knew I had awoken in the rehabilitation centre, watching dead Mother snooze in the armchair beside my bed. When she woke, I said: 'Sorry I over-cooked the lamb, Mother.'

"'That's ok," she told me. 'I just want you better, my love.'

"'How did we get here?' I asked her.

"'A raven-haired woman brought us. An enchanting beauty. Oh, how I wish you weren't gay.'"

Randolph looked around the room with a wry smile. "You may all think that I'm insane, or you may think I was hallucinating in a fit of alcohol withdrawal. But I assure you that Mother was as real to me that day as any of you who sit before me right now. She is the manifestation of my higher power. She is the unrelenting force that has kept me sober and thriving in this world. Thank you all for lending your ear. God bless and keep coming back."

"THANKS, RANDOLPH!"

"Yes, thank you for that very vivid story, Randolph," said the session chair. "Would anyone else like to share?"

The meeting ended and Earl rocketed for the door. He was almost free when a man gripped his arm. "Hi, Earl," he said. "Have we met before?"

Earl thought about the janitor's warnings as people began milling around him, murmuring his name, blocking the exit. He was found, trapped, doomed. The wound on his face itched and throbbed like a flashing red beacon. He used all his will to resist the urge to tear at it with his fingernails and mangle his jowl into a clump of forcemeat.

"Surely we've met. Even your dog seems familiar."

"Earl's an aspiring film actor," said Randolph, swooping into the conversation. "But he has had to make do with television commercials lately. It's a tough business, isn't it, Earl?"

The man blanched at Randolph's arrival.

"I've urged him to throw himself into theatre," Randolph continued. "That's where the real actors work. They toil night after night, spilling their blood and sweat onto the stage, exposing their flesh and souls to the audience."

Earl felt his body quail under the heat of the spotlight, naked and bleeding in front of a packed house.

"Film actors can hide themselves behind the cold glass of the camera lens," Randolph said. "They can deny their audience intimacy. Not to say that there haven't been many fine films, but they are mere entertainment. Theatre transcends into the realm of the spiritual. It can open eyes. It can change lives. It can alter the trajectory of the universe."

"What commercials have you done, Earl?" the man asked.

"Uh, Tundra Glass Vodka," Earl shrugged.

"How inappropriate."

"Earl and I have a dinner engagement and we mustn't be late." Randolph patted the man's hand that still clutched Earl's arm.

Past the boob shacks and porn shops of Yonge Street, Randolph led Earl and Sigmund deep into the heart of Toronto's Gay Village. They walked under moon-shaped streetlights and up the shark tooth brick path that snuck its way between evergreen shrubs to the front door of his home. The path was freshly shovelled but quickly accumulating a new blanket of snow. Flanking them were ancient oak trees, robust even as winter nudes. Crows skittered through the branches, cawing and raining acorns down upon the trio, cracking them on the brick path and avoiding the soft snow.

The house was two stories of red brick, covered in vine veins and dead brown moss. Earl looked around the cul-de-sac. Similar structures populated it, covering every square foot of real estate except for the property that sat kitty-corner to Randolph's. That space was empty.

Randolph led them up the steps to the front door where he riffled through his mailbox, grumbling with displeasure at what he found inside. "Bills, junkmail, fundraising appeals," he reported. He held up an envelope with a picture of a baby chimpanzee with a hypodermic needle in its eye. "This summarizes the human condition," he said. "Barbarism and cries for money.

These fundraisers don't seem to realize that most people don't give a hoot about baby animals. They may say they do but in reality, they care about Lamborghinis." He pointed to the vampire black car with gull-wing doors parked across the street. "Is that fatalism I speak? Or realism? Fatalism, I think, because surely a car like that is a death trap in winter. But I suppose yuppies will forever suffer for status. Please come inside, Earl."

Randolph offered to take Earl's jacket but Earl insisted that he hang it up himself, careful not to expose the bulge of the rye bottle. He placed his backpack on the floor and unlaced his boots as Randolph called into the house: "Vinnigan, I brought a friend for dinner."

Randolph removed his suede coat and Canadian wedge hat as Vinnigan flounced into view. "Good," Vinnigan said. "Because I'm cooking more crab legs than Randolph and I could ever eat." He extended his hand to Earl. His eyes rested on the bloodied bandage but only momentarily before he turned his attention to Sigmund. "And who is this handsome beast? Crab legs might be a little refined for your taste. How about I cook you up some brown rice with ground turkey and carrots?"

"That would be nice of you," Earl said.

"Vinnigan," Randolph said. "Did you shovel the front path?"

"Yes. I did the Smiths' driveway too."

"In the middle of a blizzard? What is the point?"

"Exercise, my love. I need to keep this hot young body desirable, don't I?" He laughed and Randolph did too.

Randolph gave him a kiss. "What's that on your breath?"

"It's nothing."

"Vinnigan?"

"I had a scotch while I waited for you. That's all."

"You brought scotch into my house?"

"I'm sorry. I can get rid of it."

"It's too late to be sorry. I should string you up." Randolph grabbed Vinnigan by the neck and forced him into the living room.

Earl watched from the foyer as Randolph pointed to the noose hanging from the ceiling and said: "That's my fate, Vinnigan. You'll kill me."

Vinnigan's eyes welled up. His mouth opened but no words came.

Randolph softened. "I'm sorry. Maybe I didn't make it clear enough to you the severity of my disease." He embraced his lover, who was now sobbing. "I take my sobriety very seriously. It is the only thing of importance in my life. Without it, everything else goes away."

Vinnigan nodded.

"Now, go back to the kitchen. That meeting made me ravenous."

Randolph invited Earl to sit at the kitchen table. Vinnigan was busy about the stove top as he composed himself. He heavily seasoned a large pot of boiling water before dropping in a bundle of long spindly crab legs.

"Sorry, Earl. My temper can get the better of me at times," Randolph said as the two men sat across from each other, one with excellent posture and one without. Randolph's elbows rested upon the table-top that hid under crisp white linen. His clean chin sat upon his hands that folded like an inverted steeple as he smiled warmly. His clear eyes surveyed Earl, who looked ill, sallow, pale.

Randolph's gentle expression momentarily quelled Earl's anxiety. But what was he doing here amongst gorgeous men? He should be unconscious in a ditch somewhere with winter mites crawling over his frigid genitals. Earl thought about asking to leave when Vinnigan said: "May I please have the privilege of fulfilling your requests today?"

"What?" Earl asked.

"Yes you may my fine young friend and thank you very much," Randolph said. "We will have your finest bubbling mineral water, two tall glasses, a bucket of ice, and a bowl of sliced limes. And I think we shall have something to chew on also. How about . . ." Randolph took a moment to read an imaginary menu, his chin and eyes pulled down towards it.

"Crab legs. Lots and lots of crab legs. Yes Earl. I hope you like crab legs."

Earl wondered what kind of cruel conditions the crabs must have suffered during their journey from the depths of the wide and wonderful ocean to Toronto's concrete wasteland.

"Excellent, gentlemen. My name is Vinnigan, and if there is anything you need, anything at all, please do not hesitate for one second to ask." Vinnigan looked at them as if they best not disobey him, then turned back to the stove.

Randolph adjusted the pressed collar of his green blouse and asked: "What's your poison, Earl?"

"Alcohol."

"What kind of alcohol?"

"Whatever I can get my hands on."

"But you must have a preference."

"Rye."

"Mixed? Muddled? On the rocks? Straight?"

"Straight."

"How disappointing," Vinnigan laughed.

"From a glass or from the bottle?" Randolph asked.

"Bottle."

Randolph winked approval. "Your wound looks painful."

"I got hit by a train," Earl replied. He shifted uncomfortably in his seat.

"How long have you been sober?"

"I'm drunk right now."

"I wondered," Randolph said as the mineral water and accessories arrived. He clinked four ice-cubes into two tall glasses, then aggressively squeezed the juice from three lime wedges into each. He dropped the rinds in, allowing the zest and ruptured juice sacs to further flavour the ice. He poured the sparkling mineral water. Carbonation explosions leaped like electrified pinheads. The liquid boiled with lime-green energy, but its surface had adopted a poison-dart yellow from the overhead lamp.

Randolph handed Earl his beverage and said: "Take a small sip but don't swallow. Let the cold water bubble in your cheeks and pour around your tongue. Be aware of how it feels."

Earl swished it like mouth wash.

"Slowly, Earl. Take the time to enjoy the moment. Ignore everything else. Close your eyes if you must. There is nothing but the bubbling liquid. Think of it as a crystal stream flowing through the pitch darkness of a cave. There is no light or sound, apart from the trickling of water and the detonation of bubbles. There is nothing to distract you. No pain or misery. No desire. Only darkness and bliss. Now swallow."

Earl opened his eyes. "Bubbly," he said.

"Yes, bubbly. It's lovely isn't it? It's gorgeous."

"I suppose."

"What lengths would you go to achieve sobriety, Earl?"

"I don't know. I haven't given it much thought."

"Well, you must have given it some thought if you came to the meeting today. You must have reached a particular depth of desperation and realized that you have no power over alcohol, and that it's a cunning beast that has taken control of your life. Am I right?"

"I'm not sure." Earl paused. "I don't know." He thought for a moment about his shattered existence. "Ok. You're right. I can't control my drinking. I can't not drink."

"Yes, Earl. You speak like the true alcoholic that you are. You can't not drink. This negation of phrase is what we alcoholics hold to be true. It's a kind of madness that has killed swaths of good people. But we must live, Earl. Because surely, life is better than death."

Earl shrugged. "Is it?"

"Surely."

"Life is only death's waiting room. It's a cage run by the rules of others where the insane or sick are tormented. This world isn't made for people like me."

"You don't understand the freedoms life can afford because your addiction has you circumscribed," Randolph said. "But you can be extricated. By the grace of God, you can. But it's far too powerful a demon to be defeated by one mortal man. It takes an army and I would like to enlist. I want to help you defeat the evil scourge that has annexed your soul. You must be reclaimed, Earl. Can I help save you?"

"I guess so."

"It will take much more conviction than that. So I will ask you again. Can I help save your life?"

"Yes. Thank you."

"You're welcome. Good. We're on our way. Before we begin, you must understand your enemy. You know it's powerful and cunning, and that it has total control of your life. But did you know that it's alive and calculating?"

The crab legs arrived. Vinnigan's young face betokened pride and gratitude to the sea for offering such weird and wonderful creatures. "Enjoy, gentlemen."

"Thank you, Vinnigan," Randolph said. "Would you please join us?"

"But it is very bad etiquette for a server to eat with his guests."

"But I insist."

Vinnigan giggled and pulled up a chair. Sigmund was beside him, digging into his meal.

"It is very much alive and is most definitely trying to kill you, Earl," Randolph continued. "Just look at the wound on your face. Just like any effective disease, alcoholism feeds upon its host until there is nothing left. Its mission is not unlike that of the human parasite: to lay waste, and in doing so, annihilate itself in the process."

Earl considered this and said: "How do I beat it? I don't think I can beat it."

"You're right. You can't beat it," Randolph said. He dug into the mountain of crab legs and cracked open a huge Dungeness claw to suck the flesh out. "But *we* can beat it, Earl. By the Grace of God, *we* can."

"God doesn't owe me any favours," Earl said.

"That may be, but it's irrelevant. This has nothing to do with favours. I'm talking about the Grace of God. Do you know what Grace is?"

"I think Vinnigan is quite graceful."

Vinnigan blushed.

"The Grace of God, Earl. The Grace of God. The unsolicited and unmerited *Grace of God!* You're right that God doesn't owe you anything, but God will nevertheless save your life and redeem your soul if you allow it."

"I don't know," said Earl. "I've never been the Godly type. I don't go to church. I don't pray."

"What do you think of when you think of God?"

"I think of an old guy with a beard masturbating on a cloud. I think of the Bible as prescribed dogma—a large pill that causes severe internal damage."

"Forget all that, Earl. For God is a higher power of your own understanding. Think about God in this way and *your* God can save your life. Maybe your higher power is this mineral water." Randolph took a slow pull from his glass. "You must embrace the light, Earl. Otherwise, you die."

"I'm going to die anyway, Randolph."

"Of course you are. But your higher power has greater purpose for you. It wants to see you thrive in this world before your time is up."

Randolph grabbed Earl's empty glass and once again performed the ice and citrus rigmarole. Earl took it and sipped slowly, closing his eyes. He felt the cold liquid bubble and slide in his mouth. He swallowed slowly. "Maybe you're right," he said.

"Dig in, Earl. You haven't touched the crab legs."

"I'm a vegetarian."

"Plenty of vegetarians eat seafood."

"They're not vegetarians."

"Then what are they?"

"Carnivores."

"I strongly suggest you eat protein. Detoxification is a terrible ordeal and you will need all the strength you can muster." Randolph placed a crab claw on Earl's plate and cracked it open. "It'll grease your bowels," he said.

Earl stared at the soft white flesh revealed within. He noticed how it had molded itself against the shell that encased it, conforming to the claw's serrated edges and contours. It was tinged around the edges by the exoskeleton's leaching colourant. He said: "It looks alien."

"It is alien," Vinnigan laughed. "We understand less about the ocean than we do about Mars. How is that possible?"

Randolph raised his hand for silence, and said: "Earl, the way you sit slumped and woozy suggests a lack of earnestness. You do not exhibit the steely resolve necessary to achieve sobriety at any consequence. Yours is a mindset of any addict with young and wriggling tentacles, desperately flailing for salvation in the deep murky darkness."

Earl blinked.

"Will your suckers find purchase? Do you have conviction?"

"I don't know," Earl said, honestly.

"Do you have a plan?"

"A plan?"

"Do you posses a blueprint for revival?"

"Maybe," Earl said, pulling the brochure the janitor had given him from his pocket. He handed to Randolph. "I'm going west."

Randolph's eyes widened as he turned it over in his hands. "We leave at dawn."

Randolph showed Earl to the guestroom and offered him a toothbrush still in its packaging. Earl was grateful because his mouth tasted like sewage, but the brushing of his teeth was unpleasant. Every stroke ratcheted up the pain in his face until his entire head and neck throbbed. He found a bottle of peroxide and took a sip. He tilted his head to let the antiseptic run across the wound. Tears welled in his eyes and mucus dripped from his nose. The sting escalated quickly, to the point that his cries alerted Randolph, who said through the bathroom door: "Horrors tend to subside with time."

Earl snuck down to the foyer after Randolph and Vinnigan retired for the night. The old house was built solidly, and his footsteps didn't creak upon any floorboard or stair. He retrieved his half empty bottle of rye from the inside pocket of the janitor's coat and headed back upstairs. He stopped outside Randolph's bedroom and pressed his ear to the door. He could hear arguing, but of a gentle variety. Vinnigan said he would be lonely in the big empty house. He wanted to know if Randolph found Earl attractive. He asked if they would be sharing a tent. Randolph calmed his woes with cooing words and grinding bed springs.

Earl found Sigmund in the guestroom stretching and yawning. He jumped onto the foot of a tightly made bed and was quickly asleep and dreaming. His legs began to sprint through the air. Sorrowful groans. Whining. Panting. What sort of terror was he running from? Earl wondered. Or what was he running towards? A bitch's heat?

Earl looked around the tidy space. It was simple, modern, pretentious. The window curtain was thin and white. It exposed his silhouette to the dark street. Come morning it would welcome every ray of sunlight. But Earl wouldn't be there to experience that illumination. Randolph promised to wake him before daylight broke, to drag him from his warm cocoon and guide him westward.

Artwork hung from the walls of such prudent minimalism that it teetered on the edge of non-existence. Its projection was a stark contrast to that of the creature staring at Earl through the glass of a full-length mirror. If his reflection was art, it would be surrealist. For in what dreamscape did that creature exist? The light had twisted itself violently to create this foul effigy. This freak. Leper. Societal outlier. Pitiful and lonely. Sanity breaking free. Humanity evaporating into the sky. His love burrowing deeply, petrifying with inertia, waiting patiently for the death of his body. Only then could it be released back into the world, free to choose a new and auspicious host: a wriggling infant clamped onto her mother's breast.

Earl sat down on the bed and drank to his higher power. He contemplated what remained. There was fear. And there was alcohol: the undisputed champion of the Earld. He wondered if his ruin stemmed from fate—the world's system of culling the feeble and forcing those of inconsequence down through the cracks of existence where they cannot affect the world at large. For if every human possessed great strength and influence, the world would become overwhelmed. Earl helped keep the aggregate of human ambition manageable. He felt around the murky depths and looked up through these cracks of existence. He caught glimpses of people pushing forward. People that had left Earl behind. But at least he wasn't alone in this static. There were millions of others with him, wading through the muck.

But is fate even real? Earl wondered. Or is it a mental concept used to excuse failures and shortcomings? And if one believes in fate then they must also believe in luck, for it is the lucky ones whose fate unfolds favourably. But what of those born unlucky? Must they accept a dour destiny? Or is innate fortitude effective enough apparatus to combat doomed trajectories?

Earl looked at Sigmund's severed ear, the bite marks around his thick neck and shoulders where the fur never grew back, his docked tail, and the scars that lined his rib cage. He had escaped his unlucky fate and found a new way to live: loved, cozy, and sleeping peacefully. He had outrun whatever had been exciting his dreams.

"Hey, buddy. Who do you belong to?" These were the first words Earl had said to Sigmund when he saw him in a park where he liked to get drunk and smoke cigarettes. He held out half a sandwich that Sigmund ran off with. "Come on out," Earl said but Sigmund ignored him, eating in the bushes. The next day Earl returned with liver snacks that Sigmund devoured. Sigmund pawed at his leg for more as Earl patted his head and slipped a collar around his neck with a leash attached. Sigmund growled and fought. He barked, snapped and defecated. He bit Earl's hand, drawing blood. Then he sat and quivered, looking up at Earl with wet eyes. Earl said: "You can come live with me. Does that sound ok?"

"What the hell is this, Earl?" Samantha said when she got home to find Earl drinking on the couch with a canine brute beside him, mouthing a teddy bear.

"I think I'll call him Sigmund," Earl told her.

"Get that fucking dog out of my house."

What a loveless wretch, Earl thought as he yanked open the bed sheets and squeezed himself in beside Sigmund. He removed his wedding ring and placed it on the bedside table, where he found the television remote.

The evening news was on and Earl stared at it blankly, taking long pulls of rye. The news man was saying: "New developments have unfolded in the murder of a livestock distributor and former underwear model in Toronto's east end. Murphy Rampart was found dead by his wife in front of his home late last night. Mr. Rampart was a loving husband and father. He was a highly regarded community volunteer who worked closely with at-risk youth, new immigrants, the homeless, the elderly, and injured squirrels and raccoons. Police say they have a suspect named Earl Qume. His whereabouts are yet unknown but he was spotted earlier today at a twelve-step meeting. He left with a man named Randolph—last name unknown—and they are believed to be located in the Church and Wellesley area. Earl Qume's wife reported to the police that the man caught on CCTV on the night of the murder was indeed Earl Qume. He disappeared from their home the night of the murder and she has not seen him since. She provided his picture to police."

A photo of Earl and Sigmund in summer daylight filled the screen. Earl recognised the picture that had been taken by Samantha on a camping trip at Algonquin Park. He looked happy and healthy. There was flesh on his face and his cheeks glowed. His hair was messy after an uncomfortable night in a tent, where-in a tree root dug into his ribs and Sigmund and Samantha had snored and farted all night. Earl stared at the photo for as long as the newsman allowed it. He wondered in what dreamscape that version of himself existed.

Earl turned off the TV and rolled around in the sheets. He drained his bottle of rye and turned off the bedside lamp. He was immediately asleep. And he began to dream.

Earl pukes badly in the badlands and reaches for his empty, forsaken bladder. His last energy drops below him, and he vomits again. The yellow bile beads upon gold and black sand that spreads about him with endless mirth; centillions of grains swimming and swooning together to create a single boundless organism, lining the horizons and absorbing sunlight. Earl looks up at the sun. Maybe if he stares long enough he can blow it up. The sun remains huge and daunting and continues to drop heat bombs on him, soaking him with plasma. His eyelids blink rapidly. He feels his optical nerves twitch like eels. He looks down but cannot see anything except sparks. It does not matter whether he can see in the desert. It does not matter whether or not his eyes are bleeding. Earl screams and something happens. The atmosphere changes. Wind carries a civilization of sand across the sky. A dust devil lifts Earl and shoots him. He hits the ground hard and ponders misery. Is it a symptom of desperation? A bone protrudes from his arm. He looks around to see if the devil is whirling back but he cannot tell. There's too much blood in his eyes. He listens to the wind howl in the darkness and imagines being blasted into the sun. He smiles through blood and feels the presence of a monster. A shadow envelopes him. He hears the loud breath of a beast. He shivers and looks up. His vision only allows him to see the silhouette of a hairy giant, murky in the sand storm and breathing blasts of hot putrefied air. It makes a low guttural noise as if trying to detect signs of life. "I'm alive," Earl says weakly. The monster grunts and lifts Earl in its hands. Earl lies motionless, feigning death, regretting he admitted to life. The monster turns him upside down and back over again, like a little girl with a floppy bunny. Earl grimaces with the pain in his arm. The monster seems to notice and stops. It carefully lays him in its palm. Earl lounges as if in a hammock. The monster begins to walk. As bloody sparks gradually dissipate and his vision begins to clear, Earl inspects this massive lumbering beast. It stands twenty feet tall with powerful slumped shoulders. It is covered in grotesque dreads of sandy brown hair that sway as it walks. Its massive eyes are the colour of space. Its ears are floppy like a beagle's and it has the snout of a fox. It walks upright like a Sasquatch. Its odor is putrid from the rotting flesh between its jagged rows of shark teeth. The palm of its hand where Earl sits is bare and black like a gorilla's. The fingernails are humanoid, cracked and pale. "Where am I?" Earl whispers, appalled by his reflection in the monster's eyes. "Your breathing is deep and ragged," Earl says to the monster. "It sounds phlegmy. My arm is shattered. What do you think about that?" The monster looks down at him and says, "Urrg Hlug." "Are you going to eat me?" "Grunt." "Grunt once for yes and twice for no." "Grunt Grunt Grunt Urrg Hlug." "Where are we going? We could walk forever and still be in the desert." "Urrg Urrg." "I think I'm dying. Can you wait until I die before you eat me?" "Grunt." "Was that a *yes*?" "Grunt." "Are you going to cook me?" "Grunt Grunt." "Are you God?" "Grunt." "I'm delirious." "Grunt." Smoke rises in the distance. The monster lumbers towards it. Earl stares ahead at the black, gaseous smoke. The monster increases its speed towards the wreckage. "Was I on that plane?" "Grunt." "Are there other survivors?" "Grunt Grunt." The monster puts Earl down and rips the plane cabin open with its hands. It reaches in and grabs the corpse of Randolph. Earl looks up at the monster as it pops Randolph into its mouth. He listens to the crunch of bone and squirms his body in the sand until he finds a comfortable groove. "Do you only eat dead people?" "Grunt." "Good. I need a few minutes to reflect."

I Wish You a Present Fright

Days of Sobriety: 1

"Alcohol is a depressant that forces vitality downwards," Randolph said as he captained his Cherokee 180 aeroplane through Canadian airspace. "The nervous system of an alcoholic depreciates over time. From a lively system of flashes and broadcasts, it transmogrifies into to a sick and desperate predator lurking in the body's murky recesses. When the beast becomes starved, it lashes out and the effects can be severe: heart attacks, strokes, lurid hallucinations. In your case, Earl, severe panic."

Earl writhed in his seat, and screeched.

"That sounded like propeller malfunction," Randolph chuckled. "It must be grinding to a halt." He put his hand on Earl's, which was white-knuckling the arm rest. "The water in your brain is boiling but there is nothing to be afraid of, Earl. We both know that the screeching was organic and not mechanical. It came from your tonsils. Use your powers of reason. We are in an aeroplane. That is all. We are participating in a very normal and safe activity."

"We're miles in the sky." Earl screeched some more.

"Earl, focus on your breathing. Take slow, deep breaths, in and out. In and out."

Earl clenched his eyes shut and felt the nose of the plane drop ninety degrees as its thrust succumbed to Earth's gravity. His spatial perception went into a tailspin.

"Your fear of reality is consummate," Randolph said. "I imagine that you have never before experienced the threat of such a concentrated, omnipresent enemy."

"I need drinks." Earl clutched at his chest and felt his heart race. He doubled over and emptied his stomach of green slime.

"Stewardess? Oh stewardess? Could we please have some mineral water for my friend and I?" Randolph was smiling at Earl, who sat bunkered in his seat. "Calm yourself, Earl. Keep breathing. That is life-giving air that's circulating around us. Suck it into your body. You don't need alcohol. Remember that alcohol is trying to kill you. It's the genesis of your fear. Don't feed the terror, Earl. Concentrate on your breathing instead."

"I'm suffocating."

"Focus inward, Earl. Imagine oxygen. Be mindful of your body parts in space."

"In space? Oh no, no, no."

"Think of the blood in your head flowing through the muscles in your scalp. There is a calmness dripping down your face and neck, your front and back. Can you feel your shoulders loosen? There's fluidity in your rotator cuffs. Pay attention to your breathing. Easy in and easy out, Earl. Easy in and easy out." Randolph took several audible breaths. "With every exhalation, notice that a bit more relaxation has come over you. It is spreading and deepening, calming your body and mind. Listen to your body. Take your time. Enjoy the pleasure of it. Not often enough do we take the time to enjoy the bliss of existing in our bodies. Think of your chest responding to breath. Up and down, up and down, in and out, in and out. Your heart is powerful, Earl. Think of warmth and pleasure as blood easily flows through you. Feel it run down your arms and into your hands and fingers. Feel it in your abdomen as your stomach and intestines slowly digest. Imagine a ripple of water on the surface of a calm, cool lake. Can you see how it quietly spreads? One little ripple when you breathe in, and one little ripple when you breathe out. Relaxation has reached your pelvis and hips, your penis and testicles, down into the muscles of your thighs and calves, ankles, feet, toes. Notice the whole of your body becoming calmer as you breathe in and breathe out. Easy in and easy out. Think about a pleasant place, Earl. Can you imagine one?"

"Algonquin Park," Earl snapped.

"Good, Earl. Imagine yourself camping. You emerge from your tent in the very early morning light. You stretch your body and survey the pristine wilderness. You start a fire to heat some water and then you jump in a crystal blue lake. The water is so cold and fresh. You feel yourself invigorate. Sigmund runs in after you. Imagine cavorting with Sigmund in the water. Think of the beauty that God has given Sigmund. Now return to your breathing again. Imagine rivulets of calm flowing down your body like beads of lake water, relaxing your spine and lapping up upon your shores in a timeless rhythm. Intensify these feelings, luxuriate in them."

"This isn't working," Earl yelled and scrambled into the back cabin of the plane where Sigmund was in a wrestling mood. Sigmund crashed Earl up against the cooler box, scattering bottles of mineral water. Earl felt the weight of the great dog pinning him to the floor, licking his eyes, nose, ears. Randolph laughed as he flipped dials and eased off the throttle. "Flying is easy," he said.

Earl squirmed free, only to be thumped by his romping mutt into the back corner of the plane. He felt something under him. It was a nest, made of clothing strips, feathers, snake skulls, and shredded Playgirl magazines. He pushed Sigmund off and rummaged through it. He pulled out ear plugs, playing cards, a little chewed-up book titled Twelve Steps and Twelve Traditions, a pill-box in which he found three little skittering white pills. He ate them.

"Doug, you rascal. I thought I got rid of all those," Randolph said, craning his head back. "You can never trust an obsessive-compulsive ferret."

Earl felt an instant lightness in his head and an opening up of the chest. He sensed endorphins swimming throughout his entire body. The relief felt planetary, as if the entire biota of the cosmos could breathe easy for at least this moment in time. "What is this stuff?"

"Ativan," Randolph said. "It might help you in the short run but you should understand that the relief you feel isn't genuine."

"What's it doing to me?"

"Rearranging the chemicals in your brain."

"It's a miracle drug."

"No. It's just another vice."

Earl picked up the little book and flipped through it.

"You will find nothing but divine wisdom in that book," Randolph said. He quoted the first paragraph: "'Who cares to admit complete defeat? Practically no one, of course. Every natural instinct cries out against the idea of personal powerlessness. It is truly awful to admit that, glass in hand, we have warped our minds into such an obsession for destructive drinking that only an act of Providence can remove it from us.'"

Randolph patted the seat beside him. "Grab me one of those mineral waters."

Earl handed Randolph his beverage and sat back down. He opened his own bottle and poured some in Sigmund's mouth. Sigmund smacked his lips as he experienced carbonation.

Randolph took a long drink and said: "It's an act of Providence that Doug left that little book there for you and Sigmund to find. You should keep it. It will shine brightly for you in the dark days ahead. And be mindful of Providence, Earl. You must first open yourself up to it in order to be cognizant of it."

"It was an act of Providence that Doug left those little pills," Earl said. He looked out the window at the micro-world below. Snow-covered prairie stretched westward until the momentum of geological boredom rumbled the Rocky Mountains into the clouds. Directly below he saw a providential black hole—the tar sands of Alberta—muddled like a crude, infectious penis that festered to the southeast, scarring the planet. Sulfur smog billowed into the atmosphere, fogging Earl's view of the Lego-sized earth movers that crumbled the land into lifelessness. Tailing ponds dotted the landscape and squelched poisons, killing migrating birds by the tens of thousands. Westward, pipelines slithered towards the Rocky Mountains and British Columbia's coast— overrun by Asian oil tankers and flooded with the black horror of economic progress. More pipelines ran south for Texas. Earl hoped they would wipe out the southern fundamentalists in a black pestilent death while they prayed for the mercy of their wildly misinterpreted God. He took a sip of mineral water.

"It's the grace of God, Earl," Randolph declared.

"It's a pit of sin."

"I suppose it's a matter of perspective."

"I'm talking about the tar sands."

"Ah. I wish you would call them the oil sands."

"But it is tar. You could pave roads with that stuff."

"It's trapped energy. Ancient sunlight."

"The planet buried it for a reason . . . Nature's Providence."

"And we unearthed it," Randolph said. "It's human nature. As infants we instinctively suck nipples dry. Then we grow up and do the same to everything else. That's why black *tar* is spouting from the ground like the seed of Satan."

"Is that a justification? I thought someone with your sensibilities would be more concerned about the Devil incarnate."

"There's nothing we can do about it, so why worry?"

"Because the planet is reaching its boiling point and all life is doomed."

"There are forces in this world too powerful to change."

"Like addiction?" Earl asked.

"Yes. Addiction in its multitudinous manifestations. That's black gold down there. It means jobs and profit, economic stability, mortgage payments."

"It means the end of days."

"Possibly, but we're a myopic species."

"At the meeting, you talked about wants verses needs. You said you judge people caught up in desire. Economic stability is a desire. And the economy is a fabrication. It has no bearing upon reality."

"We need creature comforts to keep our minds stable, Earl. So, we invented a system based on currency and value that affords this. And I do judge. And then I judge some more. But that doesn't mean that I can do anything about the evils of this world."

"Apathy lets evil off the hook."

"It's not apathy. It's homeostasis. I am at peace with the world. And what would you have me do about these problems, Earl? Join rallies? Vote Green? Do you want me to donate to all the charities that stand against sticking needles into the eyes of baby chimpanzees so I can deem myself a decent citizen?"

"At least it's something," Earl said. "Charities are necessary to clean up the mess left behind by corporations run amok. They exist to help heal the planet's wounds and to save the lives of people spat out the tailpipes of capitalist machines. But we need to go further than that. We can't continue to clean up after an ever-escalating scourge. We have to get in front of the problem and tackle it head on."

"These are big themes, Earl. Revolution?"

"Violence is often an answer. And it's happening right now. I know a guy who's orchestrating a global economic meltdown."

"You're thinking too big. At least for now. There's a long dark road ahead and you need to heal yourself before you can heal the planet. You must regain your strength and return your mind and body to equilibrium. Your sobriety must be your priority at all cost. In the meantime, the world can burn."

"And it will burn," Earl said.

"Yes. But you must achieve sobriety before you can examine the problem with clarity. Only then can you don your cape and mask."

Earl felt his stomach rise into his throat as the little plane dropped through an air pocket. He looked at Randolph and tried to imbibe his cool. He watched him flick the glass of his gauges and check his maps. Earl tried to form his opinion of the man but could not. It was shrouded somewhere in the expansive valleys that bridge love and hate.

"Tell me about yourself," Randolph said. "You're a bit of an enigma."

"What do you want to know?"

"Who are you? Where do you come from?"

"I grew up in Toronto. I've lived there all my life."

"Tell me more, Earl."

"I grew up a privileged only child in North York. My father is a wealthy investment banker. He spends his days commuting in his silver car. He doesn't talk to me."

"Is this a result of your drinking?"

"I'm pathetic and embarrassing."

"And your mother?"

"She died when I was young."

"I'm sorry, Earl."

"She had it coming. The only memories I have of her involve eating and flopping around like a walrus."

"You shouldn't talk about your mother that way."

Earl looked at the ferret-gnarled photograph of Randolph's mother that dangled at the front of the cockpit. She was slight, big breasted, and dark in shadow on what appeared to be a glorious sunny day. Her eyes were large and beautiful, but their focus was ambiguous, their intent was distorted through the lens of the camera. "Did you take that photo?"

Randolph nodded. "It was only ever Mother and I. There was no one else to take her picture. You should reach out to your father, Earl. Family is vitally important."

"He wants nothing to do with me. And it's not just my drinking. Our politics are severe and polar opposite. He's anti-abortion, pro-guns, anti-welfare. He's pro-immigration though. He thinks immigrants will bring old-world conservatism with them and drown out people like me. He hates what I stand for."

"What do you stand for?"

"Self-righteousness," Earl shrugged. "Or something intangible that doesn't exist yet."

"Something beyond the status quo?"

"There's no such thing as a status quo. The world evolves too rapidly."

"Your father must love you on some level."

"He loves his silver car more than he's ever loved me. The last time we were together I kicked the tail-lights out of it."

"Your drinking has affected him, hasn't it, Earl?"

"He doesn't understand what it's like. Same as my wife. Ex-wife."

"That's the nature of Earthlings," Randolph said.

"Earthlings?"

"People that can look at a drink and take it or leave it. They can order a beer and abandon half of it on the bar. Their opinion of alcoholics is something we have to contemplate retrospectively during our days of sobriety. Earthlings agonize over many things, but their minds are free of alcoholic obsession. They see a drink as something to socialize around, something to relax with, something to enjoy with a meal. They don't see it through desperate eyes like we do. They cannot empathise with our disease. That's why they will abandon you in your greatest time of need. Tell me about your wife, Earl."

"We were happy once," Earl said. "Our life together was scripted and sterile but that was ok. We did domestic, civilized things. We were routine, neutral, and I was complacent in mediocrity because that's what people do. But things changed."

"You mean your alcoholism escalated?"

"Yes, but I don't know why. If I was molested as a child I could pin it on that. Or if my parents were alcoholics I could at least blame it on something."

"You don't have to blame it on anything, Earl. You were destined to become an alcoholic. Every alcoholic is. It's not a matter of if, but when. You're a young man, Earl. You're fortunate to catch it early."

Earl pulled out a pack of cigarettes. Randolph shook his head.

"The past is gone, Earl. It no longer exists. You have shifted into a new reality and embarked upon a journey into the great wilderness and into the loving arms of sobriety. You will miss your wife of course, but you will also survive. God willing, you will even thrive."

"You make it sound as if I'm cured already."

"You're on your way, Earl. But you have an awfully long way to go. From here on out it's taking things one day at a time. One moment at a time. You will experience much pain, fear and anguish, but you must learn to press through it. Otherwise your sobriety will overcome you."

"Wouldn't that be a good thing?"

"Yes," Randolph nodded, "but only if you can come to terms with the agoraphobia of endlessness. Sobriety must be forever, otherwise, it's only a reprieve. To achieve immortal sobriety, you must adapt to a new universe by shifting your inner defaults. You must reframe your mind and learn to live all over again." He was staring straight ahead at the Rocky Mountains that loomed in the distance. "I had a friend who failed in sobriety. I don't mean he couldn't stay sober, I mean his sobriety killed him. He was a jovial sort which made it difficult to identify his inner turmoil. He was a laugher and a singer. He was a mushroom cloud of charisma, a conversationalist, a polyglot, a cultural chameleon who under-stayed his welcome wherever he went. He attempted to replace his alcohol dependency with social activity, and it ultimately became clear to him that he couldn't stand to be alone while sober. He became reliant on twelve-step meetings and attended as many as he could cram into a day. But not just meetings for alcoholics. He attended meetings for sexaholics, love addicts, hoarders, gluttons, gamblers, smokers, incest and rape survivors, workaholics, asexuals—which he told me are meetings where ugly people get together to commiserate and fuck. He joined dragon boat and ultimate Frisbee clubs; Dungeons and Dragons clubs, chess, anime, and communist clubs. Book clubs, running clubs, foodie clubs. Eventually, he realized that his efforts could not fill the void that alcohol had left behind. He chose not to participate in his existence any longer. He took his own life." Randolph looked Earl in the eye. "There are many dangerous vices in this world waiting in line to empty your soul. The key is to move beyond materialism, temptation and become enlightened, spiritualized. You must disarm yourself against epiphany and divine revelation, and understand that God and temptation are diametrically opposed. One will doom you and the other will absolve you. You have to decide which path to take. But always remember that you cannot live with both. Their colossal polar might would rip your guts to shreds. And it's humanly impossible to survive with neither. You must make a choice."

Randolph pulled his phone from his pocket. It was the latest in technology, fashion and government spyware. "I watch this sometimes," he said, handing it to Earl, "to remind myself why I chose God."

A shaky video played on the screen. It was old with flickering black dots typical of damaged film, but modern technology translated it with clarity. There was a large gathering of people laughing and conversing. Some were singing and all were drinking. Coolers, picnic tables, and barbeques were scattered about the grass. There was a game of limbo with people falling on their backs when the bar got too low. There was a pick-up game of softball. 'Every time you strike out you have to drink,' someone said out of the camera's frame. 'No wait. I change that to every time a pitch is thrown everyone has to drink.' The camera shook violently then recorded the ground, a thigh, the sky, before it panned towards a barbeque where Randolph was flipping burgers. He was a young man. Maybe twenty-five, and very handsome. He wore a summer dress shirt open at the collar where his deep black chest hair tumbled forth. He was talking and laughing with whomever passed by to top up his libation. He held a tall drink on ice in one hand and a toddler in the other. The girl was three, maybe four, with brown curls piled on her head like spaghetti and meatballs. She laughed and giggled every time Randolph tickled her with his whiskers. The videographer dropped the camera and yelled 'Fuck.' Someone else said: 'Watch the language, Granny. There are fucking kids around.' Granny cackled and sputtered before refocusing on Randolph and the little girl who were now joined by a blonde woman. She was tall and beautiful, graceful until she tripped over a cooler and vomited. Randolph helped her to her feet and sat her down on a chair. 'Is mommy sick?' asked the little girl. 'Yes,' said Randolph. "But don't worry, sweetheart." Randolph poured the woman a tall glass of vodka on ice before he refilled his own. The camera moved away with granny, who tripped and fell. She could be heard screaming as the video camera tumbled through grass. The picture went black.

"Granny died that day," Randolph said. "She snapped a rib that punctured her lung. We rushed her to the hospital but she was dead long before we got there. We were all having so much fun—laughing and carrying on like we did at every family reunion. But behind it all, alcohol was doing what it does best to people like us. It was picking us off one by one. It killed generations. Everyone filmed in that video is dead now except for my daughter and me."

"That was your daughter?" asked Earl.

"Yes."

"And the blonde woman?"

"My wife."

"You were married? To a woman? But I thought you were . . ."

"Gay? You can say it. Gay gay gay. Faggoty faggoty fag. It's not a bad word. Not anymore at least. Homosexuality has come a long way in thirty years, Earl. But back then I had to bury it. I had to wear the mask of the alpha male while secretly flouncing my way through life."

"Where is your family now?"

"My wife died not long after that video was filmed. Car crash. Drunk."

"And your daughter?"

"Beautiful Suzie. She paints landscapes and nudes in the Territories. After her mother died, I did what I could to raise her. I did the best job any raging alcoholic could. She ran away at fifteen and I didn't see her again until I got sober. I found her and she forgave me. What a beautiful soul she has. What a forgiving child. And she lives clean and sober. Can you believe it? She broke the alcoholic chain that decimated my family lineage. She lives free in the Arctic Circle with her girlfriend and Inuit son. It's a beautiful life they have. She is my single greatest accomplishment, even though I had nothing to do with her success." Randolph flipped through his phone. He showed Earl a nude portrait of himself standing stoically before a great glacier dotted with trees and arctic fox.

Earl smiled at Randolph as the aeroplane banked north-west. The right wing dipped towards the hard Earth. Earl looked straight down through his side window at where the Rocky Mountain range began its surge into the sky. Randolph pulled the yoke to gain altitude. They rose through wispy clouds. Snow began to dot the plane's glass and creaking metal. It was a crisp,

earthen familiarity that spattered the windows. Earl's nerves still
jangled with pangs of panic, and the diversion of conversation
had ebbed. His mind darted towards its obsession and snapped
shut like a bear trap. He emptied his bottle of mineral water. It
tasted hollow and inane. There was a deep thirst drowning out
his mind and there was nothing in the cockpit to satiate it. There
wasn't a drop of alcohol for unimaginable distances. He thought
about huffing gasoline. He needed a cigarette. He needed to
knock himself unconscious. He could hear a suicidal solution
percolate through his brain. He breathed deeply and tried to calm
his accelerating thoughts—but there was no way this little aeroplane was going to make it up and over the Rocky Mountains.
It was a microbe against the backdrop of ancestral rock behe-
moths, like a satellite moving across the sun. He looked below at
ice and snow covering the jagged rocks that climbed ever higher
into the atmosphere. The Cherokee 108 was hurled through the
sky and its single propeller chopped madly for purchase.

The weather was relatively clement, but inherently zealous
in these irregular undulations at such vertiginous heights.
Swirling winds, born as moon breaths upon the Pacific, made
the most of the freewheeling altitude before dropping into the
endless depression of the prairies. Earl looked at Randolph who
was grimacing and gripping his controls. The veins in his hands
and forehead bulged from his skin like surfacing hydras. "It's
going to be a fun ride," he hollered as they pitched, rolled and
dropped hundreds of feet before regaining control. Earl reached
back for Sigmund who was rag-dolling in the back cabin. He
grabbed his collar and pulled the hulking beast onto his lap. He
wrapped his arms around his panting dog and breathed in his
familiar musk.

The plane crept higher through the wind and thinning
atmosphere. It sputtered and coughed. Earl could see minute
details on the rock face now: ice patterns, sparse vegetation, the
whites of the eyes of mountain goats scattering in fear of the
UFO, their beards whipping in the wind. Randolph jammed the
throttle forward and screamed at the barometer. He was sweaty,
giddy, wild-eyed. He let out a bellow as the plane gave him

everything it could. Then, with the zenith of the continent meters below, he winked at Earl and said: "No problem."

Earl lost his breath as they breached the summit and the world opened up into eternal rock, forest and sky. It was too beautiful to exist. Its scale was too massive to comprehend. He put his hand on his chest and felt the racing of his heart through his breast plate. He wondered what perpetuated and inspired this determined muscle. Was it love? Faith? Desperation to keep up with the immensity of existence? Earl took a breath. Easy in and easy out. He looked ahead at nature's infinity.

As Randolph checked his coordinates and pointed at a landing strip in the distance, Earl looked below and saw a golden eagle stretch its three-meter wingspan to harness the energy of frigid wind blasts. The eagle's crystal vision surveyed the highest peaks of the jagged mountains and watched the Cherokee 180 become smaller and smaller in the distance before it disappeared into the snow-laden forest. The great bird spent the remaining hours of daylight circling and swooping above a natural masterpiece; blissfully freewheeling in a place crafted over eons, where the sky is punctured by spires of rock that steeple from the ground as Earth's dominant plates grind and compress. As the sun began its slow dip into the Pacific Ocean and the shadows of the forest stretched for the mountains, the eagle glided west. Lesser peaks emerged below and small trees began to poke through the snow where soil dusts the rock. The ground flattened out and the trees grew larger and denser until the teeming forests of the British Columbian foothills claimed their borders.

The golden eagle peered through the dense sea of green pine, searching for movement and opportunity. It caught a glimpse of darting black eyes, skipping along the white forest floor. The eyes were erratic, panicked, moving at speed. The eagle dove with its razor talons extended, its mouth open and its eyes intense as the sun. But a lynx broke through the forest cover and pounced, silver on white. It landed with its head in the snow and its legs pedaling in the densely frozen air. It remained there seemingly stuck, writhing, until it emerged with what appeared to be a convulsing snowball in its mouth. With a whip of its neck, the lynx paralyzed the snowshoe hare, which was now another victim of the frozen landscape, brought down by a foe mightier than he. Above, the golden eagle cried and changed course. It returned to the high skies.

The lynx dropped the hare from its mouth and watched it spasm in the snow. Wind threw horizontal snow-blasts over the hare, which stopped moving, save for eyelids that blinked in sad acceptance. The lynx licked the hare and tasted its blood that was the only blemish on the perfect white canvas. Its eyes confidently swept the landscape before falling once again upon the prey. Its jaws closed on the hare, which made a shallow, low groan as the life which once flourished within it escaped like a breath in winter. The lynx lifted its bounty and was gone.

"Did you see that?" asked a man with a beard the colour of thunderstorms. He stood with an awed group of spectators, staring out the window of a tilted cabin that was hemmed by snowed-in garden beds and creeping, barren grape vines. "That was incredible. I'm stunned. I'm shocked. I've never been so excited in my life." The man with a beard the colour of thunderstorms began to dance around the room, warm and snug from a fire that haunted the space with trembling shadows. Between inspirited lunges and gyrations, he said: "What luck has befallen us on this day to see such a miracle? This is a tremendous omen for our adventure. We are the luckiest people on Earth. I haven't seen the elusive lynx in a decade at least. And I've never seen one engaged in such a wonderfully gruesome activity. That hare didn't stand a chance. Could you feel the power of the grimalkin? Goes to show what clean living and fresh air can do for you."

The others in the room looked bewildered as they watched the man with a beard the colour of thunderstorms do the watuzi about the flickering room.

"Come. Everyone around the blue and orange fire. Let's sit and talk. Let us get to know one another a little bit before we undertake such a terrific journey tomorrow in the very early morning." The man with a beard the colour of thunderstorms sat down in the coal-black inglenook with his legs crossed and his back to the fire. He watched the new faces and bodies as they moved from the window and found old chairs and benches made of coniferous lumber, moulted whooping crane feathers, and deer hide. As they sat, dust plumes billowed about and lit up like holograms in the fire light, emanating from a grand fireplace that looked luxurious within the knobbly log cabin that ensconced it.

"You will have to excuse me if I seem a touch peaky," said the man with a beard the colour of thunderstorms. "I'm convalescing from a wicked bout of food poisoning." He patted his stomach. "Now, before we make introductions, let's brainstorm. We shall think up a team name. It will be a sobriquetical representation of solidarity amongst strangers who are currently eyeing each other across this wee room with inquisitiveness. It will bridge the gap between our strange singularities with spider's silk. Peace amongst friends is as beautiful in spirit as the landscapes of this wilderness are in physical prowess, and positively more powerful than any mean force in this world."

"How about Clovis Redux?" a man cloaked in Gore-Tex offered. A band of silver hair was wrapped around his head. His chin was pointy, his nose slightly upturned, his eyes wide and friendly. He was smiling and looking around the room, seemingly poised to modestly accept compliments for his suggestion. He sat snuggled on a chair with a much younger woman, who was equally waterproof. Every time they shifted, Gore-Tex swished. Her head was leaned against his zipper-vented armpit. Strands of her long wheaten hair stood straight up into the air with static electricity. They waved and squirmed each time the man in Gore-Tex jarred her to improve his own level of comfort. She was staring into the fire, watching flame bursts which astringed her pupils. Black speckles orbited these pupils, and dotted her Dutch-blue irises which were feathered with gold. Earl was close enough to realize that these eyes were distant and starry masterworks in inspired colour, bled edges, sprinkled salt.

"Interesting," said the man with a beard the colour of thunderstorms. "But what does Clovis mean?"

The man in Gore-Tex explained with excitement: "The Clovis formed ancient civilizations and are the ancestors of all the indigenous peoples of North America. They are known for the arrowhead fossils they left scattered about the continent. They used these arrows to hunt great beasts like saber tooth and woolly mammoth."

"How mysterious," said the man with a beard the colour of thunderstorms. "How incredibly brave these people must have been. Imagine hunting such animals. The terror of it would bring any mortal to his knees. These people were Gods. Masters of the land. Symbiotic Neopagans. But let's keep brainstorming, shall we. Does anyone have another suggestion?"

A long silence crackled in the fire until someone said: "How about Team Douchebag?"

"Ok then," said the man with a beard the colour of thunderstorms. "Clovis Redux it is. I love it. Thank you for the winning suggestion." He motioned towards the man in Gore-Tex. "What's your name?"

"James."

"Welcome, James," said the man with a beard the colour of thunderstorms. "What brings you here?"

"Well," James began, "I'm here with my beautiful and brand-new wife." He squeezed the taciturn woman in his arms whose expression was inscrutable and diverting. "This is Inertia and we just got married. We're here on our honeymoon."

There was applause and congratulations from the room. Randolph could be heard above the din. "What beautiful news. My deepest felt felicitations to both of you."

The man with a beard the colour of thunderstorms focussed his attention on Randolph. "And who might you be, good sir?"

"My name is Randolph and I have no idea why I'm here." Randolph laughed, rapid and infectious. "I made a rash decision to join my friends Earl and Sigmund on this trip." Randolph laughed again.

The man with a beard the colour of thunderstorms turned to Earl and asked: "Are you Earl or are you Sigmund?"

"I'm Earl. This is Sigmund." Earl reached down from his chair and patted Sigmund who sat at his feet.

"It's a tremendous pleasure to meet you, Earl. And Sigmund too. What brings you here?"

Earl could think of no reason to lie to this group of strangers. He could only think of reasons to lie to people he knew. "I'm here to find sobriety and clarity and any powerful emotions that you may have on tap."

"Excellent," said the man with a beard the colour of thunderstorms. "You will be met with purpose and success in this wonderland of forgiveness. Your cup will overflow with nature's intoxicating brew." He stood and walked over to Earl. His smile a slash in a soiled shag carpet. He bent down to pet Sigmund behind the ear. Sigmund blinked at the strange being that had materialized before him. "I love you, Sigmund," said the man with a beard the colour of thunderstorms. "I'm so glad you brought him, Earl. He will inspire us to consider the wonderful wolves of the wild with whimsical familiarity. We will tie this bell around his neck so he will scare away the big, beautiful, bashful bears before we come upon them. As the planet warms, many are tardy to hibernate and they become cantankerous. Their berries are long gone and the fish are safe in their frigid kingdoms, protected by a frustratingly pellucid mote of ice." He tied the bell around Sigmund's neck. "And hopefully the ringing will attract Sasquatch." He rubbed his hands up and down Sigmund's body and said to him: "Your purity will be our glowing beacon in the dark cold nights. Your playful purpose will be our ultimate inspiration. And you will be a great hunter."

"I don't think he's much of a hunter," said Earl.

"He will be," said the man with a beard the colour of thunderstorms. "For he's a Clovis Redux."

"Do we know each other, Earl?" James asked.

"I don't think so," Earl replied.

"We must. You look awfully familiar. Do you belong to any yachting clubs?"

"I hope not."

"But surely I know you. You're too familiar to possibly be a stranger."

Earl shrugged, willing the wound on his face the power to dissolve.

"And you?" asked the man with a beard the colour of thunderstorms, turning his attention. "What's your name?"

"My name is Kyle. And I still think we should be called Team Douchebag considering how the evening is progressing."

"Why are you here, Kyle?"

"I needed to escape the cellulite flooding the streets."

"So, you want to replace chunkmunks with chipmunks?"

"Exactly. I had to flee the sea of human flesh polluting my field of vision twenty-four-seven. I couldn't fucking take it anymore."

"That may be the greatest reason I've ever heard for why someone would embark upon this journey," said the man with a beard the colour of thunderstorms. "But Kyle, could you please refrain from using the word fuck, or fucking, unless you are referring to copulation in which case it is appropriate. Otherwise, the aggression of the word brings the belligerence of your society into this delicate ecosystem. Let's adopt an intensifier more reflective of our surroundings. How about flower or flowering?"

"I couldn't flowering take it anymore," said Kyle.

The man with a beard the colour of thunderstorms nodded his approval. He looked at the final man in the room. "And you? Tell us your name and story."

"My name is Paul. I'm here to get away from the real world for a while."

"Excellent. Thank you, Paul," said the man with a beard the colour of thunderstorms. "But you will find that you have just entered the real world, and what you left behind is but a cartoon."

"And what's *your* name?" asked Paul.

"My name is Wolfgang Yellowbird," said the man with a beard the colour of thunderstorms, "and I am here to guide you, my intrepid travellers. You are all very welcome at my tilted cabin in the woods. It's from here that we will embark upon our great adventure. Don't drink any alcohol tonight because I need everyone at their most alert in the new pre-dawn." Kyle guffawed and Wolfgang Yellowbird continued. "It is important that we get an early start so we can all witness that around here, the night melts away into soft, buttery morning light. This light is but one of the many steadfast condiments that flavour this forest's magical bedrock. There is nothing better for the soul and there is no better way to commence our travel. Therefore, it is without a doubt imperative to be early risers."

Earl's cabin-fevered alcoholism palpitated with the possibility that there was alcohol on the premises. He tried to push these thoughts away by focussing on the resentment he felt towards the janitor for sending him to this strange place, sparsely populated by strange people. He wanted to be drunk somewhere, anywhere. He missed the accessibility and abundance of urban alcohol, and the justification for alcoholism through billboards, television ads, and plethoric bars and liquor stores that overwhelmed Toronto's downtown landscape. He looked over at Inertia who was in mid-yawn. Or was it a silent scream?

"I am so happy for all of you because you have embarked upon a life changing journey," said Wolfgang Yellowbird. "You have come here as a group of strangers but by the end of this daunting and perilous journey, you will leave as soulmates with a bond as indestructible as lightning."

"Is it actually perilous out there?" asked Kyle. "The brochure said it was very safe and the terrain moderate. That mutant house cat didn't look friendly. And what's this about wolves and bears? And Sasquatch?"

"Danger is in the eye of the beholder, Kyle," said Wolfgang Yellowbird as he eyed the wary man. "Cavernous forests and wild beasts may spell danger to some, but pure, outrageous joy to others. You will have to wait and see if this journey is of a dangerous ilk in your mind's eye."

A Mouthful of Blood

Days of Sobriety: 2

"Awaken, Clovis Redux. New light is creeping upon us." Wolfgang Yellowbird pranced around his cabin in the nude. He hit a rusty pot with a rusty ladle. "James, brew the gourmet coffee that you were talking about last night. The kind processed through a weasel's digestive tract."

Bleary eyes cracked open to view Wolfgang Yellowbird's anus as he stooped to rekindle the cabin's fire that had diminished to embers in the night. He clanged the rusty pot again to ensure that everyone in the room was stirring in the dusty air. Sleeping bags rustled and squirmed in morning consciousness.

"Fuck off, you nasty hippie," said Kyle.

"Flower off," Wolfgang Yellowbird corrected.

Earl did not need the wake-up call. His night had been long and unforgiving. He was curled in a ball with his eyes open, as they had been much of the night. He could not shake away the hideous images that had haunted his darkness.

Many times during the night he had snuck outside to smoke in the frigid air. The trees creaked and swayed like silhouettes of shaggy monsters, lit dimly by a sickle moon. Earl heard distant wolf cries, and the *Who Who Who* of an owl, asking questions of night's introspective occlusion. He looked into the darkness and the darkness glowered back, gauging the potency of the toxins pulsing through his veins. Blood rivers whisked oil slicks from mountain to ocean, deluged lakes with algae blooms, intoxicated hissing trees with carbon dioxide. To be in such a place was not something Earl had yet accepted as he exhaled ghostly smoke into the snow-shrouded night. The picture absorbed through his eyes did not seem real. It felt like a scene from a very distant time;

a future or past when the world was at peace and Earl wasn't a murderer on the lam. He thought that maybe he should kill some more to gain serial killer status. He would be known as The Blackout Butcher: a deranged human mind biding its time in the deep woods.

Earl looked at the moon that floated like a blade in the sky. It was a slash of illumination in darkness, cultivating malignant selenotropic germination. He wondered if James would eventually recognise his laceration and realize he was the murderer depicted on TV. He touched the mess of stitches on his face that caged the killer inside. Was it for pleasure? Self defense? Was it he or the alcohol that killed Murphy? Or a toxic collaboration, conspiring to summon a dormant demon unencumbered by morality?

Sigmund scratched on the inside of the cabin door and Earl let him out. They sat quietly together in their new environment, while Earl's mind wandered thousands of miles away. He probed the blackness of his memory, searching for a flash of a blade, an expression of terror, a corpse in the snow. But there was nothing. Maybe it never happened. Or maybe Samantha had killed Murphy. She framed Earl to achieve her ultimate revenge and knockout punch. It seemed unlikely to Earl that she possessed such criminal guile, but it wasn't outside the realm of possibility. She could have been planning this for years, patiently calculating the demise of her husband, eroding his will, encouraging his self-loathing, accelerating his downward spiral by constantly replacing the bottle of rye in the kitchen cupboard. Was her manipulation responsible for his feelings of worthlessness and despair? Was it because of Samantha that he couldn't function as a productive member of society? He couldn't hold down a job. He was an under-achiever in every aspect of his life. He felt no pangs of aspiration. He had no self-worth. His existence was grey and devoid of colour. And why did she so readily provide his picture to the police? Why *that* picture, taken when he was happy and healthy in the summer sunshine? It was probably to remind him of their era of relative contentment, a time of marital partnership, when Earl and Samantha would spend their weekends together wandering the city streets and trying out new coffee shops. "Ooooh, let's try the Rwandan blend," Samantha would say and then complain it was too bitter. So they ordered something Columbian to take aboard the ferry to Toronto Island, where they sprawled naked upon the fine sands of Hanlan's Point. Samantha would playfully flick Earl's penis. Her red hair dazzled in the sunlight and her freckled body was a mosaic of constellations that Earl enjoyed mapping along the contours of her breasts and bottom, and around the corner towards her flaming supernova. They watched well-endowed gay men trawl the beach for ass. Techno beats blared at the volleyball nets. Human walruses unfurled their globs of lard beside uninhibited female beauties who were elfin by comparison and lounging in clusters, rolling deeply bronzed bodies like dripping rotisserie meat. Pink parts flashed for the eye of the opportunist as they settled supine. Bubble-gum nipples, hot and gelatinous under an azure sky. Men with good etiquette submerged their erections. Naked children rollicked in the shallow waves. A curious toddler reached for her father's penis. Boaters looked through binoculars at the sea of human flesh, and fully clothed creepers prowled the tall fescue. Samantha giggled. "All shapes and sizes," she said.

Sunburnt, Earl and Samantha would board the late ferry back to the city and head for a smoky-blue bar in the Esplanade where lone musicians sat on stools and crooned deprecating songs. They drank beer. Samantha said: "You look good in this blue light. You should have been a smurf." Earl replied: "I am a smurf and you're my smurfette. That blues guy is Gargamel. He's going to smuggle you off in his guitar case. I'll miss you. And I'll curse that rotten Gargamel for the rest of my life."

"Would you move on?" Samantha asked.

"Eventually. But I would always worry about you."

"You would have to trust that Gargamel was caring for me."

"Could you ever be happy with Gargamel?"

Samantha looked at the musician. "I could."

"Are you sorry that you never slept with anyone else before we married?"

"Yes."

"Me too."

Earl stroked Sigmund's back and pondered why he had never cheated on Samantha. It wasn't a matter of loyalty or fear of being caught. And like every human, Earl was a hyper-sexualized primate, aroused by the slightest of notions. But he was racked in the societal chains of monogamy and sexual properness that stemmed from jealousy: a highly evolved emotion rooted in fear of sexual inadequacy. The real reason behind Earl's chastity was that he was intimidated by the sexuality of others. He only knew Samantha's sex and this crippled his confidence. He had no experience in adapting to new sexual situations so he lacked the courage to seek out physical contact. But the cloying desire was always in his mind. Ever since Earl's teenage lust for Samantha had burned off, his sexual desire had forged alternate cranial outlets—often freaky and outlandish, sometimes romantic. Always desperate.

Earl stood up and led Sigmund back inside the tilted cabin. He lay down and closed his eyes. His muscles twitched and nausea came and went.

In the darkness, alone with strangers in a strange place, his imagination was assaulted by demonic alcoholic spasms in flickering horrors and tortures. A picture show, on a glossy black canvas spattered with dripping yellows and reds, plastered the walls of Earl's skull and choked the flow of life through his medulla oblongata. His brain churned and blended to a pulpy pink puree in which an old giraffe ran against wind and sleet and was decapitated—its neck crudely severed above the shoulders by a flame-red manta ray that shot through worm holes in the pulpy slurry. The giraffe's neck squirmed with dying nerves before it stopped rigid, its eyes wide and its tongue hanging into red dirt. The body kneeled as if in prayer as a blood fountain sputtered. The manta ray crashed in an explosion of cartilage that swept over a diameter of melted flesh and blew open the side of Earl's skull, shooting bone shards into the cabin's fire.

"These are hallucinations, Earl," Randolph purred into his ear. "Everything is ok. Your heart is still beating."

Earl reached for Randolph but he had vanished into a mass of wet women, scrubbing chrome and steel with soapy suds. Their tanned skin glistened between small slashes of clothing that bounced with their breasts and slipped inside their buttocks when they bent over buckets of hot, soapy water. Earl watched as they laughed and threw suds at each other. They hollered delight until the soapy water turned vitriolic and their flesh melted into heaps of smouldering gruel and hair.

"Is your heart still beating, Earl?"

Earl didn't know. He was distracted by the stirring in his loins. He looked down and watched his penis elongate twelve feet, grow scales, and wriggle into the air above him where it spread a narrow hood around its coffin-shaped head. It opened its ink-black mouth, exposing two-inch fangs dripping with venom. It hissed and coiled. Muscles rippled along its shaft. Then it struck at Earl's throat and face, injecting a profusion of necrotic poison that corroded his flesh into bubbling globules, constricted his oxygen, and dissolved his spine. It reared up again, stretching to its full height before plunging into Earl's chest, cracking through his ribs and grinding them down to ivory dust. Earl could hear the slick sounds of his innards as his penis dislocated its jaw and consumed his heart.

Earl opened his eyes and slunk outside for a cigarette.

The caffeinated group emerged from the tilted cabin in the forest. Earl was glad that Wolfgang Yellowbird insisted on a very early start so he could distance himself from the horrors he had witnessed in the night. The patter and spray of heavy snow clumps falling through branches could be heard all around them. The weight of the forest emerged from the darkness as morning light sprang through the cold air, igniting breath mists. The air grew orange and tingled with energy as the sun peeked its fire above the Rocky Mountains. "Look at that," Inertia said. "It's like a giant rubbing the shoulders of a mammoth." A clear blue sky opened up above them.

"Thank you for that decadent coffee, James," Wolfgang Yellowbird said. "I've tried growing coffee beans in my garden but they don't seem to take in this climate. I have everything I need here, but I must admit that I sometimes desire the luxuries of the tamed world, alien and unnatural as they may be. Speaking of which, may I have one of your cigarettes, Earl?"

Earl sparked his lighter for Wolfgang Yellowbird as he watched Inertia up ahead. She raised her arms and jumped into the air. Her face was alight as she pirouetted. She said: "It's as if God herself is ejaculating huge globs of seraph dust all over us. Look how it's matting in our hair and fur." She looked up at the trees, then added: "and fir." She laughed. "This light makes me think of lava flows on distant planets."

"Try to keep your emotional outbursts in check, dear," James said. "As the only female representative here, don't you think you should act respectably?" He got no reply. Inertia bounded ahead with Sigmund who kicked up powdered snow and pine needles in energetic bliss. He proudly ding-a-linged his new bear bell.

"I do apologize," James said to the others. "Her exuberance lacks masculine reason."

Wolfgang Yellowbird gave James a befuddled look and Randolph said: "I don't think there's anything to apologize for, James."

"She is still young and will mature in time," James continued. "I will have to persevere in the meantime. I only wish she would find direction. She spends her days at home working on her creative projects. It's a cute hobby but the problem is that she obsesses over it as if it's important. She needs to . . ."

James was drowned out by Sigmund's barking, his face the picture of primal joy as he jumped and rolled with Inertia. He stopped to lick the blood mark in the snow where the snowshoe hare had taken its last breath the night before.

Wolfgang Yellowbird passed them to lead the way. He was dressed like an earthen wizard, in a brown cloak with a hood that lay slack and wrinkled around his neck. He walked with his spear lashed against his back and a knobby staff that left a holy trail in the snow. His beard, that was the colour of thunderstorms, was multi-purposed. It provided voluminous insulation and doubled as a facial fanny pack in which he stored his compass and snacks. Honey candies protruded from his beard and looked like fluorescent boils growing like fungus in nutrient-rich soil. Occasionally he would pluck one from his face and pop it into his mouth. "The jolts of energy they give me are as intense as their flavour," he declared. He led the group deeper into the wilderness and the tilted cabin disappeared from view behind thick towers of pine. "Would anyone care for one?" Wolfgang Yellowbird asked.

Inertia eagerly plucked a honey candy from Wolfgang Yellowbird's beard. She put it in her mouth and let it rattle around her teeth.

"I make them myself."

Inertia's eyes grew wide. "The sweetness kicks up my endorphins like dust."

"I harvest the honey from my bee hives," Wolfgang Yellowbird said. "They are so generous with their golden honeycombs. Did you know that the industrious honey bee only lives for six weeks? And in that infinitesimal lifespan they produce only one-twentieth of a teaspoon of honey? Think of the amount of effort and death it takes to fill just one honey jar. And of course, it's taken for granted. Nature strains to produce its magic and humans just eat it all up. People give no thought to the toils of nature. One appreciates the food one eats much more when one hunts and harvests one's own." Wolfgang Yellowbird poked the snow with his knobby staff. "There is a path here that I've beaten down over the years, but we can't see it for the snow. Don't worry though. I know this land as well as the beasts that inhabit it. I know every frozen creek by its ice texture and I know every tree by name."

"What's this tree's name?" asked Paul.

"That's Bruce," replied Wolfgang Yellowbird. "And this is Seymour." He knocked on the bark as if to see if anyone was home. He pointed. "And that spiked power plant up ahead is Jesus."

"You spiked it?" asked Paul. "And why did you name it after Jesus?"

"I didn't name it *after* Jesus. It *is* Jesus. As I said, I know this land very well, and it knows me. We have the same mother after all. No need to leave a trail of crumbs. But do leave a trail of essence. That way, none of you will ever be forgotten by these woods."

"I think I'll deposit some essence right now," said Kyle. He unzipped his pants and urinated upon Jesus. Inertia laughed and James reddened.

"Well done, Kyle," said Wolfgang Yellowbird. Kyle zipped up and they continued toward the impassible mountain range that stood monumental to the east, but shrouded by forest.

"Where's your gun?" asked Kyle.

Wolfgang Yellowbird swung around and peered at him. "To what end would I require a genocidal agent? Do I look like someone hell-bent on wiping out all life on Earth?"

"Surely we need protection. The brochure said that this trip was safe."

"It is safe, Kyle. The beasts are not here to harm us. This is their home and we are their guests. They're very hospitable you know."

"But the brochure said—"

"Forget the brochure, Kyle," Wolfgang Yellowbird said. "That thing is something made up to lure people like you. It doesn't mean anything here. It's something imaginary from the land you have left behind. What's real is what we see around us." Wolfgang Yellowbird patted the trunk of a tree named Penelope before continuing onwards. "We are as safe as the wilderness allows us to be. And that should be comfort enough for you. Now, let's keep going. We have much ground to cover today."

Kyle followed and said: "That's real reassuring, Wolfiebird."

Randolph passed Jesus with his eyes gawking upwards, his mouth open and his eyes wide. The great tree towered above the forest canopy, clutching thousands of tonnes of caught snow in its branches. Its trunk was twenty-meters across, and it groaned deeply in a strong breeze, communicating to its colony of squirrels one· thousand, nine hundred and eighty-five years of accumulated wisdom. Randolph said: "Look at the beauty around us." His slack jaw widened. "How can this be?"

"How can what be?" asked James.

"How can you not fall to your knees and wonder? What kind of design is this? What kind of masterpiece?"

"This is nature's way," said Wolfgang Yellowbird. "This is the power of it."

"Yes, nature," said Randolph. "But what else? Who else? This cannot have just happened. Who planted the seeds of this forest?"

"There are no answers to such questions," said James. "So why do people keep asking them?"

"Because it's the meaning of life, James," Inertia retorted. "How can people not ask these ancient, primeval questions? What's the point of existing without wonder of the great unknown?"

"These questions are too big for you, Inertia," said James. "It's silliness."

"I don't understand how you can endure yourself. If I were you I would have killed myself long ago." Inertia stared at her husband's Gore-Tex back and his crown of silver hair as they ambled single file. His cranium's half-moon turned to face her.

"I'm sorry, honey, but I'm right. These are not things worth worrying about. It will only cause stress, dear."

"Don't call me dear. And don't call me honey."

The group moved on in awkward silence before Kyle said: "So, Paul. You must be a sports fan."

"What? Why?" Paul asked, adjusting his thick orange-tinted glasses that blended with the morning light. His eyes were magnified like a gecko's.

"Your clothes, genius. You're draped in vintage sportswear."

Paul looked down at his Starter jacket with the Vancouver Canucks logo circa 1993 emblazoned on the back. His sun-bleached Buffalo Bills earmuffs sat on his head awkwardly. The high-top Air Jordan sneakers that he wore had little basketball pumps on the tongues and were full of snow. "I hate sports.

What a stupid question." Paul turned his attention. "Hey Wolfgang Yellowbird, do you think we'll run into any Happy Rainbow Energy personnel out here? My radio said they're increasing their security presence in the area due to eco-terrorist attacks."

"We'll run into them," Wolfgang Yellowbird replied. He looked Paul up and down. "You're dressed poorly for this terrain."

Earl struggled in the rear while his herd proceeded into the day. His lungs ejected black tar and his muscles burned with slag. The snow was heavy. His vision was unreal. The sparkling brightness was painful. He needed God to dim its intensity, or dim the anxiety it incited within him. Each time he stopped to vomit, Randolph rubbed his back and the others waited patiently.

They stopped to rest and eat by a small frozen waterfall that hung like a memory. Cold days had slowed down the stream's flow and crystallized it until its ultimate ice-over. The water's meandering pilgrimage to the Pacific had been put on hiatus.

Randolph, James, Kyle and Paul enjoyed an impromptu potluck, while Wolfgang Yellowbird whittled a fresh branch and sang a song:

When the moon, is shining high,
And the trees, yearn for the sky,
Oh how I'll cry, oh how I'll die,
When you come home to me,
Come home to me.

When your spine, is lying broke,
The forest looms, but for the smoke,
The flames pour by, oh how you'll die,
When you come home to me,
Come home to me.

You're too far gone, too far to see,
And you'll think, think of me,
I will die, oh how I'll cry,
When you come home to me,
Come home to me.

But in this place, in this life,
You're too alone, to be my wife,
Please let me know, when I die,
If you'll come home to me,
Come home to me.

Earl sat on a stump and swallowed. Sulphuric blooms escaped his stomach. The heat was corrosive in his throat. He watched Inertia's wheaten hair and soft face in the full midday light. She was sitting in the snow away from the group with her legs crossed. She was hunched over a notebook, writing with a pencil. Earl stood and moved to her. He sat beside her, careful not to guide his breath in her direction.

"I wrote a poem," she said. "Would you like to read it?"

Earl nodded.

I'm envisioned by no one in the night,
Who tastes me until morning light?
I bestir to no one,
But I feel his needling upon my naked skin.
Night became a blanket of snow,
An icefall silty in my mouth.
My ardour will echo from tree to tree,
Frozen between his vision and me.

Earl read it twice. "What's the point of poetry?" he asked.

Inertia smiled. "To preserve moments," she said. "Moments are all we have. They are fleeting milliseconds that build our world. Poetry traps them in bell jars for others to see."

"What about stories?"

"Stories are different. They run head-long into the unknown universe while poetry introspects. Are you a reader?"

"I used to be." Earl remembered his days as a bibliophile, when the decision over which book to read next held great importance. Countless hours were spent in bookstores, where he slunk through the fiction section, pained to narrow down his choices. He brought his new books home to cherish like dependents. The arrangements of his collection were tidal and influenced by the gravity of many competing moons. He ordered them alphabetically by author, or chronologically. He divided them by genre, sub-genre, geographic or emotional setting, author nationality, author politics, author socio-economic class, author gender, author sexuality. He arranged them in order of descending emotional impact, strength of dialogue, description, characters, prose. His bookshelves were fluid mosaics made of small rectangular universes. Ever expanding. Never contracting.

"Why did you stop?" Inertia asked.

"Alcohol turned my imagination to stone."

"Do you remember any of the stories you read?"

"Yes."

"Tell me one," Inertia said.

Earl mined his memory, hoping for the haze to clear. "I once read a book about an innocent sent from the heart of the world to save humanity." Earl struggled for details. "He was a creature. A munchkin with angel wings. He could fly, but not very well. It was more like bouncing than flying."

"Like a chicken on steroids?"

Earl nodded.

"Who sent him? From the heart of the world?"

"Others like him. His elders. They feared the end of times."

"Did he succeed?" Inertia asked. "Did he save humanity?"

"He failed."

"How?"

"He tried to get his message across through spiritual rock music. He emulated Jesus and John Lennon, and his band was successful. People bought into his plea for world peace and ecological harmony. They were drawn to his message and his strangeness. And he ignited a great international groundswell that demanded change. But this threatened the global corporate hegemony. He was captured and experimented upon. They fried his brain and concluded that he was an extraterrestrial bent on human destruction. They locked him up in solitary confinement. He was able to escape but he couldn't cope. He tried to get home but his mind was too damaged to remember where he came from. He fell victim to temptation. He became addicted to drugs and pornography. He became a murderer and a rapist. His semen was phosphorescent."

"That reminds me of Frodo Baggins."

"Phosphorescent semen?"

"No. How innocence can be corrupted."

"Frodo became deranged with power," Earl said. "In this case it was vice and primitive desire."

"It sounds like a good story. The best art questions morality. What happened to the mystical munchkin in the end?"

"He died. Shot by police with a bazooka."

"And what about humanity?"

"We continued living as we do, harming ourselves and others, and destroying the planet."

"So, the mystical munchkin wasn't sent to save us from an outside threat. He was sent to save us from ourselves."

"Yes, I suppose so," Earl said.

Wolfgang Yellowbird's voice boomed across the snow. "Arise you slothful sinners. Let's get a move on."

As they stood Inertia asked: "Have you ever tried writing?"

"Yes. But only sophomorically."

"It's cathartic, isn't it?"

"I enjoyed your poem," Earl said. "I'd like to read more."

Inertia smiled. Her cheeks speckled rouge through the wheaten hair that draped across her pale face.

As owls began to hoot questions in the tree tops, and darkness spread through the forest in a way that reminded Earl of encroaching doom, Clovis Redux set up camp.

They sat huddled around a fire that Wolfgang Yellowbird summoned from bark chips, dollar bills and flint.

"Are you burning money, Wolfgang Yellowbird?" James asked.

Wolfgang Yellowbird ignited spark showers with his breath and squinted his sun creased eyes against the growing heat. "Indeed, I am," he said.

"Why?"

"To start a fire so I can cook dinner."

Flames spread and engulfed a small pocket of oxygen. They consumed crackling twigs and discarded branches. Soon the flames were towering and distorting the forest through heat waves.

"You could have used it to buy dinner," James said. "That's what civilized people do."

"I have no use for your civilization, James. I have all I need here in the forest. My garden keeps me full of berries and vegetables in the warm months, and the forest provides me with bush meat in the cold."

"You know burning money is illegal?"

"Call the police!"

"I can't get any cell phone reception out here." James shook his head. "Why did you charge us for this trip?"

"To spark this fire, James." Wolfgang Yellowbird held up a burning bill so the others could watch Queen Elizabeth melt in polymer. "Also, to take your foul cash out of circulation so it can no longer do any harm."

"Harm? Do you mean the harm that allows people to buy food and shelter?"

"Yes. That harm exactly. That people must be *allowed* food and shelter, but only if they can afford it. Money is the perfect representation of our human shortcomings, James, because it is designed to be hoarded. What people don't understand is that we can all be happy if everyone has *enough*. But greed is as much a part of human nature as love and wonder. We strive to multiply wealth only to learn that this does not multiply happiness. Rather, it leads to destitution in others."

"You're a ridiculous man, Wolfgang Yellowbird."

"No, I am not."

"You shouldn't have charged us if your motive was so absurd."

"James, would you accept a free guided tour of the wilderness?"

"Of course."

"From a stranger?"

"Well . . ."

"It sounds sketchy doesn't it? As if I was luring people into the wilderness to sodomise them. But fear not." Wolfgang Yellowbird chuckled. "I'm just a pseudo-hermit with a penile disposition in need of some company."

"Do you get lonely out here on your own?" Inertia asked.

"It's not loneliness I feel, Inertia. It's omniscient aloneness. And this is a gift. For in this verdant expanse, I've learned great lessons in solitude. I've found many answers by gazing at my soul. The way it absorbs colour and light. Why it trembles in absolute quiet. How it escapes my fragile confines to flit about the planet only to return to me with greater knowledge." Wolfgang Yellowbird stared unblinking into the fire. "But I admit that I sometimes miss contact, intimacy. I yearn for the scent of my other." He glanced around at the flickering faces gazing back at him then sprang to his feet. He referred to Sigmund as the K-9 unit. "Come. We have little time before we are all consumed by darkness." He disappeared into the trees with Sigmund bounding along beside.

James looked around the fire and asked: "Is it just me or does anyone else think Wolfgang Yellowbird is a little off?" When no one replied he added: "Can we trust him?"

"He's just a nasty hippie," said Kyle.

"But can he keep us safe? We are putting an awful lot of faith in a guy we know nothing about."

"It was your idea to come on this trip, James," Inertia inserted.

"I imagined someone a little different."

"What did you expect?" Paul asked. "He lives by himself in the middle of the woods, completely cut off. He's bound to be odd."

"I thought he would be more like a lumberjack," James said. "Or a frontiersman. But instead, he's a lunatic who lured us here to burn our money."

"It's not our money anymore," said Paul as he threw a snow-covered log on the fire. Water vapour hissed. "It's his. He can do whatever he wants with it."

"But doesn't it seem crazy to you?"

"Not in this context," Paul replied.

"What context?"

Paul widened his gecko eyes, surveying primitive surroundings. "This context," he said.

Four snowshoe hare dangled from Wolfgang Yellowbird's hand as he returned to the fire. Sigmund's snout was red with blood. His grin was crazed.

"Sigmund's a natural," said Wolfgang Yellowbird. "He ravaged that warren with terrifying blood-lust. I told you he was a hunter, Earl. I could tell by his keen eyes."

Wolfgang Yellowbird shucked root vegetables from severely recycled mason jars as he prepared roasted hare stew with wild mushrooms in a pear cider broth. "The Dalai Lama once said, 'Approach love and cooking with reckless abandon.'" Wolfgang Yellowbird jumped into the air, performing 360 seasonings. He flashed his genitals with karate kick herb drops. "The historical fabric of this forest is as bloody as it is ancient. If you will allow it, this old raconteur would like to share a chapter."

"Are those mushrooms safe to eat?" asked Kyle.

"Yes. But I have a different batch that will turn your world slanted and electric if you're interested."

"What about food poisoning? You said last night that you had food poisoning."

"That's nothing to worry about, Kyle," Wolfgang Yellowbird assured him. "That was the consequence of a very peculiar food experiment."

Wolfgang Yellowbird stirred his cauldron, releasing the ambrosia's aromatics that made mouths water and stomachs bubble. He hung the hare hides from a tree branch. "Once these have dried, I will use them to fashion you some suitable footwear, Paul." He asked Kyle for a drink from his whiskey bottle.

Earl watched the bottle pass from hand to hand like an oil tanker stalking inlets. Accessing it would require covert movements in the night. He could feel Randolph's eyes on him.

With the exception of James, who sat snuggled between Inertia's legs, and Sigmund, who lay curled around his teddy bear, everyone had their back against a tree trunk. They encircled the fire, comfortably mesmerized by the flames, excited for delicious food after a long day's march, and subdued by Wolfgang Yellowbird's voice.

"This forest was unmarred by human ambition until the early eighteenth century when intrepid British wayfarers happened upon it. In the dead of a night like any other, while these trees stood silent and resolute, a British legion embarked upon an imperialist crusade, launching their vicious whaleboats from the Port of London's drizzly moorings. They massacred their way across the Atlantic Ocean and around Cape Horn, wiping out entire pods and flaying plundered blubber tonne by tonne. They sailed north, finally alighting where the city of Vancouver teems today. By the hundreds they chomped their way northeast, through tree, river and mountain until they reached this forest's southwestern flank.

"Native peoples would not come here because they knew of the danger that dwelt within. Ancient stories had passed through the generations, warning of a great and wary power. But the British marched oblivious into what lay in wait. Such is the nature of imperial arrogance. The great British Empire never heeded whimsical, savage folklore. They brushed the natives aside, spewing small pox and ginger warts. And they broke the dense epidermis of this dark wood.

"The bumbling incision of boots and the grinding of steel horseshoes on rock sliced and echoed deep into the forest, turning the ears of beast and tree. It cut the darkness within, swirling sounds and blackness. Little did the British know as they trounced along confident in destiny that their feet were sending tectonic warnings towards the heart of the forest. It was in this nucleus that Sasquatch clans began to gather with breakneck urgency. At the first sign of the intrusion, the Sasquatch Overlord let out a clarion call to arms that spawned avalanches in the east.

"The Sasquatch defence was exact. And the forest was cleansed.

"One Briton survived, however. He broke the Sasquatch ranks on horseback and galloped back the way he had come. As the Sasquatch bellowed their victory and devoured human flesh, this man blazed from the forest, heading for the coast and his motherland. He reported to King George I, who in response, ordered an army of twenty thousand of his finest redcoats to follow the survivor back to this forest to rain vengeance in the name of God and country.

"The Great Sasquatch War was long and brutal. The Sasquatch held the early advantage, utilizing guerrilla warfare to whittle down the numbers and fortitude of a formidable opponent. The telluric horde overwhelmed the British who were disembodied in a strange land, uselessly firing their muskets into the trees, screaming at their ghostly enemy. They listened helplessly to the distant cries of their compatriots as they were torn limb from limb, their bodies crushed by boulders, and their skulls split by the blows of tree branches. The Sasquatch used camouflage and manipulated sound and light, picking off stragglers, defectors and defecators. They stalked the edges of the firelight, tearing out the throats of the night watch and smothering soldiers in their sleep. They set ghastly traps that saw soldiers fall hundreds of meters through the forest floor, or catapulted a kilometer through the sky, or decapitated in the blink of an eye by a chiselled granite slate. And they would bombinate in the darkness, their guttural drone unleashed an insanity upon the redcoats. It was an all-consuming noise that crippled their minds, confused their bearings, and incited murder and cannibalism.

"It was the infected mind of the original survivor that turned the tide of the Great Sasquatch War. He lit himself on fire to quell his madness, which coincided with a tremendous windstorm of biblical proportions. Fire proved to be the Sasquatch's greatest fear, and their Achilles' heel. It spread far and wide, scattering the Sasquatch and burning them alive. They panicked and lost discipline. They attacked the British head-on only to be cut down. In spite of their own charred casualties, the British took advantage. Their assault was a bombardment and their momentum was unrelenting.

"The Sasquatch fought bravely. Females joined the defence and reinforcements arrived from the American northwest. They battled the redcoats back, hurling boulders and swinging branches. They clobbered the British legion, but their numbers fell too low. And ultimately their firepower in open combat proved too effective. The Sasquatch were wiped out with grenades and continuous volleys of artillery fire. Their mighty bodies were blown to shreds.

"Of the twenty thousand men sent by King George I, only fifty survived. They rounded up the remaining female Sasquatch with their young and burned them together in a pit of fire. The Sasquatch Overlord was the last to survive. He was forced to witness the eradication of his kind before he was beheaded. His head was delivered to the King.

"It is said that the war wiped the Sasquatch population from the face of the Earth. But I know some still remain. The slaughter created a fearful pedigree that exists deep in this wood, shy and elusive. They are here, shrouded in mystery."

"Have you ever seen one?" asked Inertia.

Wolfgang Yellowbird paused before answering. "I've heard their songs," he said. "I thought I caught a glimpse once, but it vanished into space before I could be certain of what I had seen."

Kyle coughed up whiskey and asked: "What kind of acid are you on, Wolfiebird?"

"A concoction I blended myself but would not recommend to virgins of the forest." Wolfgang Yellowbird stirred his cauldron. "The food is ready. Dig in! Eat! Gormandize!"

Clovis Redux eagerly obliged.

Kyle swigged his whiskey and stared at Earl. "How about it, Scarface?" He offered the bottle and Earl reached for it.

Randolph shot to his feet and Inertia interjected: "How dare you, Kyle." She wrestled herself out from underneath James and grabbed Earl's outstretched hand, pushing it away. Earl felt a subtle squeeze and a brush of her thumb before she let go and returned to her food.

Kyle took another drink—slurping, obnoxious—and told everyone to relax.

Earl put his hand in the pocket of the janitor's winter coat. It was warm in there, cozy even—a sharp contrast to the cold that stung his cheeks—but he preferred the feel of Inertia's mitten. He had sensed the power of her body beneath it. A singular strength, unique in the world. It was a wisdom of sorts, feminine and resolute, transferred through gesture, a tiny shared moment, invisible in plain sight. The woolliness of the mitten hid her hand, but he could still perceive it. Cold, dry, fidgety. Always feeling, searching, relaying secrets to her brain. Secrets about him? Secrets of passion? Pity? Stillness? He sensed her irenic energy. It was the kind that threatened fire. She was an equator between antipodes, capable of tilting the planet towards lightness or dark. Earl knew which direction she would choose. War is over, he thought. Give peace a chance.

He looked at the bowl of food on his lap. It reminded him of writhing disembowelment. Hot and steaming, fresh from the gut. As he snuck his stew to Sigmund, Wolfgang Yellowbird asked: "Is everyone enjoying their meal?"

Sigmund barked and heads nodded in agreement.

"It's exquisite," said Paul. "It's magic. What's your secret, Wolfgang Yellowbird?"

"It's nature's secret, Paul. That's a question for the Earth."

Paul chewed and said: "There are many questions I've asked the Earth. But I've never received a satisfactory answer."

"Can we please not get into this again?" asked James. "I want to enjoy my meal without being inundated with hippie psychobabble."

Paul continued: "For example, why does the Earth allow humans to rip it apart? Surely it possesses a mechanism for self-preservation. Why not wipe us out?"

"Like the dinosaurs?" asked Inertia.

"Don't encourage him, honey," said James.

"The Earth didn't wipe out the dinosaurs," Paul said. "They were killed by a space rock sent from the other side of the universe. That was beyond the Earth's control."

"Maybe the Earth still has hope for us," said Inertia. "We're still evolving."

"No, we're not," said Paul. "We're devolving. We have transcended evolution and this is what separates us from nature. We have reached a level of technological advancement that has slowed down our brains. We no longer have to worry about our next meal or fight for a sexual mate. We don't have to be physically strong. We don't even have to think for ourselves. Everything is offered to us, and everything is done for us. Our adaptation is now guided by neural and cerebral atrophy. A hundred years from now we'll all be massive drooling amoebas."

"You're grossly generalizing, Paul," said Inertia. "Not everyone is like that. Not even close."

"But the vast majority is. And it's the behaviour of the majority that determines genetic trajectory. We're evolving badly." He pointed at a light-seeking moth incinerating itself in the campfire.

"Why would the Earth kill us off if it can just wait for us to destroy ourselves?" Inertia asked.

Paul nodded. "One has to wonder what the point of it all is."

"The point is to exist," Earl said.

The others waited for him to continue but he did not.

"What do you mean?" prodded Inertia.

"Exist in the present. Like animals do. Not get depressed about the past and anxious of the future. Or worry about what's happening in all corners of the globe. We try to control everything but we can't because everything is indecipherable. We should paganise the world. Get back to the elements."

Kyle sputtered. "You all need to chill out with the metaphysical."

"That's my point," said Earl.

"Is this a personal mantra?" asked Inertia.

"No. It's something I thought of right now."

"Do you think we're here for a reason?"

Earl shrugged.

"Do you believe in God?"

"I believe in something," Earl said. "But I don't know what."

"You will, Earl," said Randolph. "For God reveals himself on an individual basis. One soul at a time."

"For the love of God," said Kyle. "I'm going to go piss in the woods."

"You're not going to find the love of God in there," said Paul.

"He might if he looks," said Randolph.

"There's no God," said Paul. "Only Mother Earth."

"Semantics," Inertia said.

"Shhhh, dear," said James, unspooling a meter of dental floss and wrapping it around his fingers with practiced vigour.

"Thank you, Inertia," said Randolph. "For God's grace is different for everyone."

"I think you're right," Inertia said. "God can influence us however she pleases."

"Honey, stop."

"But it also depends on our individual acceptance of God," said Randolph.

"I don't think so," said Inertia. "We don't posses the power to influence God's will. We might have the arrogance to think that we do, but it's a delusion."

"But we do possess the agency to accept or dismiss God," said Randolph.

"God holds all the agency," said Inertia. "She sparked the universe."

"Then what sparked God?" asked Paul.

"I'm just about sick of this," said James.

"Shut up James." Inertia stood. "I can't stand the sound of you." She walked to her tent.

Kyle stumbled back from the trees and into the firelight. "What's the chick's problem? I bet it has something to do with bloody Old Faithfuls spewing from her blowhole."

James stood and took a swing at Kyle, knocking him to the snow. He knelt down and punched him in the eye.

"Separate." Wolfgang Yellowbird sprang to his feet and swirled his knobby staff, bending a spectrum of firelight that flashed like butterfly wings. Two days later, a slow turning pair of category five hurricanes, named Deirdre and Clive, would spawn in the Atlantic Ocean and submerge the southern United States.

Earl felt a presence outside his tent. A breath fell hard and dewy against the canvas. A crunch of undergrowth underfoot. The displacement of snow. A grin through a mouthful of blood.

He lay inside his sleeping bag. It was Randolph's and hotter than hell. The brown fabric was heavy and moth-bitten, and looked as though it once belonged to a soldier in the Canadian First Battalion. The tent was equally antiquated, plucked from a dank corner of Randolph's basement. Earl had wrestled with it for over an hour, trying to discern the tarp from the tent, connecting inelastic tent poles, aligning shredded flaps, finding makeshift stakes to root it in the ground—only to find that he had assembled it inside out, and the entrance zipper was rusted shut. "Let me help you," Inertia said. She cut a slit for him to use as a door. Meanwhile, the others presented their tents with the flick of the wrist, and unfurled their sleeping bags from sausage-sized capsules.

Earl shifted his cramped, itchy body. Sweat slid between his thighs. He reached out to pet Sigmund who was sound asleep after a vigorous round of teddy bear humping. He listened to the radio drone emanating from Paul's tent. The hourly news was on. Death, disease, blight. The Amazon jungle was all but slashed and burned. Planetary poles continued to thaw. People were murdering each other at the bequest of their personalized God. The newsman's voice was lugubrious, flagging, confounded.

Kyle began to snore as he fell into the depths of a blackout. His whiskey burned at the forefront of Earl's mind. He yearned to sup the warmth from it and feel its downshifting reassurance.

This was no longer a place for sobriety. He could never be sober again. He needed Kyle's blackout, complete darkness, cognitive exile. Earl removed himself from the sleeping bag and slid outside.

A shadow moved above him, blocking out the stars before lifting into the trees. There was a thrashing of branches before a fading nocturne eased itself into the distance. *My heart is still beating.* Sweat turned icy on his skin.

He moved towards Kyle's tent. The crunch of his footsteps was loud in the snow. He passed Wolfgang Yellowbird who was quiet under his makeshift lean-to, but his eyes were open and sparkling. Earl inched himself closer until someone appeared at the edge of the dying firelight. It was Randolph, moving with similar stealth. Earl pulled back into the dark and watched as Randolph looked to the stars and blew breath mist into the sky. He looked around. He was listening, watching, thinking. Then he began creeping. Creeping towards Kyle.

Randolph slowly unzipped the tent and entered. Then slowly zipped it shut. Earl heard the swishing sound of sleeping bag movement. Kyle's snoring stopped. He groaned and said: "Get off me, man."

"It's ok," Randolph whispered back. "Just go with it."

"I said get off me."

"I said go with it."

Earl listened as similar sounds began in James and Inertia's tent. Swishing goosedown. A bedding's lust. James's heavy breathing. Earl imagined Inertia's exposed body. Her pale skin's glow under moonlight. Her breasts bouncing with each thrust. He wondered about her pubic hair; its scent, its coarseness. Did it match her wheaten hair? He heard her groan and imagined the suppleness of her bottom, her inner thigh against his tongue, the muscles of her anus constricting around his finger.

If lust is a hunger, then sex is a meal, Earl thought. Love is only an ingredient. It adds flavour but isn't necessary. Earl never had sex with Samantha after they fell out of love. If passion remained it was trumped by awkward repulsion. But there was a time. He remembered the day he picked her up in his first car. A Toyota

Corolla. It was lime green with a rusted skirting. The rear bumper was dented and loose, igniting sparks off the asphalt when he geared up and jammed the accelerator to the floor. There was freedom in that car. Open highways that crisscrossed the world lay before him. The day was hot. The sky was massive and aqueous. He had just turned seventeen. He pulled up to Samantha's driveway and she jumped down the steps, laughing and singing. Her smile was as big as he had ever seen it. She got in the passenger seat and pointed north. Earl drove fast. Destination, cherry pop.

They blazed up Bathurst Street, swerving their way through taxis and SUVs, pushing through yellow lights, laughing at funny pedestrians, kissing with each pigeon sighting, singing along to Smells Like Teen Spirit that blasted from the crackling speakers, until the thoroughfare wound its way out of the city, and narrowed into a two-lane dirt road. It was in the back seat of his Corolla that he entered her. He came immediately. So did she.

Now Samantha was beyond the curvature of the Earth, three hours ahead in time. It was the dead of night in Toronto. She would be sleeping. Or was she lying awake? Wondering what went wrong and why her husband broke beyond repair. At least she's alone now, free of Earl's emotional abuse. His monstrosity. His spiritual affliction. What would she think if she knew he was sober? Standing in a snowy forest amidst the sounds of sex, feeling regret. Regret for how he treated her. Regret for hurting her. Regret for his addiction and how it ruined their love for one another. But Earl knew she wasn't thinking of him. She was thinking of Murphy. She was making love to his ghost. Her naked body writhed as the spirit moved over her, through her, caressing every cell in her body.

Paul's radio was playing classical music now and Kyle's snoring had resumed. Earl crawled back into his tent. He got in his sleeping bag and took comfort in Sigmund's heavy breaths. He closed his eyes but sleep wouldn't come. It remained distant and impossible. Somewhere deep within himself existed the gentle tugs of slumber, waiting to pull him downwards. But they would remain submerged on this night, beyond the tapestry of Earl's swirling thoughts.

Outside his tent the presence returned. But it wasn't alone this time. There were two breaths. One large and one small. Slow, deep breaths. Easy in and easy out.

Days of Sobriety: 3

Earl begged for an ounce of sleep. A dribble of it. But there was no one to implore. The weariness in his mind was a weight behind his swollen eyes, and when the light of morning inflated his tent and Sigmund stirred beside him, he was reminded of halcyon days, when life felt unassailable and the future hinted at illumination. He was warm then. He was optimistic. He wasn't brittle and hardened by ice.

Sigmund's yawn was contagious. Earl felt a great intake of oxygen that squeaked against the grip of his throat. He heard the ocean in his ears. His jaws clicked. Stars shot like water spiders across the pools of his eyes. He watched forming shadows squirm like snakes between the folds of his sleeping bag.

A clanging pot and a choir of birdsong demanded the day's commencement. Sigmund bolted through the slit in the tent, barking at the world. Earl stuck his head outside and lit a cigarette. He watched Sigmund and Wolfgang Yellowbird pandiculate beside a new fire. Coffee water began to boil inside an atmosphere of wood smoke that was thick in the early-morning air. It crept into the trees like fog, feeling for deep roots and pressing itself into textures of bark. The forest stood still and watchful, patiently absorbing the pollution through snow-laden branches.

Sigmund barked and chased his tail and Wolfgang Yellowbird mimicked him. His earthen cloak bounced and swayed, rocked and rolled. Its movement rivaled the intensity of his expression. He began to sing:

"Sigmund wakes up every morning, as horny as can be,
But he knows the Lord's unfair,

His testicles still won't be there,
The Lord's not good to Sigmund,
Johnny Scrotal seed, Amen."

Wolfgang Yellowbird cupped his mouth with his hands and trilled violently in high octaves of escalating passion. "Treeleeleelee treeleeleelee." He looked over at Earl whose head was poking from his tent.

"Merry Christmas, Earl, and good morning," Wolfgang Yellowbird said. "And what a good morning it is, would you not agree? Notice how the monarch orange light of morning dances in iridescent tandem with blue snow and green tree. Look how the world about us is illuminated after so many hours of darkness. And see how my tit songs have attracted many amorous birds." He pumped his arms like wings and pranced a self-propulsive prance. "With morning comes great vigour."

There were birds all around the encampment, hopping on branches, twittering, and fluttering in and out of Wolfgang Yellowbird's beard. They were the size of mice and very active. They were pale green mostly, streaked with red and white from their necks to their tails, and their heads were the most brilliant yellows, oranges and blues.

"Did you hear Santa Claus whip by in the night to bring cheer to the children of the world? What a strange character he must be," Wolfgang Yellowbird said before he cupped his mouth again. "Treeleeleelee treeleeleelee." He bent himself at the hips and leaned towards Earl until their noses were inches apart. Earl's cigarette smoke twisted through his alliaceous breath.

Wolfgang Yellowbird's earthen cloak swirled about in a small breeze as he eyed Earl with a look of supreme confidence. He was a man in his element, completely unfazed by the enormity of his surroundings and at peace in his body and mind. He said: "I say, Earl, with your head sticking out the bottom of your tent like that you look like a bleary-eyed tortoise without purpose. But I won't allow you to mope around. No sir. Not on a morning like this. Come out of there because I require your assistance." He plucked the cigarette from Earl's teeth and finished it with one massive inhalation. He flicked the butt into the fire and exhaled a thick exodus of tobacco smoke.

Earl crawled out of his tent like a thirsty rat. His breath was woody and steamy like a dragon's. "What can I do for you this morning, Wolfgang Yellowbird?" he asked.

Wolfgang Yellowbird put a row of protruding sunflower seeds across his pressed lips. Tits darted in and out, fluttering madly and throwing feathers into his beard as they kissed him to remove their breakfast. From the side of his mouth, as if he was smoking a pipe, he said: "Grab that butterfly net." He motioned towards a net that leaned against a tree trunk, while a multitude of tits affronted his face. "Quickly, Earl. Pick it up."

"What am I supposed to do with it?" Earl asked.

"Smack me in the face with it. Wind up and wallop me a good one. Hurry now. My seeds are diminishing at an alarming rate."

Earl looked at the butterfly net as if it was insane.

"Don't think. Act."

BAUTISTA WITH A DRIVE, Earl thought, as he wound up and swung. The net suddenly took off as two tits rocketed skyward.

"Do the twist," Wolfgang Yellowbird bellowed, now using the full orifice in his face.

Earl clenched the net handle and twisted his hips as the panicked tits strained skyward and screamed: "TWEET TWEET MOTHER FLOWERING TWEET."

"Not your hips, Earl. The net. Twist the net."

Earl finally interpreted the screaming warlock and twisted the butterfly net's handle to secure the tits inside the mesh. Earl looked down from the sky and saw Wolfgang Yellowbird grinning at him with wild eyes. Sigmund was jumping and barking in front of Inertia, James, Randolph and Paul who had emerged from their tents to see what the cacophony was about. They were all laughing and twisting their hips.

"Shut the flower up," moaned Kyle from inside his tent.

Wolfgang Yellowbird lined more seeds across his lips and said: "Right, we need about a billion more tits and we'll have ourselves a feast."

"I can't believe you people are eating sky rats," Kyle said.

"And I can't believe you're barfing on such a terrific morning," James said. He put a juicy pair of tit breasts into his mouth. "You should never drink an entire bottle of whiskey in one sitting."

"Shut up, you yuppy slut," came Kyle's response.

"Say, Wolfgang Yellowbird. What's the plan for Clovis Redux today?" asked James.

Nibbling, Wolfgang Yellowbird replied: "My friends, it's an intrepid itinerary: first we must amble for several hours through dense forest before we reach midday and break for snacks. Then we will scale the steep and craggy Black Ridge that bridges these woods and The Old Growth Crystal Valley where fairies go to die at the end of their centuries of life. If we are lucky perhaps we will meet one. We will make camp deep in the Crystal Valley. Very deep. And I have an extracurricular activity planned for us along the way."

"Sounds wonderful," said James. "By the way, this is absolutely delicious, Wolfgang Yellowbird. You're quite the gastronome."

"Thank you, James. I'm glad you're enjoying my Christmas morning meal of garlic stuffed tit skewers with a side of jellied turnip and soft-boiled turkey vulture eggs."

"Vulture eggs?" James spat.

Heads turned towards ruffling noises that came from inside Wolfgang Yellowbird's lean-to.

"Alas," said Wolfgang Yellowbird. "Have coons breached my fortress' defense?"

Kyle emerged from the makeshift shelter with alarmingly large pupils. One eye was purple and badly swollen. "Here we go," he said.

"Kyle," Wolfgang Yellowbird boomed. "Did you get into my LSD?"

"It's coming on fast," Kyle said.

"Of course it is, Kyle," Wolfgang Yellowbird said. "It will overwhelm you. It wasn't designed for virgins of the forest."

Paul sat at the edge of the fire and fondled his Buffalo Bills ear muffs. "What's that?" he asked, pointing at the ground around Earl's tent.

"I was hoping someone would notice," Wolfgang Yellowbird said. "I didn't bring it up myself because I didn't want to alarm anyone, but it seems we had a curious pair of visitors in the night. They would have been getting a sense of us, figuring out what all you alien beings represent. A reconnoitring mother and child. See how one set of footprints is the size of snow shoes and the other snow shrews? This is good news. It means they're procreating."

"What are procreating?" asked Paul.

"Sasquatch."

Earl's honeymoon with meat protein was tumultuous at best. Instead of a beach-side love shack, surrounded by golden sand sparkling with sunshine exploding off the ocean under palm trees swaying in a gentle breeze, it was a gastral tsunami. Earl had never been to the sea, but as he followed Clovis Redux through the woods, he imagined submerging himself in the endless waters. Around him swam cichlids and sea turtles, a living rainbow of sea life. Flashes of yellows and orange. Every possible shade of blue. The impossibility of the cuttlefish. He could taste the briny liquid and feel its great weight upon his body, pulling him downwards, always downwards, until the sunlight faded into the black depths of the ocean where Earl opened his mouth and drank until the ocean was dry. He could happily ingest this ungodly volume of liquid, but a morsel of bird flesh was enough to twist his stomach into steel wire cable. This reaction was as much psychosomatic as it was physical. His job had required him to administer doom to entire populations of animals with the tap of a computer key or a scratch of a signature. The only authority he had in life was to propel the hell on Earth that is factory farming. He would try not to think about it. Or convince himself that he was not responsible. But he knew that he was to blame for every cry of horror and ending of life. Each individual animal was another notch of vicarious trauma, breaking down his emotional control, welling up his eyes. Twenty thousand pigs the spreadsheet would say. One hundred thousand chickens and ten thousand cows—half of them calves. His coworkers would often make jokes to mask the horror of it, the way paramedics joke about mangled corpses. 'When will we stop eating so much bacon?' Bossman once asked. 'When pigs can fly . . . So . . . you know . . . they'd be harder to catch . . . So . . . harder to . . . ahem.'

The meat Wolfgang Yellowbird offered was different. It had belonged to animals that were wild and free. Earl had eaten the muscles and tissues that gave them the strength to thrive on this planet the way they were intended to. But even though their flesh didn't come shrink wrapped, Earl's reaction was still rejection—a hot, chunky spew that steamed upon the snow.

His nausea subsided for a short while, and despite malnourishment and debilitating fatigue, there was a jangly vigour in his limbs. He attributed this to his liver, which had taken a breath for the first time in years. He felt a calming of his heart and coldness in his lungs as he took deep breaths of air. He trailed Clovis Redux, but not by far. They did not have to stop often for him to catch up. And he might have even enjoyed the morning amble through the forest if not for Kyle's shrieks: "The forest is melting." And, "There're miasmas of skulls in the bark." Kyle darted from tree to bush with twisting expressions of disarrangement. "What the flower am I doing out here in the middle of the wilderness? Did you see that? There are Elmos in the trees. They're hopping about. Look. That Elmo is albino. The rest are blood red."

"You should save some energy, Kyle," Wolfgang Yellowbird said. "We have much to accomplish today. Everything is as it must be. It's just the acid getting a hold of you. I designed it to last for many intense hours so the best thing for you to do is remain as calm as possible within your epidermis. Don't try to fight it. Just go with it."

"Rapist," Kyle yelled. "Rectal prolapse." He climbed upon a low tree branch and lurched himself into a snow drift. He sank up to his neck and screamed: "I'm being eaten."

"You're a maniac, Kyle," James cajoled. He laughed as he helped free the terrified man from the snow.

Randolph joined Earl at the caboose and asked: "How are you feeling, Earl?"

"Ok," said Earl. "But there's still a strong chance of implosion."

"I'm not surprised to hear that, Earl. Your alcoholic mind is doing everything it can to make you feed it. It's hurt by your betrayal. It will use sickness and insomnia as weapons against you, for it has yet to successfully kill you. It will weaken in time, however, so you must keep fighting."

"That's the only choice I have. I think Kyle finished all our booze in one gulp."

"It's for the best, Earl."

"How did you cope with detox?"

"I used my addictive personality to improve myself rather than destroy myself. In doing so I was lucky enough to come down with a serious case of obsessive compulsive disorder. And I was able to replace the void that alcohol and drugs had left behind."

"What did you do instead?"

"Many things," said Randolph. "I thoroughly cleaned every inch of my home until every surface squeaked. I exercised an unhealthy amount. I read War and Peace in three days. Moby Dick in two. I watched the entire filmographies of Joaquin Phoenix and Meryl Streep. I took up axe throwing. Became obsessed with live theatre. Bought a PlayStation, a juicer, an array of herbal teas. I made a point of flossing twice a day."

"You make it sound easy."

"It surely wasn't."

"Suicide is easy."

"It surely isn't. You mustn't think that way, Earl. I promise you there's a river of joy flowing underneath it all."

Earl shrugged.

"Are you glad we came on this adventure, Earl?"

"I think so. Are you?"

"I am," said Randolph. "My soul has never been touched with such great intensity before. I'm in a constant state of awe. Thank you for giving me the opportunity to join you."

"I'm glad you're here, Randolph."

"How is your soul feeling, Earl? Is it surviving amidst your inner tortures? Can you feel it yearning for meaning?"

"It might be lost."

"That's ok. It will come back when it's ready to tell you what it has found. It will burn through your depression and show a new path. My soul is joyous. And yours will be too. I have found true glory out here, Earl. I've found but another example of the grace of God."

"That seems to be an underlying theme out here."

"It's a theme in everything everywhere."

"Does God have a plan for me?"

"God will provide answers if you ask the right questions."

"Will God tell me what to do and where to go?"

"God will guide you."

"I have no life to go back to, Randolph."

"I know, Earl."

"I don't think you do."

"Yes, I do. I saw your picture on television. It's such a handsome picture of you, Earl."

"You knew? Why didn't you turn me in?"

"You're not a killer, Earl. You're a gentle soul. Alcohol killed that man."

Up ahead, Wolfgang Yellowbird said: "We have reached the Black Ridge which separates us from the Old Growth Crystal Valley."

"Good God," said Kyle. "Its size. Its blackness. This is surely a mountain of doom. Look at the pastel boulders tumbling down the craggy ridge. They must have formed in the eighties."

Wolfgang Yellowbird said: "We will switchback up and then switchback down the other side. But first we must break for lunch."

Randolph sat down beside Earl and told him to close his eyes. "Meditation will cleanse our bodies of fear, quell our anxiety, and rid us of doubt. As you drift away, Earl, know that I am proud of you. Remember your strength and courage. Take them with you as you journey inwards along your spiritual path.

"Life is a universe of love and delight, freedom and opportunity. And we are all interconnected, sharing with each other the passion of existence. As your mind quiets and your body stills, your busyness will deactivate and you will become a recipient of peace, healing and meaning.

"Notice how quiet it is. Notice how the cold feels against your skin. Notice how your body relaxes as your muscles and nerves melt into the snow. Notice how your mind has simply let go."

Earl felt gentle tugs of slumber. Randolph paused for several minutes. When he continued his voice was so soft it could hardly be perceived.

"There is a sanctuary of absolute stillness. It has always existed and will forever more. You can sense its wisdom and see its beauty as you approach. You absorb its calmness and breathe its air. You can taste its ancient musk. Its stillness is palpable, its power perceptible. You have become immersed in the sanctuary of absolute stillness. You feel it around you, within you, all through you, now and for eternity. You have been welcomed and beckoned inside. Where do you go? What do you see?"

. . . When Randolph's voice brought Earl back to the forest, he realized that the others had joined in meditation, and that he had ejaculated in his pants.

Inertia was smiling at him. It was a toothy smile. The kind of smile that forces other smiles. She held his gaze for as long as he allowed her. Had they shared cerebral coitus? Had their thoughts entwined in the treetops, leaching secretions into one another, dripping down the branches like sap? He held her gaze once more. This time it was Inertia who looked away.

"Well that was an awful use of valuable time," said James.

"Wow," said Wolfgang Yellowbird. "You sent me around the world, Randolph. I solved mysteries. I climbed mountains. I lived for thousands of years. How did I travel so far? How can I possess such power?"

"We all possess great power," Randolph said. He leaned towards Earl and whispered into his ear: "A healthy libido is a sign of a healing mind." He patted Earl on the back as they got to their feet. Earl was thankful that the janitor's coat was long enough to cover the stain on his crotch.

"It appears Kyle is in a coma," Wolfgang Yellowbird said. "If the LSD's power has shifted from electricity to atrophy, then he could be out for some time. Probably for the best, because the acid in his mind would surely compel him to explore the Black Ridge's darkness." He strapped Kyle's dead-weight body to his back using leather twine and carabiners. Kyle's head lolled like and infant's. Wolfgang Yellowbird motioned for the others to follow.

The ascent was often a scramble on hands and knees. The Black Ridge was steep and treeless, which caused mild agoraphobia in the minds of Clovis Redux, who had grown accustomed to tunnelling through heavy forest. Earl felt ethereal under the open sky, as if the sudden absence of tree cover would send him floating away to a world even stranger than this one. He removed his mittens and placed his hands upon the black icy rock. He sensed the solar heat within it, a millennium's bounty of stored energy spreading deeply and charging the churning heart of the Earth's core. He looked ahead, watching the others struggle for footing. Each step seemed a risk. Randolph slipped on a patch of ice. His knees hit the rock face and he began to slide backwards. He let out a shrill yelp as Paul grabbed his coat sleeve and pulled him to his feet.

"Bless you, Paul," said Randolph. "I must say that this seems like an unnecessary danger."

"We must be wary of crags for they are numerous and bottomless," Wolfgang Yellowbird said. "I've seen many poor beasts fall into blackness here. But we must move forward, for this is the most efficient as well as the most inspiring route to our destination."

Earl crab-walked from where he knelt and stuck his head inside a dark scar in the rock face. It was pure black and the air inside was very cold. It smelled of decomposing flesh. "It's a tomb," he said.

Wolfgang Yellowbird said: "Let's keep moving, Earl. The Black Ridge is too dangerous to lollygag upon."

At the Ridge's apex their eyes gazed to the east. A heavily treed valley spread before them like the greatest shag carpet. It was a hinterland braced for ruination. Hewn as a single organism, it stretched into the distance, until the Rocky Mountain Range exploded from the horizon—kilometers high and white with snow.

"Surely that's the end of the world," Paul said. "It doesn't look real. It looks like macro-art." His gecko eyes bulged behind the lenses of his glasses, inflated by the spectacle before him. They darted from sky to rock to forest, then rested upon a grey snake that slimed and slithered from beyond the mountains and through the trees towards them. "Is that the Happy Rainbow pipeline?"

"It is," said Wolfgang Yellowbird, rubbing his hands together. "It's about time for our extracurricular activity."

They slid and skidded their way down the eastern slope of the Black Ridge to the forest floor of The Old Growth Crystal Valley. It felt colder than the west side, and more oxygen rich. The trees were denser and they cast more shadows. Earl peered through the forest but the light quickly turned deep green then disappeared into black. There was more forest noise—an acoustic wall of sound that could be heard above the group's crunching boots; chirps, growls and purrs amidst the hissing and hushing of wind in trees. As they moved forward, Earl watched the others look left and right, up and down, their heads on swivels as they ambled east into the darkness. He wondered why, with the countless measurements of forest surrounding them, Sigmund had to be right in his feet.

Up ahead, still dangling from Wolfgang Yellowbird's back, Kyle squirmed into consciousness. As his eyes adjusted to his surroundings, his face contorted into a slash of terror. "What the flower?"

Wolfgang Yellowbird unstrapped him and held him by the shoulders. "How are you, Kyle?"

"I was in a sanctuary of stillness."

"And you still are, but this one is made of trees."

"How the flower did I get here?"

"Clovis Redux brought you. And everything is alright. Everything is magnificent. I'm going to need you to hold it together for the next little while." Wolfgang Yellowbird looked around at the rest of the group. "That goes for all of you."

Wolfgang Yellowbird beckoned the group to follow as they resumed their march. He said: "While corporate demons and mugwump politicians are squabbling with environmentalists and Indigenous peoples, Happy Rainbow Energy rages on with its pipeline expansion through this pristine valley. As we speak, the tar sands beyond the Rockies are bubbling and shooting their poisons westward through serpentine death conductors and into delicately balanced ecosystems like this one. The infection has reached the coast where it's spreading out to blacken the world. Happy Rainbow has been victorious over the forces of good. Therefore, it has become necessary for some clandestine action on my part."

"What do you plan to do?" asked James.

"Quiet now, everyone. No speaking," said Wolfgang Yellowbird.

The group crouched behind a tree line that opened up to a clearing where the pipeline stood, hideous and unnatural. Earl looked at the sky and saw a circling unkindness of ravens. They cawed and clicked to one another, discussing the activity below.

Wolfgang Yellowbird sniffed the air as if reconnoitring through scent, then moved into the clearing. He put his ear to the pipeline and listened. He turned back to the group and said: "The Happy Rainbow security people are not far from here. I can hear their television squawk sluicing through the bitumen. It sounds like pornography. They must have built a new outpost nearby."

"So, what?" James asked. "Why are we here?"

"Remain patient and quiet. We will soon be back on our way, wandering through this glorious valley," Wolfgang Yellowbird said. He placed his palms onto the cold pipeline. He closed his eyes and breathed heavily.

As they moved slowly beside the pipeline, the chugging of a generator slowly became audible. The unnatural sound grew louder and louder, becoming more alien with each decibel. When the outpost came into view, Wolfgang Yellowbird motioned for the others to get back behind the tree line. They obeyed and watched as Wolfgang Yellowbird crouched and crawled towards the building. From his cloak he removed three sticks of dynamite.

"No," cried James. "I will have no part of this."

"Shhhhhhh." Wolfgang Yellowbird's expression was severe, ordering absolute stillness.

Kyle began to hop with excitement. He looked like he might explode. Randolph put his hand on Kyle's head and rubbed his back.

Wolfgang Yellowbird nodded at Randolph and stuck a joint in his teeth. He lit it, then attached the dynamite bundle to the outpost wall. He squinted his eyes against the skunk smoke and trailed a long wick into the forest. He crouched where the rest of the group waited. "You might want to cover your ears, every-one." He used the cherry of his joint to light the fuse, sending sparks racing towards their mark.

James jumped up and began stomping on the accelerating flame. Wolfgang Yellowbird wrestled him back to cover.

"Are you mad? You'll get yourself blown into the next universe. It's inextinguishable. It's an unstoppable force in motion."

"You're a psychopath," James hissed. He said something else but was muted by the explosion.

"A supernova!" Kyle screamed.

And then shouting from within the rubble.

"Survivors," Wolfgang Yellowbird yelled. "I wasn't count-ing on flowering survivors."

Clovis Redux darted into the forest. Earl felt Randolph's hand clutching his as he looked back to see black smoke rising above the trees where the ravens still wheeled and watched.

"Keep running," said Wolfgang Yellowbird.

"They'll be able to track our footprints in the snow," said Inertia.

"Good point," said Wolfgang Yellowbird. "Maybe we should split up to confuse them. Scatter like hatchlings, everyone. When the coast is clear I'll make tit calls. Kyle, you stay with me because you're deranged."

The group splintered into the woods. They could hear Wolfgang Yellowbird behind them calling: "Whatever happens, do not get caught. You'll be crucified for this. Take extreme measures if necessary."

Earl scampered through the snow with burning lungs. Randolph was still clutched in his grip. He coughed up battleship grey tar and kicked up snow. Sigmund barked at his heels. Trees whipped by. He heard shouting through the forest. Ravens screamed. Then rifle shots.

"Dear God, no," Randolph cried.

Earl pulled Randolph to the side and the two men crouched behind a bush. Sigmund followed, growling. Earl put his hand on his snout and heard the crunch of snow beneath big boots. It grew louder and slowed from a sprint to a walk. "I'm on to you." The man's voice was deep and powerful. It seemed to come from the tree tops. He moved closer, and closer still. Then unbearably close. He stopped in front of the growling bush that puffed plumes of breath vapour. "Come out," he said.

Randolph's expression was a question mark of terror. His eyes were huge and staring, pleading for help. He looked at Earl. Earl shook his head.

Rifle shots blasted above their heads. Randolph covered his ears and Sigmund dropped to the snow, quivering.

"Come out."

They slowly emerged from the bush. Their eyes squared on the big man. Half his face was covered in soot and there was blood on his sleeve where shrapnel had torn into his arm. His breath was heavy.

Sigmund bared his teeth and growled. The hairs around his neck and shoulders bristled on end.

The man pointed his rifle in Earl's face. He was a head taller than Earl and dressed all in black. The Happy Rainbow Energy logo was emblazoned on his breast. "Get on your knees and put your hands behind your head." Earl and Randolph complied. The man moved behind them and bound their hands together with white plastic zip-ties.

Randolph began to cry. "Please, sir, we had nothing to do with this. We didn't know this was going to happen."

"Shut the fuck up. Stay still while I take care of your bitch."

"He's not a bitch," Earl said. "He's male."

"All three of you are bitches." The man pointed the rifle at Sigmund and loaded the chamber.

Sigmund cowered. He whined and lowered his head.

"Relax, pooch," said the man. "You won't feel a thing."

Earl sprang to his feet and charged the man. He head-butted his collar bone and felt bone snap against his temple. The man cursed and slammed the butt of his rifle into Earl's face, exploding the scar stitching. Blood sprayed from the split wound and into the big man's eyes. He stepped backwards and rubbed at his face. Sigmund lunged. He sank his teeth into the man's leg and ripped off the calf muscle. He tossed it into the snow and went back for more, this time into the bone and nerves. The man screamed and fell on his back. Sigmund went in for the kill. He tore at the throat and opened the jugular. Sprinkler shots of crimson painted the white snow around him with abstract gore.

Sigmund went to Earl and chewed the zip-tie off his wrists. Earl got to his feet and walked to the fallen man whose eyes were blinking. He was mouthing words but no sound came. Earl watched the flow of blood from the man's throat diminish to a trickle. His eyes went still. "You killed him, Sigmund."

They heard a cry nearby and Earl ran towards it. Through the trees he could see Paul on his knees with his hands in the air. A rifle was pressed against his head.

"You can beg all you want but I'm still going to kill you. I've been ordered to kill terrorists," a Happy Rainbow man said.

Paul whimpered. "Please don't."

"Where do you want it? The forehead? How about through the eye?" He pushed the rifle muzzle against Paul's chest. "The heart?"

"Please," whispered Paul.

"The heart it is."

Paul closed his eyes.

Earl charged. He hit the man from the side, knocking him to the ground. Sigmund leaped at him as he fell to the snow, ripping off half his face with his canines.

Paul grabbed the fallen rifle and Earl called Sigmund off. Sigmund let go of the man and sniffed around for the severed face. He began to eat it. His jingling bear bell reminded Earl that it was Christmas Day.

The Happy Rainbow man got to his knees. His fingers traced along his exposed jaw and cheek bones, and poked at his empty eye socket.

"We should tie him up," said Earl. "Maybe we could use—"

Paul pulled the trigger.

Earl didn't have time to avert his eyes before the man's head exploded and skull shrapnel peppered the bark of a white aspen.

Paul was smiling. His vivid eyes burned through his orange tinted glasses. "Have you ever experienced such a thing?"

"I'm not sure," replied Earl.

"I can see your teeth through your cheek, Earl."

Earl looked at Sigmund who was masticating the corpse's face and licking his nostrils to clean them of blood. "We should find Randolph."

Randolph had his eyes closed. He was sitting in the snow where Earl had left him, gently rocking back and forth. Sigmund chewed the zip-tie from his wrists and regarded the corpse that lay beside him.

"We have a massacre on our hands," said Paul.

Earl knelt down beside Randolph and watched as the unkindness of ravens descended from the sky to pick apart the bodies, one small mouthful at a time.

Gunshots blasted in the distance followed by Wolfgang Yellowbird's, "Treeleeleelee treeleeleelee."

"Is everyone accounted for?" asked Wolfgang Yellowbird.

"Yes," said Inertia. "But no thanks to you, James. You abandoned me." She pushed James and slapped at his face.

"I'm sorry, honey," said James, holding up his hands in defense. "I thought you were right behind me."

"Bullshit."

"I'm so sorry, dear. I panicked."

"Not good enough, James." Inertia spat. "You left me to die. I had to smash a man's head with a rock."

"Is Kyle ok?" asked Paul.

"He was shot in the shoulder before I jumped from a tree branch to subdue these folks," said Wolfgang Yellowbird, motioning towards two Happy Rainbow security guards tied to a tree with rope. "But he seems to be taking it quite well."

Kyle was bleeding heavily and prancing about the captives like Wolfgang Yellowbird's little helper.

"Where are the others?" asked one of the Happy Rainbow personnel. "What did you fuckers do to them?"

"My guess is that we have killed them, my good sir," said Wolfgang Yellowbird. "Inertia, did you kill that man?"

"His head split open."

"Did anyone else subdue a foe?"

"I killed one and Sigmund another," Paul said. His smile had turned lurid and his eyes smouldered.

"I thought so," said Wolfgang Yellowbird, "considering how you are all dripping with blood. We'll leave them out there for the scavengers."

"You people are sick," said the Happy Rainbow man.

"It's not sickness," said Paul. "It's anarchy."

"Indeed, it is," said Wolfgang Yellowbird. "And you two should be grateful that you can enjoy life a little bit longer. You were all supposed to die in the outpost. My dynamite is getting old, I think."

James was staring at Earl. He watched as his teeth glinted through the open wound and blood dribbled down his chin. "I *do* know you, Earl. You're a wanted criminal. A murderer."

"That's some good sleuthing," said Earl.

"You're *all* a bunch of murderers." He looked at Inertia. "Even you. Come. We're getting out of this place and going to the police."

"I'm not going anywhere with you," Inertia said.

"Come, dear. We will tell the police that we were put in an extreme situation by these psychopaths and you were forced to kill out of self defence."

"I *did* kill out of self defence."

James grabbed Inertia by the wrist and dragged her in the direction of the Black Ridge. "I have to get you to safety."

"No. Let go of me." Inertia pulled at her arm and kicked up snow in defiance, but James's grip held strong and he separated her from the rest of the group.

"Leave her, James," Earl said.

"With you people? I don't think so."

Inertia wrestled her arm free and ran towards the others. Earl stepped in front of her and braced himself for the charging James. He leaned into James with his shoulder when they collided and caught him hard on the jaw. The blow forced James to the ground, rendering him momentarily stunned and giving Earl a chance to land several punches before Wolfgang Yellowbird pulled him off.

James got back to his feet and grabbed Inertia again. This time by the hair. He pulled her away as Earl intercepted. He punched James again. Solid. James fell back. Blood seeped from both nostrils. Inertia kicked him twice in the ribs.

"Easy now," said Wolfgang Yellowbird. "It's time to let James go his separate way."

James stood and spat blood into the snow. He looked over the group and the two Happy Rainbow personnel. His eyes rested on Inertia. "Please come with me."

Inertia looked away.

James picked up his backpack, turned, and walked west.

—

The others stood at a short distance and watched as Wolfgang Yellowbird circled the two captives. One was large and blonde. There were tears in her eyes and her face was flushed. The other was slight and rat-faced. His breath steamed in steady rhythm. His eyes were transfixed on the hunting knife in Wolfgang Yellowbird's hand. He said: "You don't have to kill us."

"But you have to die," said Wolfgang Yellowbird.

"We have families."

"And you feel this gives your lives value, but you're mistaken." Wolfgang Yellowbird pressed the knife against the ratty man's throat. Their eyes were level and blinking. Their breaths mushroomed as one into the low branches above. "The devil's proxy has no value."

"We will leave. You'll never see us again."

"I cannot see a benefit in this option," said Wolfgang Yellowbird. "If you live, you will spread death." He increased the pressure on the knife, causing a ribbon of blood to eclipse the blade.

The ratty man began to tremble. His breath struggled through his quaking diaphragm.

"Your deaths will be an example to those who are raping this sacred valley. Your corpses will be symbols of defiance against the hand of evil that clutches for purchase in the roots of these trees." Wolfgang Yellowbird removed the blade from the ratty man's throat. He wiped the blood on his earthen cloak. "But I am grateful for your sacrifice. And I will let you choose how you wish to die. You can choose an instant and painless death by my blade, or you can choose death by exposure."

"Exposure," said the blonde woman. She had ceased crying and now sat calmly.

"This is the better choice," said Wolfgang Yellowbird. "Prolonging your existence, no matter the suffering, is always preferable. Will it be the cold do you think? Or will the wolves have a go at you?" Wolfgang Yellowbird turned to join the others. "Maybe a sasquatch will drop by to crush your skulls."

"The blade," said the ratty man. "I choose the blade."

"Your fate has already been decided. Merry Christmas to you and yours." Wolfgang Yellowbird led Clovis Redux away, leaving the two Happy Rainbow personnel steaming in their breath.

"You're a sadist," Randolph told Wolfgang Yellowbird as they walked together.

"I'm not sadistic by nature," Wolfgang Yellowbird said. "But I am a man of conviction."

"You're a terrorist."

"Terrorists kill the innocent in the name of fantastical entities. I kill the guilty for the sake of this tangible valley."

"You have twisted ambitions."

"My ambitions are just."

"Fighting fire with fire will only create more fire."

"I am here to protect this forest, Randolph. It is my lot in life. When you leave this place and reflect on its beauty, you will understand that there are things worth killing for."

Earl followed behind them, listening to the conversation. He held his hand against his open wound and wondered what inspired terrorism and unflinching belief that what one was doing was right—that great slaughter was necessary to justify a perceived righteousness. Was it nature or nurture? Brainwashing? The allure of comradery? Earl looked at Wolfgang Yellowbird, the terrorist, the lone wolf. His cause was appealing. It seemed right.

"Taking a life can never be justified," Randolph said.

"You happily eat the meat I provide for you," Wolfgang Yellowbird replied.

"I'm talking about human life."

"A human life is no greater than the life of a bird or hare."

"Humans are higher beings."

"How so?"

"We are godly beings."

"Are not all animals godly?"

"They are not aware of God."

"Even if that is true, and I don't believe it is, it doesn't make their lives inferior to ours."

"A life devoid of God is inferior."

"What about the pagans and the atheists? Can they be justifiably killed? And perhaps even eaten?"

"Of course not."

"Then what makes their lives more sacred than that of an animal?"

Earl thought of his job as a livestock distributor. He had been an agent of genocide in a modern-day holocaust. He had been an executer of one of the world's greatest evils. "Factory farming is terrorism," he said.

Wolfgang Yellowbird and Randolph both nodded in agreement.

"The same could be said for mass deforestation," Wolfgang Yellowbird said. "Or the harvesting of cabbages. For all flora is godly too. And if someone is willing to extinguish the life of a vegetable then—" He was cut off when a black disk the size of a dinner plate buzzed his ear. "What in God's hell was that? A Martian?"

The disk levitated above, flashing lights at them.

"A drone," Paul said. "It has the Happy Rainbow logo. That damn happy rainbow."

"What's its purpose?" asked Wolfgang Yellowbird.

"It's transmitting footage."

The machine buzzed away through the trees.

"What sort of devilry was that?" Wolfgang Yellowbird said. "Technology has become omniscient." He stroked his beard that was the colour of thunderstorms and looked about. "We will camp here tonight."

"Where's Kyle?" Wolfgang Yellowbird asked as he brought a fire to life in twilight.

The group looked at one another and shook their heads.

"Perhaps he has become a vagabond," Paul said.

"That may be so," said Wolfgang Yellowbird. "That acid has been known to inspire drastic life decisions."

Wolfgang Yellowbird stood from the fire and bellowed Kyle's name. Like an obedient animal, Kyle erupted from the undergrowth. The blood from his wound had seeped deeply into the clothing around his shoulder. "A fairy," he cried. "I met a fairy."

"Did she talk to you?" demanded Wolfgang Yellowbird.

"Yes. She was so old and so beautiful. Her voice sounded like music."

"What did she tell you, Kyle?"

"She said that we all have little time."

Wolfgang Yellowbird's expression deepened. "That is the worst kind of omen. The fairies of the Old Growth Crystal Valley are clairvoyant."

"Maybe she's warning us that more Happy Rainbow people are on their way," said Paul.

"Perhaps," said Wolfgang Yellowbird. "Or maybe she means something much more ominous than that. The fairies here are ancient. They have seen ice ages. They watched as the planet was consumed by volcanic gas. They warned the dinosaurs of meteors and a poisonous atmosphere, but they were too gormless to understand. The fairies did not evolve like the rest of us, you see. They were placed here by divine power to keep watch over this place. They don't consume from the planet. They don't fornicate. They don't defecate. They simply exist."

"Fairies sent from God in Heaven," Randolph said. "This day has been too much to handle."

"Yes, Randolph, this was a trying day. But a necessary one." Wolfgang Yellowbird sat with Kyle and began tending to his wound. "How are you feeling, Kyle?"

"Fine. Is it getting warm out here?"

"How is your mind?"

"Starting to burn out, Wolfiebird. That's a potent cocktail you put together."

"I told you it wasn't designed for virgins of the forest."

"Fair enough. But I had one hell of a day."

Wolfgang Yellowbird smiled at him. "Good, Kyle. Now this might sting a little." Wolfgang Yellowbird plucked a branch from the fire and cauterized the wound.

Kyle seemed oblivious to the sear. "It's definitely getting warm. It feels balmy."

Wolfgang Yellowbird swabbed and bandaged Kyle. "The bullet passed right through you. You seem to be in fine form, Kyle."

"My armpits are damp."

Earl watched Inertia as she sat quietly on her own. He wondered if he should talk to her, comfort her. He lit a cigarette and inhaled deeply. The pleasure he felt in his clouded lungs felt cheap and unearned. He looked at the burning end that glowed as the light of day slowly evaporated. It reminded him of one of Wolfgang Yellowbird's sticks of dynamite. A death cylinder stuffed with accelerants. Light one end and wait to die. He thought about how foolish he would feel if he got lung cancer. He took another puff and said: "There are so many things trying to kill us." He pulled his carton of cigarettes from his bag and threw it on the fire.

"You'll get us all addicted," said Randolph as he coughed and waived a hand in front of his face.

"You buffoon," said Wolfgang Yellowbird. "I could have smoked all of those in one sitting." He breathed in the fire smoke.

Earl took one last drag. He offered the rest of the cigarette to Wolfgang Yellowbird, who snatched it from his hand.

Earl sat beside Inertia and pointed up at the patches of stars that had begun to speckle the sky through an opening in the trees. "Do you ever wonder about their brilliant light, surrounded by pure frozen darkness?"

"It's terrifying," Inertia said. "The scale of space's silence fills me with so much dread. It's dark energy consuming, expanding, accelerating infinity."

"Is dark energy sentient?" Earl asked.

"I hope it is, Earl. But the fact that we don't know brings into question our own sentience. We know so little. We're unaware of so much."

Shooting stars streaked the sky like paint strokes as a thin veil of clouds rolled overhead. Earl turned his eyes to the campfire that seemed pitiful in comparison to the light-show above. Tobacco and wood smoke billowed with steam from a pot of boiling water in a battle for space and oxygen. The water steam was weak, translucent, and succumbed easily to the wood and tobacco's smoky alliance. Earl breathed deeply, and exhaled without breath vapour. "I think Kyle's right," he said. "It is getting warm. Look how the water steam can't penetrate the trees."

He looked back to the sky where more clouds had appeared. Thicker now, and dark like squid ink.

The rest of the group followed Earl's gaze to the sky where a cloaked vulture was ripped across the sky by a powerful blast of wind. Ice pellets began to rattle down from the trees, and tens of thousands of fireflies lifted from wooden nooks to flash brilliantly and burn out. In the distance, a guttural bellow pierced the wilderness, followed by several more that came from all directions. "Sasquatch," Wolfgang Yellowbird said. "They're agitated. Something's coming."

Trees began to lurch violently as a rumble grew in the distance. It accelerated through the forest, escalating to a deafening roar.

"What is that?" Kyle looked up as an acorn sized hailstone smashed into his right eyeball, exploding it. He bared his teeth and went down holding his face. Blood jettisoned through his fingers, running down his knuckles like a breaching river delta. Wolfgang Yellowbird pulled him up by the collar of his coat. "We need to find cover." He was yelling. "Grab only what you can carry. Leave the rest."

They ran. Hailstones bruised their bodies. The sky grew darker. The roaring in the trees was advancing on them. Wind pulled tree roots from the earth. Lightning blasts hit close and often, burning through snow and ice.

The roar became deafening. Trees began falling all around them. Earl glanced behind and watched a tornado made of ice erupt from the trees in direct pursuit of Clovis Redux. It sliced towards them, a kilometer in diameter. "We need cover," he screamed. The others glanced over their shoulders, their faces contorted by terror.

Wolfgang Yellowbird changed course as the twisting sky followed and uprooted everything in its wake.

He led them into a cave where they cowered in darkness. The howling monster slowly faded into the night.

Wolfgang Yellowbird lit a flare. He sat with Kyle, attending to his eye. "Kyle?"

Kyle did not answer. His mouth ajar in flickering shadows. His left eye was opened wide, and his right eye, gone.

"Can you hear me, Kyle?"

"He's in shock," said Randolph.

"I think we're all in shock," said Paul. "I don't want to further alarm anyone, but there are bears in here."

"They're sound asleep," said Wolfgang Yellowbird. "They won't stir until spring. If everyone remains calm, we won't have a problem."

Two grizzly bears lay in a heap, snuggled together in deep slumber. Their breath was propulsive. Their state of unconsciousness, enviable.

Wolfgang Yellowbird finished attending to Kyle. He laid him down on his side and patted his head. "Try to sleep, my brave friend."

Kyle's left eye remained wide and staring. It did not blink for the remainder of the night. Randolph joined him. He lay down and put his arm around him, gently stroking his head. "Oh Kyle. You poor man."

Earl was seated with Sigmund under his feet. Sigmund was shaking with his teddy bear gripped in his mouth. Wolfgang Yellowbird joined them with his first aid kit, ready with sutures and disinfectant. He examined Earl's wound. "Let's get you stitched back up."

"What just happened?"

"I don't know, Earl. We will explore tomorrow when the sun comes out. Hopefully we will be able to make sense of it."

"Something tells me that's not going to happen. How did you know this cave was here? We would all be dead if we didn't find cover."

"I told you I know this place well," Wolfgang Yellowbird said. He applied tree sap to Earl's face and began stitching his cheek. "How are you feeling?"

"Numb."

"How are you feeling about your alcoholism?"

"Distracted."

"That's probably the best way to be, Earl. Ten years ago, a man came on this journey for the same reason as you. He said that the beauty of this place distracted him and inspired a steely resolve. He's a memorable sort. A big, strong man. He was eager to help in any way he could. He was always the first one awake to light the fire. He helped me hunt and cook. He was gracious and loving. He was generous. I hope he has stayed on his path of sobriety."

"He has," said Earl.

"How would you know that?" Wolfgang Yellowbird asked.

"I know him."

"How so?"

"He sent me here."

"You know Jefferson Roswell?"

"Is that his name? To me he is the janitor."

"Astonishing," said Wolfgang Yellowbird. He tied off the stitching.

"Thanks," Earl said.

"I'm glad to patch up a friend anytime."

"Not just for that, Wolfgang Yellowbird," Earl said.

Wolfgang Yellowbird smiled.

"How do I look?"

"Like a monster." Wolfgang Yellowbird wiped away dried blood. "A monster who deserves love."

Earl felt Inertia wake. Her breath quickened in anticipation of the new day and her muscles shuddered in reaction to strange energy. Her mouth opened in a yawn and Earl listened to saliva squelch against her tongue. He moved his own tongue against his teeth and felt moss growing. His mouth was sour. He felt bits of food alight from the fissures between his molars, suggesting nuttiness and decrying the hunger that growled from his shrunken gut. Wolfgang Yellowbird would know which twig variety made the best toothbrush, and maybe he carried mint leaves with him, rolled in a herbal cigar, ripened within the deep folds of his earthen cloak. Inertia rubbed her wheaten hair against Earl's whiskers, tickling his face. She whispered: "Is it morning?" The cave was lit dimly. Sunlight was searching for opportunities through the rock. It advanced little by little, spreading heat and shadow. Earl replied: "It can't be. Not yet." He looked around through the twinkling light and watched his company wake one by one, groaning with sore bones and slick with sweat. The cave had become clammy in the night.

A grumble sounded from the grizzly bears. Earl could see portions of Paul's body through an envelope of thick brown fur. He caught Wolfgang Yellowbird's attention and motioned with his eyes. Wolfgang Yellowbird moved slowly. He poked Paul's body parts that protruded like an archipelago in a roiling sea.

Paul woke and wriggled contently until reality replaced his dream-scape. He turned terrorized. His eyes stared wide at Wolfgang Yellowbird, who slowly lifted giant paws to unwrap him. Sweat dripped from Wolfgang Yellowbird's brow and streamed along concentration creases in his face, then fell from his chin into a mass of corduroy fur. With much coaxing, navigation, and manipulation of body parts, Wolfgang Yellowbird was able to detach Paul from his perilous bedding.

"I must have sleepwalked," Paul whispered.

"What a thing to do," Wolfgang Yellowbird whispered back. He was grinning at Paul.

"The fur is wonderfully soft. But the smell is putrid." Paul put on his glasses. "I dreamt of rotting leviathans."

The bears began to stir. Their breathing became stertorous and overwhelmed the cave's acoustics. Two great bodies rolled and stretched as a single canvas of fur that waved and swayed against twitching epidermis. Their arms reached out, blindly searching for the voided snuggle companion. They bleated like infants. Wolfgang Yellowbird gesticulated that it was time to evacuate. "Put yourself in their shoes," he whispered. "Imagine waking with us lot lurking like wraiths in the shadows. It would be a terrible fright."

They left the cave and stood like a patch of fescue in the transmogrified forest. The sunlight was neon and hot. It burned through psychedelic fog that hung in rolling curtains from the remaining tree tops and electrified sodden moss that swayed in a light breeze like airy green algae. Thousands of baby banana slugs slimed and levitated in a network of honeycombed icicle chandeliers that clung to the air, sparkling like crystal and shattering in gentle breezes. Melting snow chattered like swarms of masticating insects. It fell in heavy clumps from tree branches. Clovis Redux began to remove winter layers to the sounds of birds fluting woodnotes through the trees in which their tattered tents dangled and fluttered like wounded pterodactyls.

"Nights will no longer be in tents," Wolfgang Yellowbird said.

Earl rubbed Sigmund's head and looked around. He asked Randolph: "What time does your watch say?"

"Noon."

"Do you mean midnight?"

"I mean twelve o'clock."

"But it's the break of dawn."

"What the flower?" said Kyle. "Why is it so hot?" Dried blood and purple puss were smeared over the right side of his face. "There's, like, no wind-chill." His left eye was blinking and alert, taking in the light. "It's the dead of winter, dammit."

Wolfgang Yellowbird offered Kyle a drag of his joint and told him: "It's designed for maximum mellow. No paranoia. I call it Yearning Yellowbird."

"Your shock has subsided along with the cold, Kyle," Randolph said. "It has been replaced by a new emotional season. How does your eye feel?"

"I'll let you know when I find it," Kyle said, inhaling.

"Stay calm if you can," Randolph told him. "You've experienced too much."

Kyle accepted Randolph's embrace. He lightly tugged Randolph's jutting pony tail and smeared grime on him. Then said: "Get off me, pervert."

Earl watched the two men and wondered what Vinnigan would think. When he asked about it later, Randolph told him that monogamy is cruel deceit and that committing yourself to one sexual partner is like eating nothing but potatoes. No butter. No salt. He said that he was fortunate to attract younger men because he found men his own age sexually repulsive. Earl asked about emotional maturity and Randolph said that it couldn't compete with hard flesh and energetic ejaculate. Since his marital emancipation he had been spoiled with smorgasbords of ripe fruit and fresh meat.

A tremendous groaning and snapping of wood fibres tore through the forest as a great tree fell in the distance, and Wolfgang Yellowbird explained the frondescent splendour of young scions that would grow from saplings into monsters upon the fallen dead to repopulate the aggrieved biota, and how it was rare in this day and age for a tree to die of natural causes. Earl told Paul to turn on his radio.

Paul thumbed the tuner. The speakers crackled until he found a clear signal broadcasting from a high point in Prince George. The newsman's voice was strained and shaky:

'. . . POLAR WANDER, CAUSED BY A SIGNIFI-
CANT SURGE IN THE SUN'S GRAVITATION-
AL PULL, HAS INFLICTED MASS DEVASTA-
TION UPON PLANET EARTH, WHICH HAS
SPUN SEVENTY DEGREES, PULLING THE
TWO POLES INTO TROPICAL LONGITUDES
AND CAUSING MASSIVE GLACIAL MELT
THAT HAS SUBMERGED COASTAL REGIONS
THE WORLD OVER. FURTHER FLOODING
HAS BEEN CAUSED BY HURRICANES AND
CYCLONES THAT HAVE LEVELLED MUCH OF
WHAT WAS ONCE THE EARTH'S EQUATORI-
AL REGIONS. TSUNAMIS HAVE FOLLOWED
IN THE WAKE OF MAGNITUDE TEN EARTH-
QUAKES THAT HAVE STRUCK ALONG THE
PACIFIC PLATE FAULT LINE. JAPAN, TAIPEI,
THE KOREAN PENINSULA, HONG KONG,
SOUTHERN CHINA, CHILE, WESTERN PERU,
CENTRAL AMERICA, WESTERN MEXICO
AND THE WESTERN UNITED STATES ARE
SUBMERGED. MEANWHILE, MILLIONS HAVE
PERISHED IN WHAT WAS ONCE THE
SOUTHERN HEMISPHERE AS TEMPERA-
TURES HAVE PLUNGED TO SUB-ARCTIC
LEVELS, AND HUNDREDS OF THOUSANDS
OF CATEGORY FIVE TORNADOS HAVE
TOUCHED DOWN IN EUROPE, RUSSIA AND
THE AMERICAS CAUSING WIDESPREAD
CASUALTIES AND DECIMATION. THE GLOB-
AL DEATH TOLL IS UNKNOWN BUT IS ESTI-
MATED TO BE IN THE BILLIONS. SCIENTISTS
ARE BAFFLED, MANY CALLING WHAT HAS
TRANSPIRED AN IMPOSSIBILITY. PEOPLE
ARE URGED TO REMAIN IN THEIR HOMES
AND STAY TUNED TO THEIR LOCAL RADIO
STATIONS FOR FURTHER UPDATES AND
INSTRUCTIONS.'

Earl looked to the sky to catch a glimpse of the sun: God's peephole, zooming in on the reeling planet. It seemed brighter than usual. Its warmth was intense and heavy, beautiful against his bare skin. He felt the long months of brittle cold quickly melt out of his marrow. Inertia followed his glance and asked: "The sun did this?"

"It's the apocalypse," said Paul. "Nature's vengeance upon humanity has begun."

"How can it be nature's vengeance, Paul?" asked Randolph. "If scientists can't explain it, then this is miraculous. God's judgment is at work."

"Scientists are amongst the worst brands of fundamentalists," replied Paul. "They're indoctrinated by facts and figures, and secular *proof*. But you can't cram the power of the universe into a human discipline. Our imagination is finite and therefore ill-equipped to decipher the chaos of nature and the power of anarchy. Trying to define such massive forces with equations and laws is a futile exercise."

"We have been smitten," Randolph declared as the two grizzly bears emerged from the cave. They looked groggy after a poor night's sleep. Their fur shone golden in the sunlight. A male and pregnant female. Her bulbous gut was comical in comparison to the male's lean power.

"They think it's spring," said Wolfgang Yellowbird. "Their zeitgebers have been thrown way out of whack."

The bears yawned and regarded Clovis Redux with an expression of boredom. Then began great grumbling and grunting. They scooted their hind quarters along the ground. They turned in circles and bellowed towards the sky until great fecal plugs dropped from their anuses. They examined one another's efforts and ate a few mouthfuls, then lumbered into the melting woods.

"What did we just witness?" asked Kyle.

"A rite of spring," Wolfgang Yellowbird replied.

"We should head back," said Inertia.

"Yes. We will head for my tilted cabin in the woods, if it's still standing," said Wolfgang Yellowbird. "Our troubled minds require a solid structure in which to regroup."

"We should make for the air strip," said Randolph. "Perhaps my aeroplane is still in one piece."

Wolfgang Yellowbird rooted around in his beard and pulled out his compass. "The storm has disfigured the forest beyond my recognition."

"Your compass isn't going to do us any good," said Paul. "The Earth's poles are flowered, remember?"

"It's still worth a shot. Follow me."

They trailed Wolfgang Yellowbird through the unfamiliar wilderness. Trees and corpses lay scattered about. Wounded woodland creatures limped away, leaving trails of blood. Sigmund chased after them to finish what the apocalypse had started. Above in the treetops, ravens cackled and tore into an owl carcass. A severed wing fell to the ground below; a great clump of feathers that dropped like a stone.

Wolfgang Yellowbird walked with his nose pointed at his compass. He changed direction and then he changed direction again. "This is nonsensical," he said. "It seems that my compass has been tampered with by an imbecile. Tohubohu has twisted this magical valley into a cryptic ruin. It's witchcraft."

"We're doomed," said Paul. "Your compass can't lead us from the wrath of nature. Nothing will save us. Kyle's fairy was right."

"I'm inclined to agree with you," said Wolfgang Yellowbird. "But your attitude is very sour."

"You might be right, Paul," said Randolph. "Maybe this is a force of nature at work. And if this is so, then God will surely deliver us. God's grace will prevail."

"But maybe *your* first instinct was right, Randolph," said Paul. "Surely, the grim coincidence that the beginning of the end fell on Jesus's birthday was not lost on you. Unfortunately he's not around this time to die for our sins." Paul looked at Wolfgang Yellowbird and asked: "Maybe you're up for it?"

Wolfgang Yellowbird shook his head and ate some acid.

"God help us," Randolph said. "We must build an Ark. But why would God or nature, or an ungodly alliance between the two, inflict such harm upon us?"

"To kill us off," said Paul. "Then rebuild without us so a natural order can reclaim the planet. The human experiment has run its course."

Wolfgang Yellowbird stopped walking and turned towards the group. "I don't know where we are or where we're going. But at least the weather is cooperating. And this sylvan masterpiece that I call my home is still a verdant paradise."

"What are we going to do?" asked Inertia.

"Our options are few," Wolfgang Yellowbird said.

"Well, we can't bumble through the woods waiting for something to kill us," Kyle said.

Wolfgang Yellowbird nodded. "I concur." He knelt to cradle an intrepid floral shoot poking through the thinning ground layer of snow. "Perhaps a trail of floriferous ratoons will lead us to salvation."

Earl looked into the distance where black rock peaked above the shredded tree line. "Is that the Black Ridge?"

Wolfgang Yellowbird strained his eyes to where Earl was pointing. "I believe it is. It's a day's hike from here, but yes, that's the Black Ridge and the direction home. Earl, I could kiss you." And he did. Then he twirled inside a cloudburst as a woodpecker rattled a beat and a swarm of what he referred to as gargoyles ascended into the sky above him.

"We will rest here by this flowing stream to fill our canteens and bladders," said Wolfgang Yellowbird. "I'm sorry its flow isn't carbonated, Randolph, but I hope glacial-fed spring water will suffice. I'm sure you will all enjoy it and revel in your crimes, because as you know, this water has been corporatized. By indulging your thirst, you, along with every living creature that relies upon sustenance, are thieving scoundrels in the eyes of the capitalists." Wolfgang Yellowbird winked. "Lunch will be easy today. I'll take the K-9 unit with me to ferret out a carcass. Then we'll drag it back and light it on fire. Also, it's time for my poop du jour." He and Sigmund disappeared into the woods with Wolfgang Yellowbird saying: "Come Sigmund. Let's wander."

The others sat by the stream that flowed uninhibited by ice.
Easy and serene. Inertia pulled out a pencil and paper:

Earth's Moon edicts deft tidal dogged, Earth's Sun con-
veys clear wind in current,
Maelstroms vortex deeply, portside yawning, the boat
bends buoyant,
Towards Earth's Sun in gaggles of discourse, we navigate
distant alien hurricanes,
Saturn's gentle gravity allows peaceful levity, we fathom
our spec upon brevity.

With credence in physics, we embark intrepid travel
upon jeweled sea,
Our mast stands strong, sailor's sails slung slack until
Earth's Sun strangely sighs,
Charged by far flung forces, sails snap taught and onward
we go,
Onward we glide, yellow jackets in crow's nests and
porpoise beside.

Swim in vivid crystal magic blues, hemmed in Sunlight,
Azurite cubits a billion degrees, landfall a distant
uvarovite drusy,
Impossible places ensconce our small stares, otherworld-
ly reality through tactile imagination,
Human thought and human imagery, float condemned
of natural plagiary.

Down great depths a kelp bed sways, like sailor's cilia
reaching for the Sun,
Upward the Sun climbs and climbs, downward pressure
builds and builds,
A malevolent cosmic whim, catapults Earth through
ether,
A cosmic quake splits space, rock leviathan jetsam shatter
in place.

Limbs of human, whale and bear sear, hearts explode, trees succumb,
Families and loved ones vanish in heat, slashes of silver,
Bodies dissolve in Earth's Sun's flare, Earth's Moon looks on,
Anticipation of doom, fire, venom, light, a lightless vacuum.

Undeterred by dark thoughts the sailors glide on, past sunken warships,
Death, mossy with barnacles, lies forgotten, seventy-year screams agitate the water,
Old tendons snap between terrors and drowning, the ship sails by,
Hollowed cries creep by closely at pace, solemn hymns breathed quickly, Amazing Grace.

"What is this? What is this? What do I see?
What is this? What is this? Can this possibly be?"

Portside an eagle with talons drawn, plummets,
Screeching charge of war hunger, a dark dart through sky,
Screaming velocity inside accelerated gravity, torrid flight, the bird vanishes in speed,
Reappears with a BOOM to blow holes through a sail, sharp knives in the tail of a great big blue whale.

Song of crying, of shock, of alienation, the sound dies quickly in sparse molecules,
Blood from the berserk vertical zeppelin, dilutes salty aqueous that falls slowly back to sea,
Rapture in water aquamarine, the raptor lifts skyward with terrible dislocation,
Paused in profile, the animals rise, sailors mewl portside, query their eyes.

Through clouds then space, something different has begun,
The eagle brings whale to Earth's Moon and Sun.

Inertia tapped the end of her pencil on the page and looked up at Earl, who was staring back at her. She handed him the poem and said it was only a first draft, and the tenses were probably inconsistent, and her thesaurus was lost in the tornado, and the cadence was . . . well there wasn't really a cadence, it was choppy, bloated, masculine, and her mind was distracted by Earth's great upheaval. Earl said that her insecurities were conditioned by James's criticisms, and her self confidence had been eroded by his emotional abuse. He asked if she thought James was dead. Inertia turned to dunk her head in the stream and drink deeply. As she emerged, water dripped from her hair and soaked her body. The vermillion shade of her raised nipples appeared through her shirt.

Earl read the poem then asked: "Is everything a hallucination? Is anything real?"

"What exists in your mind is corporeal," Inertia said. "It's of flesh and blood."

"But we can never trust our minds." Earl became aware of his neurons firing. His thoughts skipped along in an autonomous torrent. They were active, free to explore where they wished, unencumbered by the poisonous sludge his body was purging. "It's unpredictable."

"What if nothing existed until this moment and all our memories are artificial?" Inertia asked.

"Then our minds are counterfeit."

"We might be ghosts."

Earl nodded. "We're already dead."

"We've been ghosts for eons. Floating around the edges of the firelight."

"Why should we exist?

"That's the essential question. Whatever the answer may be, we should be thankful." Inertia ran her thumb across Earl's wound. "Your colour is returning. Your vitality is shining through your sickness."

Earl felt Inertia's banshee spirit flow through her fingers and into his body. His penis slavered tears of pre-ejaculate that slimed into the hairs of his inner thigh.

"You were so sallow when I first saw you," Inertia said. "Now your vigour is gestating."

"Not gestating," Earl said. "Germinating. I'm beginning to feel better. If only I could sleep."

"You'll sleep once your mind settles into itself."

"Your mind must be settled," Earl said. "You slept deeply last night. You're a night babbler."

"Did I reveal any secrets?"

"You talked about your parents."

"I'm worried about them, you know? I hope they're surviving."

"Where are they?"

"They're nomadic. Last I heard they were travelling to Newfoundland to shoot seal hunters with pellet guns."

"Why did they name you Inertia?"

"As a baby I was very still, quiet, unreactive. They say I was inert."

"Argon is inert," Earl said. "It has existed since the beginning of time. We breathe it today just as the first amoeba did. Perhaps they wanted to immortalize you."

"Perhaps," Inertia said. "They're new age stoners who had the epiphany that I was, 'totally inert, man. She's, Inertia.'"

"You don't like your name?"

Inertia shook her head.

"It's not so bad,' Earl said. "I once met Zambian triplets named Xmas, McNervous and Small Potato."

Inertia laughed.

"You didn't mention James in your sleep."

Inertia shrugged.

"Aren't you worried about him?"

She shrugged again.

"Do you love him?"

She watched the stream's flow.

"Why'd you marry him?"

Inertia's expression turned beleaguered, as if Earl's questions were an extension of her wandering thoughts that had already exhausted this topic. She reached out to scrape dried blood from

Earl's face. She showed him the red crystals under her fingernails and asked: "How's your nicotine withdrawal?"

"Brutal. How's your James withdrawal?" After she didn't respond, Earl asked: "Do you hope he's dead?"

"I'd inherit all his money that way."

"You married him for money."

She sighed. "Security sounds better."

"You're a gold digger."

"When a man seeks to better his financial situation it's called capitalistic guile, but when a woman does so she's slandered with derogatory terms."

"But it seems parasitic," Earl said.

"It's adaptation in an unyielding patriarchy."

"But women are making strides. There's a trajectory."

"On male terms. You're lucky you own a cock, Earl, because cocks give and cunts receive and our entire society is based upon this mechanic. Cocks can bend and manipulate their environments. Even James's tiny cock that can't hold an erection."

"Did marriage give you happiness?" Earl's cock shed another tear.

"It's more a matter of surviving on my own terms. James's wealth meant that I could write. I don't have to be a starving artist, which may sound romantic, but is hell in reality."

"What about love?"

"I can love however I choose. And this is my power over James."

"What about sex?"

"I can flower whomever I desire."

"Does James know this?"

"Of course not."

"What about the sanctity of marriage?"

They both laughed.

"What about you, Earl? Have you ever been sexually unfaithful?"

"Never," Earl said, strangely ashamed.

"When you masturbate, do you always think of your current partner?"

"Of course not."

"Then you have been unfaithful," Inertia said. "The only difference is that you haven't transitioned from the psychological to the physical. Are you married?"

"Newly separated."

"You strike me as a loner."

"I was lonely. In a city of millions, I had no one."

"You had Sigmund, and maybe that was enough. Wolfgang Yellowbird lives happily with his animal friends—although, he eats an awful lot of them."

"But that's not the life I chose. It was handed to me."

"You don't believe in free will?" Inertia asked.

"It exists, but it's limited by our environment."

"That's not a bad thing." Inertia dipped her fingers into the flowing stream. "It's springtime. We can start again now."

Wolfgang Yellowbird and Sigmund emerged from the woods dragging the corpse of a young buck. Wolfgang Yellowbird was saying to the K-9 Unit: "There is a strange thirst that comes with hunger. The thirst for the juice from the rind. Or the blood from the meat. It pours around our tongues and spills down our throats. It fills our bodies and builds our strength. We are reliant upon these nutrients that we must find outside our bodies. This means we're at the mercy of elements that we cannot control, including the generosity of the sun that powers every instance of life. Imagine if we animals could receive full and nutritious meals by opening our mouths and swallowing mouthfuls of sunshine. Can you feel that warmth on you, Sigmund? As we speak the sun is electrifying the saturated forest around us. Soon the floral tapestry will pop like a loaded spring." He turned to the others, and regarding the young buck, said: "We shall dine on venison churrasco with pine bark marinade and fungal oil drizzle. Sigmund and I found this strange, low hanging fruit dangling from a tree branch, and hanging on to deer life. I ended his suffering with my spear." He lit a fire. "I told you lunch would be easy. It was my poop du jour that proved difficult."

—

"Hold back a minute, Inertia," Wolfgang Yellowbird said from the front of the group.

"I want to see," she replied.

James's corpse lay supine. Decapitated. The top of the spine was bare. Flesh of the throat torn away. The rib cage was exposed through shredded ribbons of Gore-Tex, void of skin. The offal had been removed and shredded, left in a steaming pile. The limbs were bent at grotesque angles. Snapped bones protruded from exposed muscle, marrow sucked out. The hands reached upwards towards the sky, fingers gnawed off. Bloody water stained a large area around the corpse. The head lay close by in a melting snow bank, face torn off. Ravens cawed in the branches above.

"Something has been eating him," said Paul.

"Wolves," said Wolfgang Yellowbird. "There is a large pack that hunts these woods. They're not typically man eaters, but opportunists? Certainly. The ice tourbillion must have flung him across the sky before they found him."

Earl thought he saw a rush of shame cross Inertia's features, but only momentarily. She walked over to where the head lay and picked it up. "I want to bury him," she said. "He wouldn't want to be carrion for vultures. He was fussy that way."

The ground was still frozen as they picked at it, digging as deep as they could, which was only sufficient to cover James's corpse with a thin layer of earth. "He will rest here," Inertia said, then turned and led the way through the darkening wood in the direction that used to be west.

Wolfgang Yellowbird rummaged through James's discarded backpack. He found what he was looking for: coffee processed through the digestive tract of a weasel.

That evening Clovis Redux sat around a fire at the base of the Black Ridge. Pattering rain intensified upon them.

"We'll tackle the Black Ridge at day break," Wolfgang Yellowbird said. "It's far too dangerous in the wet dark."

"It's a shame we had to leave our tents behind," Randolph said. "They were the only things out here that resembled homes."

"Don't worry yourself, Randolph." Wolfgang Yellowbird began to busy himself. "I'll build us a great lean-to as waterproof as shark skin." He gathered branches to bind with twine. "I smell dangerous smoke."

"It's the campfire, Wolfiebird," Kyle said.

"It's much more menacing than our little campfire, Kyle. We must remain vigilant tonight. I'm afraid that somewhere close by, trees are ablaze."

"The whole world is ablaze," Paul said, and turned on his radio.

'EVERY VOLCANO ON EARTH HAS ERUPTED, SPILLING HELLFIRE UPON US, AND CUTTING OUT THE SUNLIGHT WITH SMOKE AND ASH. TWIN HURRICANES HAVE SUBMERGED THE SOUTHERN UNITED STATES. SATELLITE IMAGES SHOW THEM WORKING IN TANDEM, SEEMINGLY COGNIZANT OF THEIR DESTRUC-TIVE AMBITION. OTHER IMAGES SHOW THAT OUR PLANET'S SURFACE LAND MASS HAS BEEN HALVED AS OCEANS HAVE SUBMERGED ALL COASTAL AND LOW-LYING AREAS, REN-DERING SATELLITE IMAGES OF OUR PLANET UNRECOGNIZABLE. GOVERNMENTS HAVE FALLEN AND CHAOS REIGNS. MURDER, RAPE AND LOOTING ARE COMMONPLACE. ANAR-CHY HAS BECOME THE RULE OF LAW THE WORLD OVER. GOD HELP US ALL.'

"That didn't take long. But it figures," said Paul. "We lack empathy. It has to be nurtured and enforced by strong institutions of law and order. Without them we revert back to our animalistic nature. This was inevitable. Human turpitude has prevailed. The libertarians got their wish."

"Why are we smote if we're still a work in progress?" Randolph asked. "We're still evolving towards inherent empathy."

"Humanity is a failed poem," Inertia said. "The poet has crumpled up the page."

"That's right," said Paul. "Something went very wrong along the way. In fact, we're devolving away from empathy. Technology has fostered artificial human interaction, and has led to insincere shared experience, which has balkanized civilization through the exaggeration of the metaphysics of perception. Meanwhile, our industry has poisoned our environment and sickened the primal elements that determine our evolution. We've reacted to new surroundings in weird and harmful ways. And now we're seeking shelter like a hermit crab in a beer can."

"Your opinions are self-righteous, Paul," said Wolfgang Yellowbird. "And you're overly loquacious." He admired his handiwork. "The lean-to is almost complete." He titivated it with hanging moss drapery. "How does a light dinner sound to everyone? Perhaps a rose-petal salad with fire-weed jelly." He tore disk-shaped fungi off of tree trunks and said they would make fine serving platters.

Pinecones rained down upon Wolfgang Yellowbird's head. He looked up into the tree branches where raccoons were scuttling and collecting more ammunition. "Vile creatures," he said. "They're always harassing me and stealing my raw materials. The woodling raccoons are intellectually stunted compared to their urban brethren, who can hack security systems and hot-wire cars."

"Urban raccoons evolved differently," Paul said.

"However they evolved, they are still divine creatures," said Randolph. "As are we. We're heavenly incarnations with spectacular minds, created in God's image. But it seems that we have failed God. This global devastation is the cumulative result of repeated original sin, and we have been banished from the garden of Eden, again. The Devil whispered in our ear and we listened. We drank up his every word. And just like any good parasite, the Devil is killing his host. We've hit rock bottom," he said. "Humanity is back to day one." A pinecone thudded against Randolph's temple.

"I know the Devil," Wolfgang Yellowbird said. "He lives here in these woods and I've witnessed his diabolical ways. I once saw him dim the power of the sun. I've seen him morph tree limbs and body appendages into serpents. I watched him float mountain lions into the air to thrash them through the tree tops before snapping their necks like brittle twigs. He wastes the bodies of bears by eating them from the inside, and dements their physiology with voracious hankerings. He sets fire to the trees and once to my tilted cabin. I was able to extinguish it with wizardry of my own. He possesses minds, filling imaginations with the ghastliest imagery. I've watched as he possessed the body of a rabbit to fill its guts with poisonous gas. The odours the rabbit emitted were foul beyond reason and sent my mind reeling with noxious hallucinations of sexual torture. Then the Devil regenerated these toxins into the aromas of my other. The sweet sweat of her armpits, the musk of her loins, the fumes of her breath. I became intoxicated and fell to my knees. I was powerless against it."

"Lucifer, Satan, Devil," Kyle said. "LSD."

"Who is your other, Wolfgang Yellowbird?" Inertia asked. "You've mentioned her before."

"She is my wife," said Wolfgang Yellowbird. "Her name is Rainbow Rivers and she has been lost from my orbit."

"I'm sorry," said Inertia. "Did she pass?"

"She found a companion more suitable than myself. We built our tilted cabin in the woods together and lived amorously for many happy years. She planted the gardens and nurtured the plants as if they were her own offspring. She was a black belt in wildcrafting, and a ninja arborist. She could scale the treetops with the agility of the wind. On clear summer nights, when she was at her most virile, she would howl at the moon and transform the forest into a gymnasium of sexual acrobatics. She would flitter nude through the forest canopy, light as spindrift. A nymph glowing in the moonlight. When she returned to our tilted cabin, she would use my body as a pommel horse. She spun so fast, my penis didn't know which way to look. It bobbed around with its head on a swivel, like a tennis spectator.

"Wanderland Adventures was her idea. She designed the brochure and lured many intrepid travellers out here to experience our world. Looking back, I can see that she did this to combat her loneliness. My companionship wasn't enough. Her lust for experience was too great to be satisfied by me alone. And this lust soon attached itself to the mystery of sasquatch, and escalated into zoanthropy. She spent hours every day searching for signs of them. She mimicked their songs and repeated the language she heard murmured through the trees. She studied fecal samples and adopted their diet. Our tilted cabin became littered with pickle jars containing organic evidence. And the more she studied this evidence, the more obsessed she became. Her expeditions grew in length and fervour. Eventually, she forbade me from joining her, as my imbecilic antics distracted her work. She left earlier each morning, and returned later each night, long after the fire had died and I had fallen into a fitful slumber. I would wake in candlelight to the sounds of her breathing and bombinating. She spoke to herself in a language I didn't understand. She laughed and tore through raw flesh with her teeth. She scraped her scalpel blades on glass. Then one morning, I awoke to an empty home. Rainbow Rivers had vanished into the wild. For months I tracked her footprints and essence through the forest. But like a lynx, she had become elusive. One day, while traversing the intermediate foothills of the Rocky Mountains and experiencing a particularly heavy brand of black despair whilst wallowing within the depths of psychotropic sorrow, her footprints joined another set of tracks. Giant tracks. Sasquatch tracks. For miles they lay in tandem until they suddenly vanished. Evaporated. It was as if the Earth had swallowed them up."

"Your wife left you for a sasquatch?" Kyle laughed.

"That's heartbreaking," said Inertia. "When did this happen?"

"Five years ago."

"Do you think she's still with them?"

"I hope she is," said Wolfgang Yellowbird. "And I hope she is happy, healthy and content."

—

Earl sat on a log as the others settled under the lean-to for the night. He watched them fall asleep one by one then closed his eyes and listened to the voice on the radio that flashed images in his mind of death and destruction, crumbled cities, fire, flood, pain, misery, the apocalypse. He thought about the charcoal street prophet on the streets of Toronto, and he wondered why human arrogance had persisted for as long as it had on the face of a planet that could quash it with such ease.

Rain was falling hard now. Its hush and whisper were ambience for a twiddling sasquatch nocturne that sounded close. It was airy and bright, but carried a weight and eloquence that sounded drenched in erudition, as if composed within the bubbles of Earth's primordial soup and passed along through life and time. Earl felt himself stand and move towards the source. He entered thick trees and proceeded as the song grew louder. The campfire light disappeared in the darkness behind him. He kept moving forward with his hands raised before him, feeling through tree trunks. The song grew louder still. Then stopped. He flicked on his flashlight and pointed it forward. Eyes. Long, ghost-white hair. Flesh. Saggy breasts. A streak of white through the darkness. It sprung towards him then shot into the sky. Earl watched a naked female body disappear up the face of The Black Ridge. He caught a foothold in the granite.

The climb was far more difficult this time, upon wet rock in darkness. He slipped many times, cutting open his knee and sliding meters back down towards the forest floor. But he kept going, crawling, grasping and heaving himself against gravitational coercion. He pointed his flashlight up the rock face. He swiped it from side to side, until a path of sorts—a strategy of vertical ascent—revealed itself. A Stairway to Heaven, he thought. The song reminded him of a day, years ago, when it played from the radio of his rusty Toyota Corolla. He sped along a major Toronto thoroughfare with Samantha in the passenger seat. She nodded to the song's melodious, guitar-plucking intro, and pretend-whistled along with the flutist. Earl began to say something about final exams, graduation, the future, but she silenced him with a raised hand. She wanted to hear the lyrics. When the song picked up in rhythmic verve, she said: "The concept of heaven is ridiculous. It's a children's fairy tale. Heaven is the 'live happily ever after' part. That's why it's never actually explored in fairy tales. We have to die first, in order to experience it." She looked out the window to watch the world go by and listened to the guitar solo. When Robert Plant sang '*And as we wind on down the road*,' Earl pulled into the fast lane, and Samantha talked over the music. "Why would people believe in heaven when it's such an obvious myth? I know why. It's because people need to delude themselves with hope. And they need to put the onus of achieving happiness on someone or something else. They believe that if they wait long enough, it will come to them. And they'll be born again into a brand new fluffy wilderness, where they will be loved and cared for like they were as children. It's pathetic." Earl turned off the radio to mute an annoying disc jockey. He put on a pair of mid-night-dark aviators to cut the glare of the city. "The trick," Samantha continued, "is to find joy and happiness in our every-day. To find heaven on Earth."

"How do we do that?" Earl asked.

"Make our vocation our passion," Samantha giggled, full of clichés.

"What do you want to be when you grow up?"

"I want to work in advertising."

"You want to manipulate people for a living? You call that heaven on Earth?"

"I want to open people's eyes to what the world can offer them." And she did. In her mid-twenties, Samantha got a job in a major advertising firm, and quickly climbed her corporate ladder into creative development for television advertising. She made an ad that opened with a mechanic on an aircraft carrier, who rubbed globs of thick industrial grease into the engines of a fighter jet. The jet took off from its floating runway and tore into the sky. It accelerated faster and faster until it pierced a barrier of air and exploded into mach 1. In a boom and a flash of light that filled the television screen, a bottle of Spitfire Sexual Lubricant presented itself.

Another advertisement saw a gathering of bearded Gods float upon clouds in the sky. They moved mountains like chess pieces and poured great goblets of wine to fill the seas. Then they dabbed the Earth's pulse points—volcanos, fault lines, geysers—with Ethereal Cologne.

She wrote jingles as well. One stuck with Earl, sporadically playing in his mind over and over. Its melody was not dissimilar to the chorus of Sound Garden's *Black Hole Sun*. It went:

For a wiz,
In the biz,
Of acts of God insurance,
Look no further,
Than Golding and Wherther,
Golding and Wherther.

She made hundreds of thousands of dollars every year. Earl asked her one day why he had to pay the rent when she was so flush. She told him that it was irrelevant who paid the rent because they were a unit and they shared everything. Earl asked why they didn't merge their bank accounts. Samantha told him that a certain level of autonomy from one another is healthy. Earl asked her why she didn't just buy a house. Samantha said that financial responsibilities would compromise her freedom.

Earl turned the car radio back on. Music was playing again. *Enjoy the Silence* by Depeche Mode. Earl took an off-ramp and drove south, heading for the turgid nucleus of the city. He asked Samantha: "What else constitutes heaven on Earth? Other than vocation?"

"Family," Samantha replied. "Surrounding yourself with people you love." She was smiling at Earl. She put her hand on his, which clutched the stick shift between them.

"What if you get stuck with people you don't love?"

"That would be hell on Earth." Samantha began to breathe heavily. She swallowed hard. Her eyes were closed and her mouth formed a deep frown. She told Earl to pull the car over. She got out and vomited on the sidewalk. After she got back in, and Earl merged back into traffic, she told him that she would abort the baby.

When Earl reached the apex of the Black Ridge, he looked in the direction that used to be west. The forest was ablaze. Black clouds of smoke choked the sky above a rioting inferno. Great flames reflected off the inky wet rupestrine disco floor upon which he struggled to catch his breath. He felt the heat of the burning forest upon his face and in his lungs. Thick, heavy bolts of lightning split his retinas with jagged fissures. There was no thunder. Only fire. The lightning was propulsive. It struck in legions, retreated into the black billowing smoke to crackle and regenerate, then struck again. It was a weather system under a weather system. The rain that poured from above did nothing to discourage the fire. If anything, it seemed to be feeding it. The lightning attacked the highest points of the forest; the tall trees that were the strongest and most difficult to break down. But when they succumbed to the electric fire, the smaller trees within their influence quickly incinerated. The ancient giants, with their centuries of experience and collective knowledge, had never faced such an overwhelming threat. The cry of the felling forest could be heard above the screaming blaze.

The tallest of all the trees took the brunt of the aerial assault in a futile attempt to sacrifice itself for the others. It withstood wave after wave of strikes until its scorched roots lost purchase in the earth, and the energy of the heat lifted the great tree into the sky. Earl watched as Jesus levitated above the scorched forest canopy, until bit by bit, the wizened colossus fell away in ash.

The ash floated into the sky above the black smoke. It lingered there like swarming schools of fish. Above, the rainclouds hung like a quilt of protection from the terrors of outer space, and an impasse to the afterlife. Earl thought of all the other souls of the dead floating in the mix, and wondered if it was time to join them. To let go. To consider the bottomless crags of The Black Ridge. He pointed his flashlight into the depths of a black hole. The light was quickly overwhelmed by darkness. He dropped the torch and watched it fall through chaos, littering the stone with fading light before it vanished into pure blackness.

"You were lured here by sasquatch song?" It was Wolfgang Yellowbird with Sigmund beside him. He had his teddy bear clenched in his jaws. His head was tilted to the side. Wolfgang Yellowbird's eyes were clenched against the fire. "She wanted us to see this. Maybe she hoped we could do something about it." He shook his head.

"It wasn't a sasquatch," Earl said. "I think it was Rainbow Rivers."

"Did you see her?"

"I saw flashes."

Wolfgang Yellowbird smiled. "How did she look?"

"Naked, lithe, spritely."

"Why are you contemplating a black tomb?" Wolfgang Yellowbird asked.

"The darkness compelled me."

"That's ok," said Wolfgang Yellowbird. "It's only natural to be compelled by darkness, for it consumes much of our lives. But today is not a good day to die, Earl." His voice was lilting and sing-songy, as if he was speaking to a child.

"It's as good as any other."

"Don't you want to see how the madness plays out?" asked Wolfgang Yellowbird. "I foresee fireworks ahead. And Earth-shattering epiphanies. Ride it out, Earl." He glanced skyward and said: "Look at the gloomy sky. There's beauty in it. Do you see it?"

Earl nodded as he watched the fire's orange glow ignite the clouds above.

"There's light in the dark."

"It's overwhelming."

"It can be, Earl. But it's best not to dwell on it. For if you give in to the darkness, you will darken the sky."

"I can't affect the weather," Earl said.

"But the collective fatalism of humanity can. A deluge of cynicism and despair will create a poisoned, saturnine planet where no life can exist, only sorrow. There is tremendous evil inside each one of us, Earl. We must all do what we can to combat it."

"I'm overmatched." Earl stood, watching the blaze. "I'm done. I'm tired. This world is too powerful for a microbe like me."

"But that's life, Earl. It's a constant struggle within a universe that's too chaotic to account for its own ambition. So, revel in it and embrace the insanity. And realize you're not alone in all this. You have a family here. You have people that care for you. I care for you, Earl. As does Sigmund. And Randolph. Inertia cares for you more than you know. She examines you with sparklers in her eyes. Together, we can navigate this grand quagmire."

"But what's a family without a home? I have nothing to go back to."

"You will live here with me."

"Your tilted cabin is destroyed. Your forest is destroyed."

"We can rebuild."

"Jesus is gone," Earl said.

Wolfgang Yellowbird nodded. "He will come back."

"The planet is annihilated."

"Earl, you can blame your pessimism on the floaters in your eyes, distracting you from what's important."

Earl knelt down to sit with Sigmund. He put his arm around his dog and his head on his shoulder. Sigmund dropped his teddy bear to lick Earl's face. Earl asked: "How can this fire exist in a forest so saturated by rain and melting snow?"

"Pluvial fertilizer," Wolfgang Yellowbird said. He pointed and waited for lightning strikes to illuminate a snarling gash that cut through the burning trees. It was the forest's scar where the pipeline once stood, now uprooted with scalpel-like precision. "It's a chemical fire," he said. "Water will only make it spread."

"What tore up the pipeline?" Earl asked.

"Tornadic smite."

"Eco-terrorism is God's work."

"No doubt."

"The fire is going to achieve fusion," Earl said.

"Indeed."

"We would've had a much different fate if we had respected the planet."

"It's too late to dwell on what could have been," Wolfgang Yellowbird said.

"Is it too late to learn from our mistakes?"

"I hope not."

"But I can't see a future. All I see is darkness."

"The future is darkness. It doesn't exist."

"Not yet."

"That's right," Wolfgang Yellowbird said. "Not yet."

Earl rooted around in his pocket and pulled out a sodden pack of cigarettes. "I saved a couple," he said. "Want one?"

"Fuck yeah," said Wolfgang Yellowbird.

When they got back to the encampment the rain had begun to ease. Wolfgang Yellowbird and Sigmund crept into the lean-to and joined the slumbering snuggle puddle. Earl followed. He lay down beside Inertia and put his arm around her waist. She stirred and rolled over to face him. She looked at him with wet, sleepy eyes that flickered in the last fizzling flames of the campfire. She smiled and brushed his cheek with her lips. She nestled her head into his chest as Earl closed his eyes. He felt the comfortable weight of her body against him. His mind drifted. And he fell into a deep, deep sleep.

Earl is crammed in a stifled aeroplane full of jabbering people. Randolph sits strapped beside him in the recycled, stagnant air that is heavy with carbon dioxide. Earl looks through the oval window and sees endless beige desert. Arid earth that supports only grim forms of life, much like the plane cabin that he finds himself inside, thirty-thousand feet above ground. The people around him are ugly and neolithic. Their protruding foreheads are thick with bone and their faces are obscene. Their conversations are shrill and excited, lapping over one another. Their foul breaths billow about. Earl picks up on a voice that elevates itself above the rest. "It's simple economics. The cheaper the labour, the higher the profits. And we are definitely making profits. HAHA. Who cares how many Bangladeshi girls have to grind their fingers down to bone? And who cares how many get crushed in the process? Nobody. HAHA." Someone replies: "You're right. As long as I keep flashing my philanthropic smile at the media and expressing grave concern for child slaves, the margins will keep proliferating. HAHA."

From across the aisle: "She was a sweet one. Only eight years old and tight as a drum. I tied and gagged the mother in the corner of the room so she could watch me enjoy her daughter for hours and hours." A creature replies: "That reminds me of the time I took my youth choir camping. The pleasures I encountered inside those tents full of young boys amidst their cries of pain and anguish will not soon be forgotten by this gentleman." He points at himself with both his ghastly thumbs.

"You probably shouldn't be flying, considering the state of global warming," came another voice. Someone replies: "Don't worry about it. Aeroplane exhaust reflects heat back into space. Hey, once we land, you'll have to come see my new property. It has all the fixings and is lit up from basement to attic twenty-four-seven to ensure maximum opulence. The sprinklers are always on to keep the acres of lawn lush, and the car collection is always idling so the engines stay lubricated." The other man chuckles and says: "That sounds swell."

From behind: "Hitler ist das Rheinland! Rheinland ist der Hitler!"

Somewhere else: "I like to tie them down to the table face up with a mirror on the ceiling, so they can watch as I sever all their limbs and cauterize the stumps. They usually pass out so smelling salts are required. Then I roll them over and insert their severed arm into their . . ."

Earl looks out the window. The charcoal street prophet with snapping medusa hair is sitting on a cloud. She mouths the words: 'I told you so.'

"What is this place?" Randolph asks. "Why did you bring me here?" His eyes are wide and feverish.

Crackling over the cabin speakers. A voice from the cockpit: "Grunt Grunt Grunt Urrg Hlug." Then the aeroplane nose dives, flying at full speed, at a 90-degree angle to the Earth.

Eternal Inflation

Days of Sobriety: 5

Earl half-woke. There was flashing light behind his eyelids but he didn't want to open them. He was enjoying his time perched upon the crest of wakefulness, surfing upon the surface of the deep, aware of daylight but delaying its authority—just a little bit, just for a while—so he might languish amidst the aftershocks of dreamland. Daylight, daylight, everyday daylight. Let there be light, Earl demanded as it strobed about his body and nettled his eyeballs. He thought about its source, the sun: a ridiculous fireball laboriously rotating its bulk and orchestrating power ripples throughout its solar system, altering space in profound and irreparable ways; observing its planets overlap in conjunction, dotting each other out then separating like amoebas, straining against gravity towards the outermost fringes of the sun's influence. These planets were fussy, all of them, suckling energy and using it for purposes beyond the sun's control. What was their purpose? Earl wondered. Was it to shimmer in beguiling beauty? Was it to erode themselves to dust? Was it to sprout sentient life? Does their purpose only exist if there's awareness of it? Why must the planets swim in the sun's irradiated land, like pools of micro-art, piercing the darkness of space with vivid light? Mercury stalked the solar system like a thief in the night. Venus boiled its clouds of sulphuric acid, kilometers thick. Saturn hoola-hooped for eternity. Mars froze, blood red. The gas planets traced their steps in perpetuity, forever exploring the outermost wildernesses. And Earth. A youngling. A terraqueous majestic. So spectacular. So frail. Its surface glowed like a candle in a dark window. The sun's power blew through the wispy clouds that brushed Earth's atmosphere, splashed in its oceans, climbed its trees, and allowed symphonic life to cling to the planet's surface. But the perfect harmony of Earth's biosphere has altered. It has become tilted and unbalanced. Something parasitic has evolved upon it to the detriment of all life. Something that can translate the sun's energy into forces of destruction. And this transgression has awoken the wrath of sleeping monsters.

What was that damn flashing? Was it a flashing or a flickering? Fire flickers. Fire? The boreal inferno! Earl shot awake.

Inertia was already up, sitting beside him, damp with sweat in thick, smoky air. "The sky is going crazy," she said.

"Solar flares," said Paul. "They're messing with my radio's reception."

Inertia picked crusted tears from her eye ducts and looked into a sky that was shifting through yellows, oranges, vermillions and blues. "The sun is angry this morning."

"It's angry with humanity," said Paul, riffling through his backpack. "We pollute its solar system with so much space garbage."

"Imagine the view the sun must have," Earl said.

"Yes," said Inertia. "Imagine looking at Earth, the only place you've ever known, from that perspective. It would be jolting." She patted the ground beside where she sat. "I'm happy to stay here and stare up at the stars in wonder as they carry on their journeys far, far away in complete obliviousness to my existence." She shifted her gaze from the flashing sky to Paul, who was now dumping out the contents of his backpack. "What are you looking for?"

"I'm hoping to find something useful." He unfolded the scissors of his Swiss Army knife. "But I don't think I brought anything to help us stave off the apocalypse."

"No trinket will suffice, Paul," said Wolfgang Yellowbird as he flounced resplendently nude from the forest. His long body was sinewy and strong. Lean muscles rippled about his tall angular frame. Solar flares painted his skin with iridescent waves of rainbows. "We will have to survive on instinct and resolve."

"Where did you go?" asked Randolph. "We should stay together."

"Sasquatch are near."

"Flower your Sasquatch," said Kyle. "And flower the damn apocalypse. What concerns me is that you're naked." He shielded his eyes from the fleshly beacon that pranced before him.

"The weather is too hot for clothes, Kyle. And this is how I feel true freedom. Look how my body is vibrating with liberation."

"No thanks." Kyle stood. "I'm going to collect firewood." He walked into the trees.

"We should stay together," Randolph called after him.

Wolfgang Yellowbird said: "We must keep moving today, in haste. The smoke is getting thick and it's a matter of time before the fire breaches the Black Ridge and spreads into the Crystal Valley."

"What do you propose we do?" asked Earl.

"Head for higher ground." Wolfgang Yellowbird pointed in the direction that used to be east. "We must ascend the Rocky Mountain range where the flames cannot reach us."

"Do we look like mountaineers to you?"

"You certainly do not, but it's our only option at this point. It's a good two-day amble through dense wood to the base of the monolith. We will wait for Kyle to return with kindling so we can make enough weasel-coffee to energize us for a vigorous march."

A shout rang through the trees.

"That was Kyle," said Randolph. He sprang to his feet and bolted. The others followed.

They could hear giggling. It was faint at first but grew louder as they moved closer. The giggling intensified into laughter, whooping and whistling. Then silence.

They found Kyle standing blindly in mud. He was smiling. The side of his skull cracked open. Blood and brain leaked down his neck and onto his shoulder. His remaining eyeball dangled from its socket and bounced against his cheek. He was mewling, swaying. He turned his face towards the others. His grin intensified.

While Randolph doubled over to vomit, Earl realized that this is what it meant to wander the Earth insentient. That a body without a mind can serve no purpose. But what about a mind without a body? Could it have escaped the trauma? Was Kyle watching from the treetops with a new-found freedom? He could go where he wanted now. There was much to explore. Earl looked up to see if he could catch a glimpse before Kyle disappeared in a breeze.

Randolph walked to Kyle and cradled his broken head. "Oh no. Oh God, no." He held on as Kyle's legs began to kick and his arms flailed. Randolph eased him to the forest floor. "Poor, sweet man." Randolph kissed Kyle's forehead as he died. He held his lips to the corpse and began to sob. He whispered: "Take this man's soul and protect it. Cherish it, love it, and bless it with your grace." Then his sobs overwhelmed him.

Wolfgang Yellowbird darted around the trees. His gonads flopped wildly. He examined the area around where Kyle's body lay. "A bloodied tree branch," he hollered. "And tracks. An adult and child. Kyle must have unknowingly happened upon them." He looked up from the forest floor. "This way." He motioned vigorously for the others to follow.

Earl kneeled beside Randolph, who turned his head to Earl and put his arms around him. Randolph's cries intensified. "Why is this happening, Earl? Why is God not helping us?"

Earl turned away to join the others who were following Wolfgang Yellowbird. He looked back to see Randolph kneeling in the mud, drenched in Kyle's blood.

The footprints left muddy slurs in the snow slush. They were humanoid. One set massive, one set small. From up ahead, Wolfgang Yellowbird said: "I've never been so close. I've never been so close."

"This is taking us way off track," said Paul. "The Rockies are that way." He pointed in the direction that used to be east.

Wolfgang Yellowbird paid him no attention. "I've never been so close."

"Are you sure it's a good idea to be following these things?"

Wolfgang Yellowbird increased his speed through the forest. Sigmund was close on his heels, sniffing madly.

Sunlight flared around them, alternating intensities of green in a kaleidoscopic prism of emerald, olive, lime and chartreuse— dripping with moisture and haunted by ever-shifting shadow. Earl looked up and saw ravens circling above, clicking and caw- ing. Panicked creatures darted through the trees like flames. Howling sang through the forest.

"Wolves?" asked Inertia.

Wolfgang Yellowbird's expression was alarming.

They followed the primal sounds in haste and emerged into a narrow clearing. Fifteen meters away the sasquatch stood amidst pools of diluted bitumen and pipeline debris. It was a female holding a child in her arm. She stood over nine feet tall. Her hair was brown and shaggy, dreaded with tree sap. It had patches of gold and white and covered her entire body, apart from her breasts that hung plump and black, nipples purple and engorged. She had a beard that rivalled Wolfgang Yellowbird's and her shoulders were boulders. Her free arm dangled past her knee, hand clenched in a fist. Her eyes were the size of eagle eggs, with vivid yellow irises and forest green pupils. She stared at Clovis Redux, taking them in one by one, then turned her attention to the wolves that entered the clearing and encircled her.

The pack was a dozen strong. They were big and grey, crouched with snapping jaws. The mother sasquatch backed her- self towards a tree and placed her child on a high branch. She let out a salvo of screams and hand claps. The wolves fell back in the shockwaves. Their ears bled.

"We must do something," Wolfgang Yellowbird said with his hands over his ears. "They're amongst the last of their kind."

A wolf pounced. It ripped flesh and hair from the mother's arm. She screamed and kicked the wolf away. She picked up a branch from the ground. When the wolf attacked again she swung, breaking the wolf's spine. It fell paralysed as the rest of the pack began to attack in waves, three or four at a time. She swung the branch, sending wolves flying through the air, but they kept coming, howling and barking, biting and ripping. The mother spun around and began to run. She reached a tree and began to climb it but the wolves latched onto her feet and pulled her back down. She fell on her side and disappeared under a shifting coat of bloody grey fur. With a scream she emerged, sending wolves smashing into tree trunks. Some got back up, others lay twitching.

Limping and bloodied, her torso ripped open, the sasquatch reached for her crying child and stroked his face. She said something to him before she turned once more and faced the remaining wolves. She ran at them and smashed her club into the mouth of one. The wolf's bottom jaw severed. She took out three more before she was overwhelmed and brought to her knees. The wolves were ripping at her, eating her alive. The child's crying was audible over the carnage.

"No!" Earl yelled, but it was too late. Sigmund had joined the fray. He ripped out a wolf's throat before she knew he was upon her. Sigmund's fur stood on end as he growled and barked at the remaining two wolves that turned their attention towards him. One attacked. The alpha. Sigmund darted to his left, causing the wolf to veer by him. He lunged at the other wolf and latched his jaws on her, giving the mother sasquatch time to pull her body from the ground and tear the wolf's heart out of its broken rib cage. She fell back down.

The alpha circled Sigmund and surveyed his decimated pack. Their bodies lay lifeless and scattered about the clearing. Sigmund growled and the canines locked eyes, mouths full of blood. The wolf made the first move. A lunge and an elastic jaw snap that exploded an inch from Sigmund's snout. Sigmund backed away and the wolf came again. It went for Sigmund's throat and missed. Sigmund pounced back and rammed the wolf in his flank with enough force to send him rolling in the mud. Sigmund ran at him and sank his teeth into the wolf's hind leg. He ripped at it, shredding flesh and severing tendons, using the torque in the muscles of his neck. His bear bell jingled. The wolf could not turn around far enough to get at Sigmund who was pulling backwards. His teeth drove deeper and deeper into bone. The wolf let out a whimper and used his front legs to pull forward, hastening the dismemberment. The wolf stood and hobbled. It turned to see Sigmund devour strips of his severed limb. Then Sigmund attacked again. He ran straight at the wolf then veered to get at the injured hindquarters. The wolf could not pivot and Sigmund sank his teeth into the wolf's remaining hind leg. The wolf lay down and closed his eyes as Sigmund snapped the femur. With the sickening crunch of bone in his bleeding ears, the alpha dragged himself towards his annihilated pack. He turned his eyes to Sigmund and let out a whine. Sigmund moved in to clench the wolf's throat and squeeze out the oxygen.

Clovis Redux sprinted into the clearing. Earl checked Sigmund for injuries, of which he had none. He was slick with wolf blood and bitumen. Wolfgang Yellowbird fell to his knees by the mother. "She's breathing," he cried.

The mother opened her eyes and looked at Wolfgang Yellowbird. She let out a low groan and turned her head toward the tree where her child wailed in the branches. Wolfgang Yellowbird ran to the tree and put out his arms. The child climbed into them.

Wolfgang Yellowbird placed the child in the mother's arms. She began to sing. The child's small whimpers were muffled by his mother's torn breast. She held her child's face to her own, then lifted him with her last strength to Wolfgang Yellowbird, who accepted the child against his naked chest.

Ravens descended upon the massacre and fought over the bounty. Vultures circled above and coyotes yipped behind the tree line. When they slunk into the clearing to tear meat from the fallen sasquatch, the ravens attacked in numbers, forcing them back in clouds of black feathers.

"What awful carnage," said Wolfgang Yellowbird as the young sasquatch climbed out of his arms to cling to Sigmund's underbelly like an infant baboon. "This is a sad day for the sasquatch. News of this death will spread throughout their population, relayed by birds and trees. There will be a great mourning."

Wolfgang Yellowbird knelt down to examine the young sasquatch. Big teary eyes gazed back. Its little hand reached out to touch his nose. Wolfgang Yellowbird offered a honey candy and laughed as the sasquatch stuck his head into his beard, searching for more.

"I'm terribly vexed over how his mother allowed Kyle to sneak up on her," Wolfgang Yellowbird ruminated. "If all was right in her body and mind, she would have vanished like wind in trees. Kyle would have been oblivious. But in this altered environment, she was distracted, fearful of what has transpired. Her guard was down."

"Maybe she thought Kyle was Happy Rainbow personnel," Paul offered. "Or the devil."

"Perhaps," said Wolfgang Yellowbird. "But what about the wolves that have lived in peaceful coexistence with sasquatch for centuries? Something is unbalanced in nature's equilibrium and it's sending bad waves through the beasts of the world." He shooed ravens away with his staff and lifted a wolf from the ground. He strapped it to his back and said: "Lunch."

"We should get back to Randolph," Earl said, leading the others back to the encampment.

"Wolves have no reason to molest the sasquatch," Wolfgang Yellowbird continued. "They are far too dangerous a prey, as we just witnessed. It's normally the grizzlies that clash with the sasquatch. Such titans sharing a limited space are bound to have their differences. Especially when their diets are so similar. Many epic battles have been fought over something as modest as a blueberry. Imagine the spectacle. Gladiators indeed. A male grizzly in his physical prime can defeat a sasquatch given the right circumstances, but it's the sasquatch that typically hold the upper hand. But there's a reason that their range is limited to the sub-Arctic. For with the polar bear, the sasquatch met their match."

"What about mountain lions?" Inertia asked.

"Rainbow Rivers once told me that sasquatch and mountain lions hold a strong alliance. It's much like a master and pet relationship. The lions offer dead animals and the sasquatch reward them with play and affection. They also sleep together. I mean that in the literal sense." Wolfgang Yellowbird turned his attention to Sigmund and said: "Sleeping companions provide comfort. Would you agree, Earl?"

Earl nodded.

"Where did you get Sigmund?"

"He was a stray," Earl said. "I found him."

"He must have escaped from a dog fighting ring."

"That's possible."

"It's not just possible. It's probable. Did you not see the skill he demonstrated? That's trained violence. He's a hell hound."

Sigmund was arching his neck, licking the creature that clung to his belly.

"We should name him," said Inertia.

"How about Jung," offered Earl.

"Why? Because he's young?"

"Jung with a J."

"Will Jung with a J murder us in our sleep?" asked Paul.

"He's an innocent child, and a forest treasure," said Wolfgang Yellowbird.

"Who will grow into the Hulk."

"He will grow with us, as one of us, and I will protect him with my life. Now, he's probably hungry and desires something a little more substantial than my divine honey candies. Inertia, you wouldn't happen to be lactating?" Wolfgang Yellowbird asked as he rummaged through the folds of his cloak. He pulled out a can of coconut cream and opened it. He handed it to Jung who detached himself from Sigmund and accepted it warily. He held it with his small hands and sniffed it before bringing the can to his lips. The white liquid dribbled down his chin and belly. Wolfgang Yellowbird offered venison jerky and trail mix. Jung devoured it noisily, stuffing his mouth so full that he could barely swallow.

Randolph was standing above Kyle's grave as the others returned. A cross stood from the ground that he had made with two branches and twine. His eyes were red and swollen. "All things bright and beautiful," he said. "All creatures great and small." He acknowledged Jung who had climbed off of Sigmund to explore the encampment. "What is this demon you brought with you?"

"His mother was killed by wolves," Inertia told him. "We're taking care of him now."

"You should set him on fire," Randolph said.

"Be careful with your words, Randolph," Wolfgang Yellowbird said. "There will be no more violence today."

"There is violence everywhere. Evil has shocked the planet."

Wolfgang Yellowbird stroked his beard that was the colour of thunderstorms and motioned for the others to prepare for departure.

Earl watched Randolph collect his belongings. His movements were deliberate. He folded his clothing, combed his hair, brushed his teeth. He was moving forward, blinking his eyes in the flashing sunshine. Earl wanted to offer comfort. He felt the need to reciprocate the support Randolph had so freely given him. But he could think of no words or gestures capable of quelling such impervious solemnity. All he could do was meet the man's eyes and offer silent solidarity.

Randolph grabbed Kyle's backpack and dumped its contents onto the forest floor. He picked through the pile of clothes until he unearthed an unopened bottle of whiskey and a handgun.

"What you got?" Earl asked.

Randolph weighed the objects in his hands, seemingly comparing their destructive potentials.

"Drop the gun," said Wolfgang Yellowbird. "What you do with the whiskey is up to you, but you will drop that gun."

Randolph pointed the gun at Jung and fired. The bullet missed badly, lodging itself in a tree trunk. Jung ran to Inertia who picked him up and shielded him with her back.

Randolph screamed at her to get out of the way. He fired a shot into the air then levelled the gun at her. But before he could pull the trigger, the full force of Wolfgang Yellowbird's naked mass slammed into him. Randolph hit the ground. The gun and whiskey fell from his hands. Wolfgang Yellowbird picked them up and kicked Randolph in the ribs.

"We will blame this on grief induced insanity, Randolph," Wolfgang Yellowbird said, leering down at him. "But if you perpetrate another such indiscretion, I will kill you."

Randolph was gasping. "I'm sorry," he wheezed, looking at Inertia. "So awfully sorry."

"This is no place for guns and booze," said Wolfgang Yellowbird. "I'll discard them in the woods where they can do us no harm." He cursed Kyle's name as he walked away.

Earl noticed Randolph's anguished eyes staring at the gap in the trees where Wolfgang Yellowbird had disappeared.

Jung climbed onto Inertia's shoulder and Clovis Redux began marching towards the Rocky Mountain range. It seemed like a painting to Earl. A vertical horizon piercing the sky. Its edges of snow and rock were vivid even at this great distance, and amidst the small white clouds that circled its highest peaks, golden eagles, the size of pixels, were soaring.

Randolph trailed the others at distance. Earl lost sight of him for several minutes. He called his name without reply. When Randolph appeared again, Earl slowed his pace to keep him in range. He talked to him but Randolph wouldn't answer. He shook his head with his eyes downcast and welling with tears. "You're here with us," Earl told him. "You're not alone. Shame and regret fade with time and people forgive."

"Not all people," Inertia said.

Wolfgang Yellowbird led the group. The wolf on his back had gone stiff with rigor mortis. Its eyes were wide-open and its tongue hung through its bared teeth. Blood had dripped and smeared all over Wolfgang Yellowbird's back, buttocks and thighs. He said: "I've never known of a sasquatch joining a human troop, but I've heard of the opposite. Sixty-odd years ago a family went camping in Washington state and had the misfortune of losing their four-year-old daughter in the wilderness. Search and rescue teams combed the area for many days before they were forced to abandon the mission. It was assumed the poor child had died of exposure or had been picked off by a carnivore. Several years later, a young and spritely park ranger by the name of Gwilym Cyril was responding to a call about a cougar acting aggressively in a camp site. He followed the cat's tracks for the better part of the day and this took him deep into the forest. By his account, it was nearing the twilight hour, and he was about to call it a day when he heard a noise that he described as singing. It got louder and louder until a family of sasquatch emerged before him. With them was the little human girl. The flabbergasted Gwilym froze as the father sasquatch approached him. He offered Gwilym the hand of the human child, but she didn't want to go. She cried and clung to the sasquatch with all her little might. But she would eventually calm down and say her goodbyes to each sasquatch in turn. She hugged and kissed them, blubbering all the while. Then she took Gwilym's hand and was reunited with her human family.

"When Gwilym reported to his superiors he was forced to take a leave of absence to seek psychiatric help. But, as Gwilym would tell you, there is nothing else that could account for the little girl's survival. A lost four-year-old human cannot survive the wilds.

"Gwilym, of course, became obsessed. He absconded to the hinterland to seek and study the sasquatch, only popping back to civilization for supplies and to send and receive letters from the little girl. He wanted to know all about her life. She wanted to know about the sasquatch. They grew very close over the years, and eventually, she joined Gwilym in his research."

"Are they still together?" asked Intertia.

"Over time their sexual chemistry became too strange and their ethical differences became too great. Gwilym thought her methods were too aggressive. Too intrusive. She found his to be benign and ineffectual. They had epic battles and arguments with one another. Some confrontations even came to blows. And they were forced to go their separate ways."

"How do you know all this?"

"I've heard both sides of the story first hand," said Wolfgang Yellowbird.

"The little girl is Rainbow Rivers," Inertia said.

Wolfgang Yellowbird didn't respond. Instead, he walked in silence through the tortured forest. Eyes downcast. Expression grim. His shoulders stooped, as if the weight of the Rocky Mountains ahead, sat perched upon them.

It was twilight when the Happy Rainbow drone arrived to take snap shots of Clovis Redux. It found Inertia lying on her back and looking up at the unfamiliar constellations that had begun to speckle the darkening sky. The setting sun shot flares from beyond the horizon, tricking the sky in Technicolour and morphing the forest with furtive shadows. She pointed at the moon that was reflecting the lightshow like a mirror-ball. It had spun on its head. The man in the moon was no longer there. He had been replaced by a Rorschach rabbit. Paul followed her gaze and said: "Happy Rainbow bastards. You'd think they'd have better things to do. The world is at its end and they're hung up on a petty grudge." He picked up a branch and flung it at the drone, which dip-dodged and continued taking photos. It caught Randolph disrobing. His shirt, pants and underwear dropped to the ground. The drone switched to rapid-fire shutter-speed, slowing time to capture Randolph's soul as it evaporated into the forest, and a smouldering demon emerged from the shadows to claim it. Randolph sat on a log beside Wolfgang Yellowbird and said: "If Adam and Eve were naked during creation, then I'll be naked during destruction." Wolfgang Yellowbird nodded and replied: "The devil is here. He's whispering in your ear."

Jung sat with Sigmund. He was combing through his fur, checking for ticks. He accepted a slab of raw wolf meat offered to him by Wolfgang Yellowbird. He skewered it with a stick and placed it in the fire.

"You use fire?" Wolfgang Yellowbird asked. "What's the sasquatch population of this forest? What's your life expectancy? Do you travel in packs or stick to family units? Are you balkanized? Can females give birth to litters? How far do you range? How do you remain so elusive? Are you polygamous? Was there much inbreeding after the great slaughter? Where is your father? Does the name Rainbow Rivers mean anything to you?"

Jung replied with what sounded like sass. He went back to grooming Sigmund.

Earl was consuming an entire wolf shank. The meat was tough and gristly but his hunger was insatiable. His body demanded nourishment despite the strange flavour and texture in his mouth. He felt crackling sparks of energy. There was a jangly vigour in his tendons and nerves. His stomach was warm with blood, no longer spewing strong acid up his esophagus. His heart beat powerfully in his chest and he felt its perpetuating fortitude grow in energy. His sleep the previous night was the first true rest his body had experienced in years, allowing his consciousness to fully shut down and his organs to regenerate. His liver had resumed its fight, free from the sludge that had all but shut it down, and his digestive tract was functioning again. He had experienced an epic bowel movement; a blessing upon his fundament that emerged from his anus as a single king coil, solid as oak. He took a deep breath to combat a nicotine craving. He felt oxygen flow through him, reaching every small crevice in his convalescing body.

Earl thought about flying as the sun fully extinguished itself and darkness annexed everything beyond the fringes of the campfire. Flying is easy, he thought. All you have to do is close your eyes. Earl alighted from the forest and followed the darkness through the sky. He headed in the direction that used to be east and found Toronto, flooded. The CN Tower snapped at the neck. He searched for Samantha but could not find her amongst the millions of corpses bobbing throughout the city streets. He kept going. The British Isles were submerged, leaving sharks to pick at the bloated corpses that found their way to the surface. Siberia was melted. The Asian sub-continent, marooned by earthquakes, slowly floated out to sea. Australia, incinerated. Sub-Saharan Africa, frozen. South America, gone. What kind of agent would pen such a narrative, Earl wondered. What kind of psychopathic malcontent could conflate this concatenation of destruction? What kind of bloodshot eyes could envision such a massacre? Gone were the polar ice caps, the elephants and snow leopards. Gone were the jungles, the vipers, and the chirping tree frogs. In their stead was a nightmare, unconcerned with the insufferable sadness of death and the unbearable weight of grief. This careless rage went beyond biblical proportions. It wasn't a suite of plagues or forty days of rain, because those slaps-on-the-wrist allowed for the propagation of humanity through the survival of the righteous. This, on the other hand, was eradication. Extermination. Annihilation. Obliteration. Humankind wiped out in swaths. Then, stragglers were picked off in turn; like the little girl in Istanbul holding her little brother in the eye of a tornado. Or the old man in Albay negotiating a lava field with his wife in a wheel barrow. Or the woman taking her chances at sea to escape a New York City ravaged by rapists, marauders and murderers. And what about the boats scattered about the seas? Those weren't Arks. They were shrieks in the dark, quickly getting pulled towards the Algeria-sized maelstroms churning the oceans. Earl began to fear for his soul as he flew around Earth's tattered panorama. It could so easily be lost in the terror, leaving his body-husk to topple into the campfire. As he made his way back to the Crystal Valley, he wondered why he couldn't see the souls of others floating in the sky with him. Had they transcended this nightmare to dwell upon a different plain? Or had they simply deliquesced into the ether? On a brighter day, this would be a question for Randolph.

When Earl returned to the forest, Wolfgang Yellowbird was yelping. "A mosquito bit the lip of my urethra," he bellowed. He hopped about the encampment until Randolph sat him down to apply raw honey to the stinging prick mark. "I'll have trouble urinating through such a thick balm," Wolfgang Yellowbird said. "But the sensation is staggering."

A broken signal crackled through Paul's radio speaker.

'DOOMSDAY THEORISTS . . . RIGHTEOUS-
NESS . . . WORLDWIDE . . . DESENTERS
CLAIM . . . INEVITABILITY . . . PIOUS PREDIC-
TIONS . . . HATE . . . INTERGALACTIC GENO-
CIDE . . . THAT THE SOLAR ACTIVITY . . .
DYING OF THE SUN . . . END OF DAYS . . .
MAY GOD HAVE MERCY ON OUR . . .'

The transmission turned to static and Paul switched it off. "If Earth is going down, it's a shame the sun has to go with it," he said.

"What do the flares mean?" asked Randolph.

"It means that at any second the sun is going to implode."

"But surely God could breathe more life into it."

"Have you ever heard of the anthropic principle?" Paul asked.

Randolph shook his head.

"A universe is destined to be conducive to the existence of life. It doesn't need a God to bestow it. And we aren't alone. Our universe is one of many in a colossal multiverse that stretches and stretches far beyond the scope of our collective imaginations."

"What's going on in these other universes?" Randolph asked.

"Nothing, mostly. The vast majority of them lay bare and empty. But all of them have the potential to create and sustain life, because nature allows this to be. Soon, our sun will collapse backwards without limit. The black hole it creates will consume and scramble all the matter of this universe and blast it out the other side. What happens next is anyone's guess."

"That's the afterlife," Earl said. "That's how it happens."

"In a way," agreed Paul. "The sun displaces all the energy from this universe into a new one."

"There had to be a starting point for this multiverse," Randolph said. "It's a physical law that something cannot be created from nothing. Something had to start the whole process."

"And that would be God?" Paul asked.

Randolph nodded.

"What if there was no existence? Would we need a God to create that too?"

"God is eternal."

"The idea of God in your mind cannot diminish the merits of nature."

Randolph stifled a sob. "We have forsaken God and we are smote. Look at the damage we have inflicted upon the planet, the hatred and fear we feel towards others and ourselves. I don't think I can stand it."

"We just have to be patient, Randolph," Earl said. "We can try again on the other side."

NATURISM

DAYS OF SOBRIETY: 6

Jung chewed on Earl's hair, matting it into wet clumps. He put his ear against his chest and mimicked the sounds of breath, heart beat and stomach gurgles. His little fingers plugged Earl's ears and nostrils, curled in his beard, poked his torso, thigh, scrotum. The sensations coaxed Earl into a wakefulness, in which he was unsettled to learn that the pleasures he was receiving were being administered by a grinning primate whose teeth were glowing in violent new-dawn light.

Inertia's body was pressed against him. Her breath was hot and moist against his neck. She was groaning, dreaming in a world far away from this one, where possibilities were only restricted by the limits of her mind. This saddened Earl, because an imagination like Inertia's should have infinite range and unlimited freedom to explore and express. Otherwise, it was a caged bird, moulting before its captor; singing sad songs of longing. He kissed her mouth and felt the soft flesh of her lips. He tasted her saliva. Small bubbles glided across the tongue. Her breath was sour. Her teeth mossy. Earl wanted to live here, forever treading light in her warm aura of sleep. He caught the curiosity in Jung's eyes which snapped him back to reason. His kiss was a violation—an assault upon her body that deprived them both of the gratification of mutual consent.

Inertia stirred and woke. Blinking. Recharged. Electrified. She studied Earl's face and gauged his expression. "Good morning?"

"I kissed you. I'm sorry."

"I wish you hadn't told me," Inertia said. "You killed the mystery in your eyes." She leaned forward and brushed her lips across the wound on Earl's cheek. She kissed his eyelids, his neck, his lips. "You're forgiven," she said.

Jung began to chatter and pounce on their entwined bodies. He pointed at his penis.

"He's hung like an elephant," Inertia said.

"I think he has to pee." Earl stood and accepted Jung's small hand in his own. Jung led him into the trees where they emptied their bladders. He climbed onto Earl's shoulder and pointed through the gaps in the tree cover. Flashing sunlight had breached the shrouded Rocky Mountains in pulses of kaleidoscopic power. The last star in the sky twinkled out.

Jung's nose sniffed energetically. He growled and became rigid. He jumped off Earl's shoulder and climbed a tree. He began screaming, panting. Tears wetted his face.

"He smells smoke," Inertia said. "His senses are acute."

Earl reached his arms into the air. He took his time coaxing Jung down from the tree.

Earl shook Wolfgang Yellowbird awake.

Through a mass of hair and tree-sap-dreaded beard, the old man stared back, taking a moment to determine his whereabouts in the multiverse. "What dimension are we in?"

"There's smoke," Earl told him. "Jung is panicked."

"Indeed," Wolfgang Yellowbird said. "The sasquatch's fear of fire is justified. The inferno has breached the Black Ridge." He rose and prepared breakfast. Oatmeal infused with cinnamon sticks and vanilla beans. "I'm going to throw in some horseradish for kicks." He stirred the pot with his rusty ladle, staring blankly, lost in thought. The porridge began to soften and congeal. "It's a dark day," he said. "But as the old bones of the forest rattle awake and inhale deep breaths from the sky, the primal elements will fight for the requisition of our planet. These trees are angels and the birds in the branches are the angel's eyes, watching over us."

"Lucifer is an angel," Randolph said, stretching his naked body and tying his hair back. He accepted his bowl of oatmeal with thanks. "He was once the brightest star in the sky and the Son of the dawn. But the morning star can never reach the highest point in the sky before fading out in the light of the rising sun."

"Now he lives here with us," said Wolfgang Yellowbird. "Prowling through the smoke with smouldering eyes."

Randolph nodded. "Cast down to Earth to unleash the deadly sins, and raise a satanic legion in this bloody sewage of transgression." Randolph took a bite of oatmeal and looked up at the flashing sky. "We're beyond deliverance. God's grace no longer exists in this place. Perdition waits for us beyond the sun. Life waits for death." He noticed Inertia, scribbling poetry with her pencil. He asked if she would read it aloud.

Feel this: it breathes like we breathe,
A wilderness taller than cities.
Time: 14 billion years
Past and future water through your fingers.

Crumple the page,
Shake the branches with eggs to the floor.
Shine fire in the crevasses,
Grind the world to seeds.

The ocean floor is simpler,
Coruscation, this seahorse, features
Unglimpsable.
Beasts grow fat from carrion in the water.

Without a beginning or end, life cheapens
Though not one volunteers for slaughter.
Our memories are clear as glacial melt,
Pressed flat like dried flowers.

The past is the tree's shadow,
A future is the way landscapes form.
In this spell upon the great serpent's back
We have achieved enlightenment. We have walked on
the Moon.

—

By early afternoon everyone was slick with sweat and the river was a welcome sight. It was wide and breaching with melted snow. Wolfgang Yellowbird waded in to his knees. "It's painfully cold," he said. "But a vigorous ablution and shampoozling is well earned. We're awfully ripe." He dove in. Sigmund and Jung lunged in behind. The current moved them downstream as Wolfgang Yellowbird hollered, laughed and praised the 'magic of this blessed forest.' Sigmund howled. Jung screeched. Randolph eased himself in, and groaned at the frigidity and his 'aging gonads that aren't as hardy as they used to be.'

Earl watched Inertia disrobe. The details of her ink-work were intense against her pale skin. There was a fairy on her shoulder whose wings blurred like a hummingbird's. On her heart-shaped buttocks a fawn lowered its head towards a patch of grass. The wind-bent tree on her upper thigh shed arrowhead leaves that feathered down her leg. A raven extended its wings across her shoulder blades, and the spider that had weaved its web on her stomach left a hole for her belly button to peek through. She noticed Earl's gaze.

"Do you like my tattoos?"

Earl nodded and noticed that her pubic hair *was* wheaten.

"James told me that for my next birthday I could get them all removed with lasers. As if that was something I wanted." She dove into the water and came up spitting. "Holy hell that's cold."

Earl stripped. He could feel the others watching. Why was it that he could sprawl confidently naked upon the sands of Hanlan's Point before the eyes of thousands of strangers, but be unnerved by the judgment of friends? It wasn't the skeletons in his closet he was unveiling. He wasn't disclosing dark mysteries of his secret life. He was merely exposing a sexual organ. He whipped off his underwear and dipped his toes in.

"You have to jump in," Inertia told him. "It's the only way."

Earl followed her advice. He lost his breath and felt layers of grit alight from his body to be captured in current and swallowed by churning silt.

Paul stood alone on the water's edge. He slowly took off his hare-hide moccasins.

"Nothing to be afraid of, Paul," sputtered Wolfgang Yellowbird. "It's time for you to truly embrace the freedom this wilderness affords."

Paul disrobed. His penis looked like a purple grape, lost in a great jungle of pubic hair. "It might as well not exist," he said. "It's a curse from God."

"There is no God," said Randolph. "You only have Mother Nature to blame for your tiny munchkin."

"We're all made differently is all," said Wolfgang Yellowbird. "Take Jung for instance. He stands as high as my knee but his penis is quadruple the length and girth of mine."

Paul jumped in the water. He surfaced to find that two grizzlies had emerged from the forest, puffing heavily in the torrid heat. A cub ran from the trees to join them at the water's edge.

"It's Jesus," Wolfgang Yellowbird cried. "He has returned again. We must protect this creature from yet another grizzly death." The bears sniffed Paul's pile of clothing. "Paul, they remember your musk from the night you spent snuggling with them in the cave."

The bears entered the water and swam up to Paul.

"Don't try to get away, Paul," Wolfgang Yellowbird said. "It'll excite them into a fury."

The bears surrounded Paul and sniffed at him. They licked his face and body.

"Help," Paul whimpered.

"They're showing no aggression. Your scent must have melded with pleasant dreams they were having during hibernation." Wolfgang Yellowbird chuckled as the bears began to lumber excitedly. They chased Paul through the water and took turns tossing him into the air. Paul's expression contained both terror and joy. It was an exhilarating harassment. "Nature's balance is most surely out of whack," Wolfgang Yellowbird said.

Earl felt Inertia against his back. Her fingers curled through his. She led him to the river bank and they entered the trees.

They found a bed of moss, which they drenched with river water, fresh sweat, and reproductive lubricants. Saliva flicked off their energetic tongues. Through the writhing of limbs and quaking of muscles, Earl noticed the orchestra of birdsong that fluttered through the trees and charged the forest with resplendent sound. He imagined the birds hopping in branches and staring down with angel eyes at the exotic novelty of human canoodling. Why are these strange, hairless bipeds ravaging one another on the forest floor? Earl felt the heat of their twinning beings. The friction of flesh. Pummelling heartbeats pounded the forest floor and scattered pine needles. There was great energy surrounding them. Propelling them. Propelling the birds. Propelling the trees higher and higher into the sky. Reaching for the horizons, the core of the Earth, the core of their bodies where desire overcame them. But desire was only a symptom of this energy, which emanated from a much deeper source. It was the awakening of their fundamental humanities, recharged by the decomposition of loneliness. It was the energy of friendship. The energy of love.

"That was the big bang," Inertia said. "We just created a new universe." They lay beside one another. Earl was on his back and Inertia was on her side with her head perched on the palm of her hand. Her other hand ran along Earl's body until it rested on his penis, which she held like a newborn animal. "Do you think your wife is still alive?"

"I hope she is." Earl could feel his penis hardening again. "But she might have drowned."

"She could have escaped."

"I'll never know."

"Maybe she's happier now than ever before. She's on her own Wanderland Adventure."

"She deserves that," Earl said.

"What would've made you happy?"

"A child. A daughter."

"Would the responsibility of fatherhood have kept you sober?" Inertia asked.

"I think so. It would've given me meaning."

"Could a child have saved your marriage?"

"Samantha never wanted a child. She would've resented her."

"What about in this new reality, with the world left behind. Could you have started again?"

"I poisoned her, emotionally. There could be no coming back from that."

"Do you miss her?"

"Not since I saw the speckles in your eyes."

Inertia smiled and said: "We found each other."

Earl laughed. "We have something to live for."

A massive noise came roaring through the trees. They looked up to see Jung riding Sigmund like a pony, with Jesus in hot pursuit. The three of them crashed to the forest floor where they engaged in epic arboreal wrestling that enticed great howls from Jesus and Sigmund, and high-pitched shrieks from Jung.

Then a gunshot. Loud and close.

Randolph sat with his back against a trembling aspen. Kyle's gun lay in his hand. The emptied bottle of whiskey was cradled in his lap. The bullet had passed through his mouth and blown open the back of his head, from which brains sluiced through patterns of tree bark.

Earl looked into Randolph's eyes. They were wide and devil-red. His final moment of life stared back at Earl, eclipsing any light Randolph may have left behind. His body was slack, as if resting away the heat of the afternoon upon a soft patch of undergrowth. But the edges of his respite had torn open and its contents spilt into the mercy of peaceful eternity. Randolph's head lolled downwards and Earl put his hand against the wound to cover the pain. He wished for it to disappear.

"God dammit," Wolfgang Yellowbird shouted. "I can't lose anymore fucking Clovi."

Earl couldn't stop his tears from flowing when Randolph's body was covered in earth and shielded from the visible world. "He was my great friend," he said.

"He still is, Earl," said Wolfgang Yellowbird. "His flesh will nourish the valley. His spirit will find new life and a great energy will explode through the trees. Just like tomorrow's new dawn sun, Randolph will find us again."

"I should have saved him."

Inertia embraced Earl. His tears rolled down her shoulder.

"I should have been with him."

"Nothing could have stopped this," Paul said. "Not after his God left him." He picked up the gun. "I'm taking this."

Wolfgang Yellowbird nodded grimly. "We should press on." Smoke was filtering through the trees, catching rays of flashing sunlight. He turned his attention to where an otter and ferret emerged from the undergrowth. "It appears a domesticated ferret is in our midst," he said. He stooped down to examine the tag dangling from the ferret's collar. It read: DOUG.

"Doug?" Earl asked.

Doug pawed at the loose soil of Randolph's grave. His nose burrowed deeply. He went to Randolph's backpack and emptied the contents. He crawled inside. Earl picked it up and slung it over his shoulder. "He's been tracking Randolph," he said. "He was minutes too late."

They crossed the river, leaving piles of clothing on the other side. "It's a natural firebreak," Wolfgang Yellowbird said. "It will buy us some time."

The otter emerged from the water with a rainbow trout flapping in her jaws. She dropped it on the river bank and tore out the skull. Earl remembered what Randolph had said about this otter. That her power was a great inspiration to him, and that she was put on this Earth to thrive. Randolph's power was also an inspiration. His compassion for Earl had saved him. Without Randolph, Earl would be a corpse by now, floating down a Toronto avenue, or starved to death in a forgotten jail cell. But Randolph had brought him here instead, to thrive in this fantastic wilderness.

The otter brought the trout to Wolfgang Yellowbird and placed it at his feet. Wolfgang Yellowbird picked it up and took a bite. He thanked the otter and passed the fish to Inertia.

"What a strange posse we've become," Wolfgang Yellowbird said, watching the fish pass from being to being, until Jesus swallowed it whole. Wolfgang Yellowbird ate some LSD then turned to lead the others deeper into the Crystal Valley.

An opalescent tear-drop of light floated down from the tree tops. It stopped its descent at eye-level and hovered throughout the company of travellers. When it spoke, its voice emanated from the sky.

"Hello, Wolfgang Yellowbird."

"Crystal. It has been so long. You look tired. You've aged greatly."

"These are hard times."

"What's happening?" Wolfgang Yellowbird asked.

"We're losing loved ones." Crystal landed on Jung's shoulder. "My poor child," she said. "The trees told me what happened to your mother. Be brave my sweet." Jung cooed. He closed his eyes and Crystal caught his tear. She held it in her arms like a boulder before it broke and spilt to the ground. She rose back into the air with wings treading light. "Our world is angry," she said. "But we're not without hope." She pressed herself against Inertia's belly. "There is new life here. We must cherish what's left. Love one another. Be good stewards of the Earth."

"I've tried," said Wolfgang Yellowbird. "But I failed."

"You have been this valley's great protector, Wolfgang Yellowbird, and you are not alone anymore. You have many friends here that have come to understand the ethos of this forest."

"Where are the others?" Wolfgang Yellowbird asked.

"They have moved on," Crystal said. "I'm the last to remain."

"Why did you stay?"

"The devil is thriving. I must temper its diabolism."

"You're losing."

"I am."

"What do we do now?"

"Continue onwards," said Crystal. "Live your lives and let experience enrich your souls." She floated back upwards into the tree tops. "Bless you Wolfgang Yellowbird," her voice was fading. "Bless you all."

Wolfgang Yellowbird called after her but there was no response. "So cryptic," he muttered. He turned towards the others. His beard was black in shadow. "I've dedicated my life to this place. But it's burning up now. The world is too evil to allow such beauty to exist."

"We can try again," Inertia said.

"But how many attempts has humanity had to gets things right?" Wolfgang Yellowbird asked. "How many planets have we already destroyed?"

"Things will be better next time," Inertia said. "There will be no pipelines or chemical fire."

"Will I still be needed here?"

"You're always needed here, Wolfgang Yellowbird. We all are." She squeezed Earl's hand. "We have a child to raise."

"If only we could watch her grow up," Earl said.

"We will. It might be fourteen billion years from now on the other side of the sun, but I can wait. Can you?"

Earl nodded. "Do you think Randolph will be there?" he asked.

"Yes."

"He will make a great god father."

"He will."

"You're all whacked out," Paul said. "The chance of life existing in the next universe is infinitesimal. And if by some miracle it does evolve it will be nothing like this world. Chaos won't allow it. The world as we know it is over. This is the end of it."

"But life is possible?" Earl asked.

"Well, yes, but—"

"So shut up, Paul."

Wolfgang Yellowbird stopped walking. "We're getting close now," he said. "But I can't go any further." He lay down on the ground and closed his eyes. Jung snuggled in with him and they were both instantly asleep. Paul slouched against a tree with the grizzlies. The otter joined Doug in Randolph's backpack, which was transformed into an extravagant nest during the night, brimming with things Doug deemed important: pine cones, Paul's radio, samples of Wolfgang Yellowbird's beard, honey candies, grizzly feces.

The sun had set but there was still a bounty of light from the ever-intensifying solar flares that rippled across the atmosphere. No stars were visible on this night. They were engulfed in light. Earl lay down with Inertia and Sigmund. Slashes of silver and gold burned though his eyelids and illuminated his darkness.

Earl watches sand flow through his fingers. He sees the individual grains. Heat waves distort the horizons. The glare off the aeroplane metal is too bright to look at straight on. The sun is flaring here too. The monster stands before him, eating people. Some he swallows whole. Others in bite-sized nibbles. A head, a torso, a shoe with a foot inside. The sounds of crunching bone and snapping cartilage sicken Earl. His shudders catch the monster's attention as he pulls the corpse of Adolf Hitler from the torn plane cabin. He pops it in his mouth and chews. He savours this one. It is especially delicious. "Do you eat children?" Earl asks. "Grunt." "Women?" "Grunt." "Will you eat anybody as long as they're dead?" "Grunt Grunt." "You only eat evil people." "Grunt." "I'm evil?" "Grunt." "Why did you eat Randolph? He wasn't evil. He wasn't a murderer." The monster lifts Earl from the ground and begins to walk. "Randolph was a good man. He saved my life." Earl sighs. "He was a rapist?" "Grunt." "Is rape worse than murder?" The monster bobs his head as if to say: 'It depends.' "There are grey areas in your righteous judgement." The monster bobs his head again. "You should consider my transgression. I didn't kill Murphy. My hand may have wielded the blade but I was possessed at the time." "HLLLUG HRRMPH GRUNT GRUNT." "I couldn't stop it. I couldn't not drink." The monster continues walking. "I've been getting better. I'm sober." The monster looks down at him. His breath is sweet. Earl is silent for awhile, enjoying the oblique beauty of beige. "Did you eat Samantha?" "Grunt Grunt." "Is she still alive?" "Grunt." "Will you eat her when she goes?" The monster doesn't answer. He's staring into the distance at shapes emerging through the heat waves. Two shapes. Both human. One large. One small. The monster stops to pick them up. "Thanks for the lift," says Jefferson Roswell. "Where are we headed?" asks the yellowing man. The monster points to the strobing sun.

FOR THE TREES

DAYS OF SOBRIETY: 7

When a flaming snowshoe hare ran past, it was time to start moving. Wolfgang Yellowbird roused his company and screamed of fire. Doug, the otter, and Jung dangled from his arms. Sigmund and Jesus nipped at his heels. The air was hot. The forest was a monster's stomach, sealed fast but letting light through. Solar flares were pooling in the ozone layer. They had scorched the moon.

Earl was alive and blinking through the smoke. It was thick and vivid. It burnt the back of his nostrils. Inertia's naked body moved against him. He looked around at the others and imagined them all burning together in a heap of melting flesh. Their screams wouldn't be heard above the roaring flames. The pain would be intense until the nerves were gone and their bodies were left to char. There are worse ways to die. Like starvation. A body cannibalizing itself, and watching its family suffer the same torture upon the cracked earth that was once lush with sprouting maize and mangos while the western world throws away its billions of tonnes of cosmetically unappealing food. What about death by animal? Earl wondered. Shredded by a lioness. Liquified by fire ants. Scrunched by an anaconda. Perhaps the most peaceful way to go would be in palliative care, surrounded by loved ones, loaded with opioids and enjoying a splendid window view. Would a plane crash be the most exciting death? The ultimate adrenaline rush that grants you precious minutes to experience primal fear and reflect on successes and failures, accomplishments and regrets. Or death by imploding sun? There is nothing so instantaneous. Earl's mind felt around, sprouting stems that reached into the past, seeking the cosmic equation of preceding incident that had created this exact moment in time. Memories of alcohol and rage scuttled into the dark areas of his brain. His time in the deep woods had eroded them. Before him lay his Eden. It was a vast expanse where he had his second chance. He watched Randolph walk naked into the trees. He turned to Earl and smiled before vanishing into the light of the sun. Earl felt his love. He felt his sobriety.

Clovis Redux were on their feet and moving. Wolfgang Yellowbird led the way. Jung hung around his neck, bouncing in stride and baring his teeth in grimaces. "We're close," Wolfgang Yellowbird panted. "I can see the whites of the mountain's eyes glaring down at this bloodshot valley."

Inertia was trailing. Falling behind. Earl took her hand.

"So much of this beautiful forest has passed us by," Inertia said. "We're too busy staring at our feet, worried about tripping over roots. We're lost in the understory."

"We must keep moving," Earl said.

"We can't control anything." She allowed Earl to pull her along. "All we can do is burn through time. I wanted to write one great poem that could change the world. But I'm far too small."

"You don't have to write it," Earl said. "Your expression says it all."

"But no one will see it but you."

"Isn't that enough?"

"Not if we're dead."

"You can try again."

"What if I can't?" Inertia asked. "What if things never improve and people like me continue to get crushed by the weight of gravity? We die because we feel too deeply. We're too sensitive to survive in such a terrible world because we understand its sickness. Imagine all the great works that were never finished or even started. These were gifts never realized because they weren't allowed to exist. Sylvia Plath. Vincent van Gogh. Elliot Smith. David Foster Wallace. Philip Seymour Hoffman. Virginia Woolf drowned herself in the Ouse River. She filled her pockets with rocks."

"That would be a painful death," Earl said.

"It would be cleansing. You could watch the sunlight dance on the surface as sentience slowly faded from your mind." Inertia tripped on a fallen branch. Blood poured from her knee. Earl pressed the wound as she recited Woolf's suicide note: "'You have given me the greatest possible happiness. You have been in every way all that anyone could be. I don't think two people could have been happier till this terrible disease came. I can't fight any longer . . . If anybody could have saved me it would have been you. Everything has gone from me but the certainty of your goodness.'"

"Love survives. Even in great sadness." Earl kissed her. He tasted the salt of her tears. He held her face in his hands. They embraced and vanished in grey smoke.

Sigmund was barking. There was panic in his voice. When he found Earl and Inertia he was panting heavily, willing them to hurry. They caught up to the others who stood in a cleared area that a tornado had rampaged through. It opened their view of the snow-capped mountains ahead.

Wolfgang Yellowbird was bent over at the waist and heaving oxygen. He stared at the mountain and pointed at a plateau above the tree line. "See that slab of retardant rock? That's where we need to go."

Sigmund's fur raised on end. He growled as a creature emerged from the trees in a cloud of billowing smoke.

"What the flower is that?" said Paul.

Wolfgang Yellowbird raised a hand, demanding silence.

It stood a meter tall on two bent legs. Its skin was deep brown and piebald. Patches of coarse black hair sprouted sporadically about a body that stooped at the shoulders. Its spine was unnaturally long, stretching the skin at the tailbone and the nape of the neck. The arms were heavily muscled, hanging slack and slowly swaying. Ribs protruded through taut skin that pulsed with the beating of its heart. Its ears were long and dangled below a mass of black curls piled high on its head. It opened its mouth in a dark oval, baring yellow teeth, and stared at Clovis Redux with darting black eyes. It walked to Sigmund and patted his head. It ran its long fingers down his back. Its lips curled in a ghastly smile. It furrowed its tall brow as a woman entered the clearing, accompanied by a massive male sasquatch.

"Hello, Wolfgang," said Rainbow Rivers.

Wolfgang Yellowbird stared at the woman who stood naked before him.

Rainbow Rivers put her hand on the creature's head. "This is Gunter."

"Is he . . . ?"

"Mine? Yes. And this is his father, Yusuf."

Yusuf walked to Wolfgang Yellowbird. He stopped in front of him, dwarfing him, and put his hand out. Wolfgang Yellowbird stared up at the hulking massif that towered above him and filled the entire forest.

"He was curious about human customs so I taught him some," Rainbow Rivers said.

Wolfgang Yellowbird put out his hand and Yusuf enveloped it in his, gently shook it and said: "Noys tmeeeeeetyuhhh." His voice sent tremors into the ground. He walked towards Jung, who was hopping on the ground with his arms reaching into the air. His little fingers wriggled. Yusuf lifted him and cradled Jung's little head in the nape of his tree-trunk neck. His booming laugh shook the forest as Jung scampered about his shoulders. Yusuf turned to Sigmund and said: "Tshaaankoo wroolfok."

"He thanks the wolf-fox," Rainbow Rivers said. "The forest informed him of the dog's bravery. How he saved Job from the wolves."

"Job?" asked Wolfgang Yellowbird.

"Job is Yusuf's son," said Rainbow Rivers. "We've been tracking him ever since we heard what happened to his mother. I'm glad you found him, Wolfgang. I assured Yusuf that he was being well cared for."

"So, they are polygamous," said Wolfgang Yellowbird.

"Not necessarily. It was more a situation of species propagation. Yusuf and Grendle were close friends but never lovers. She wanted a child and Yusuf helped her with that. Mates have been hard to come by since the Great Slaughter." Rainbow Rivers embraced Wolfgang Yellowbird. "I'm sorry," she said.

Wolfgang Yellowbird ran his hand through her white hair. "I missed your body. I missed the crinkles by your eyes." He breathed deeply. "I missed your smell."

"I missed you too, Wolfgang."

"Why did you leave?"

"You know why."

They let go and Wolfgang Yellowbird smiled. "I'm happy you found your sasquatch, Rainbow."

They held one another by the finger tips, gazing into each other's eyes. Two souls, seemingly designed for one another, but lost in the wilderness.

"Time to go." The voice came from a man emerging from the tree line. "Wind has pushed the fire across the river. It's coming on fast." He was very old, hunch-backed, and dressed all in khaki. He carried an injured fawn in his arms. "Hello, everyone. I'm Gwilym Cyril."

"Nice to see you, Gwilym," said Wolfgang Yellowbird. "I thought you were long dead."

Gwilym Cyril tapped the glass box attached to his belt, from which cables ran under his shirt. "Solar powered pace-maker," he said. "It has kept me virile. With the sun acting so strangely of late, I've never felt so sprightly in all my life."

"We found him the other day," said Rainbow Rivers. "He was hollering in broken Sasquatch. You would think he'd have a handle on the language by now."

"I was terribly lost," said Gwilym Cyril. "This valley isn't recognizable to me anymore." He looked towards the Rockies that reached into the sky before him. "We must go now. In haste."

Earl looked up at ravens circling above. They clicked and cawed, adjusting their flight patterns to avoid the foreign body that invaded their air space. "Happy Rainbow drone," Earl said.

The drone dropped down into the clearing, snapping photos, relaying footage. It zapped Yusuf between the shoulder blades with a laser taser. Job jumped from Yusuf's shoulder into Inertia's arms.

Yusuf screamed as the drone moved in on him again. He jumped and swatted it out of the air. It crashed to the ground. Buzzing metal shards exploded in sparks.

In the distance came the sound of chopping blades. It grew louder until the sound overwhelmed the forest and a helicopter emerged from the smoke.

Paul pulled Kyle's gun from his backpack and fired a shot into the windshield as the helicopter landed in the clearing, sending forest shrapnel flying though the air. Clovis Redux ran for the tree line.

The blonde woman and ratty man jumped from the helicopter. They opened fire.

Earl could feel bullets thud into the tree trunk he hid behind. Sigmund was at his feet, shaking, growling. He grabbed him by the collar. "You're not going in, Sigmund. Not this time."

Wolfgang Yellowbird crouched behind the tree next to him. He was clutching onto Rainbow Rivers. Gunter was between them. "I should've finished these bastards off when I had the chance." He hollered between rifle bursts.

Inertia sat with Job clutched to her neck. She stared up at Earl. "We can't die this way," she said.

Earl peeked around the tree trunk. He had an open view of the clearing. Doug and the otter were still out there, pressing their bodies to the ground and bobbing their heads. They cried out after each gun burst. Behind them, the trees were ablaze.

"Paul," Earl yelled. "I need cover fire."

Paul's eyes lit up through his orange-tinted glasses. Kyle's gun was in his hand. "I'll see you on the other side, Earl." He broke cover, firing round after round. Earl ran after him. He saw the ratty man buckle when Paul blew out his kneecap. Earl reached Doug and the otter. He lifted them into his arms as Paul's magazine emptied. He watched as the blonde woman levelled her rifle and fired. When Paul hit the ground, Yusuf charged. Bullets pounded into his chest but he didn't slow. He reached the blonde woman and swatted at the gun with enough force to tear her arm from her body. He ripped the skin off her face with his teeth. She stood still for a moment. Then slowly

walked into the burning trees. The ratty man was on his back,
firing bullets. Yusuf stomped on his skull.

"We need that," Wolfgang Yellowbird yelled as the helicopter lifted from the forest floor. "The fire is here."

Yusuf ran at the aircraft and jumped. He grabbed onto the
landing skids. The helicopter dipped against the sasquatch's
power and fell back to Earth. Yusuf reached inside and pulled out
the pilot. He threw him to the ground and pinned him there
with his foot.

Fire surrounded the clearing. There was nowhere to go but
up. Wolfgang Yellowbird ran around, pushing everyone inside
the helicopter. He grabbed Earl by the shoulder and forced him
towards the aircraft.

"Paul," Earl yelled.

"He's gone." Wolfgang Yellowbird said. "It's the price of
anarchy."

They moved for the chopper as the ground began to quake,
knocking them over. Trees began to fall. They smashed into the
ground and exploded in flames. Massive crevices opened in the
earth around them. Earl looked at the others in the helicopter.
They were screaming at him. He clutched Doug and the otter
tightly to his chest and ran. He made it to the helicopter and
tumbled inside. He jammed himself in beside Yusuf. The great
primate was breathing hard. Sucking oxygen. Bullet wounds
were leaking blood upon his chest and torso.

Wolfgang Yellowbird squeezed in and screamed at the pilot.
The helicopter struggled against the weight of the wildlife. It
slowly lifted into the air. The grizzlies were panicking. They
bleated and roared. "Where's Jesus?" Wolfgang Yellowbird
yelled. He told the pilot to: "Hover dammit. Hover." He pointed at the scene below. Paul was on his feet. His body was on fire.
In his outstretched hands he held Jesus. "Drop down," Wolfgang
Yellowbird yelled. "Jesus will not burn." Yusuf secured
Wolfgang Yellowbird by the legs as he reached out the door of
the helicopter. He strained his body towards Paul, who was
nothing but a ball of fire. Wolfgang Yellowbird grabbed Jesus by
the front paw and hurled him upwards and into the cabin, where

Clovis Redux smothered the flames that had singed much of the cub's fur.

The helicopter lifted into black smoke. Earl watched as Paul disappeared in the swaying inferno below where huge fissures opened up in the ground. The forest was collapsing in on itself. "Imagine the scene at the epicentre," Wolfgang Yellowbird said over the chopping blades and engine roar. "The coast of British Columbia is no more." He pointed at the plateau of retardant rock. The pilot followed his direction.

They landed in a small meadow of woodland pinedrops and prickly rose. Wolfgang Yellowbird dragged the pilot from the cockpit and crushed his skull with a large rock.

"We might have needed him," Earl said.

"We won't." Wolfgang Yellowbird looked about his company. "Despite our losses, Clovis Redux is stronger than ever. Our number has grown. Especially if we include the little urchin growing inside Inertia." He joined the others as they gazed across the valley. They watched silently as a tsunami encroached from the horizon. It submerged the Black Ridge and flooded the Old Growth Crystal Valley. All flames extinguished. All life displaced. It crashed into the base of the Rocky Mountain range. It boiled and foamed. Maelstroms raged and churned, until the new borders of the Pacific Ocean were defined.

"Randolph would have liked this," Earl said. An aftershock buckled his knees. "He always wanted to live by the sea." He looked out towards the horizon. The world and its brevity had never been so vivid. In the loaded heat the ocean was at its darkest blue, filling the air with briny oceanic flavours. A thousand water-spouts swirled in the smoke. The sky was filled with an unkindness of ravens, tits, vultures, hummingbirds. They swooped and circled, gazing down at their strange new world. A golden eagle glided down from the rocky peaks above. It soared far out above the ocean, surveying its Atlantis. It dove and disappeared below the water, resurfacing with a sockeye in its clutches. Beyond, blue whales breached the surface. A mother and calf, off course in their epic migration to the North Sea, meandered through tree tops that poked above the water's surface. They flopped on their backs, waving their flukes in the reflections of the flaring sun. The Pacific was lit with a galaxy of sparkling stars, intensifying under the ever-brightening atmosphere. The flares were advancing and melding together. The heat became painful. The sky turned white.

Earl put his arms around Inertia and Sigmund. It was the physical contact that he needed. Doug and the otter curled up beside them. Rainbow Rivers leaned her head against Yusuf. Gunter sat with Job in his lap. Gwilym Cyril stood holding his fawn. The grizzlies licked the singed spots on the body of Jesus. Wolfgang Yellowbird stroked their great bodies and lifted the young bear into his arms. He walked to the edge of the plateau and reached his hand into the sky. "It's a good day for it," he said.

Earl looked into Inertia's eyes. He was aware when it happened. But only for an instant.

Epilogue

Jose Bautista

It was a Sunday. The first day of October. The last day of regular season baseball. The Blue Jays were playing the Yankees, wrapping up a dismal year.

"Two straight ALCS appearances and then, garbage." Murphy was watching the game on the television above the bar. "Why were the Jays so miserable this year?"

"It's Bautista's fault," Earl said.

"You can't put the blame on one player."

"If he played as well as he should have then he could have carried the team to at least ten more wins." Earl took a pull of beer. "That would have put them in wild card contention." He waved at the bartender and ordered rye shots.

"He's not the only player to underperform," Murphy said. "And they had a bad injury year."

"Bautista is old." Earl drank the rye and ordered another. "He should've retired in the off-season. Made way for fresh faces."

"You have to look at his legacy." Murphy's speech was slurring.

"Lightweight." Earl took another shot.

"He's one of the greatest Blue Jays of all time. And that homerun against Dyson. The bat flip."

"*BAUTISTA WITH A DRIVE!*" Earl said. "I'll give you that." He had finally agreed to meet Murphy for a drink. He'd been avoiding it because he didn't like bars and preferred drinking alone. And there was something about the guy he didn't trust: he liked the job. Anyone who enjoys executing animals for profit is deranged.

"It doesn't really matter, does it?" Murphy sipped from his shot glass. "It's just a game. It's a stupid sport."

"Baseball is the finest sport."

"Sure, it may be. But it still doesn't mean anything. It's entertainment. Idol worship."

"We need that," Earl said. "It's a distraction from the mundane."

"Right. It pacifies us so we'll keep grinding. We'll keep the machine running."

"That's life, Murphy."

"No, it isn't. Life's not supposed to be like this. We've been sapped of our humanity by the greed of powerful puppet masters." Murphy ordered more shots from the bartender and looked up at the television. Bautista drilled a long single to left field. "And where has this got us? People are miserable and disillusioned. Animals are going extinct everyday. The planet is on the brink of ecological collapse."

"You seem to be doing your part in all this, Murphy. You're the company's bright new face."

"It's a ruse." Murphy belched.

"What's your end game?"

"I'm working my way into upper management. Into the global offices. I've got Bossman wrapped around my finger."

"So, you'll be a big shot in a mega multi-national. You'll make high six figures. I'm not picking up on the ruse, Murphy."

"Can I tell you something, Earl?"

"You can."

"You're a bit counter-culture. You're anti-authority. You're malcontent."

Earl shrugged.

"I'm working on something. I think you might be interested."

"What is it?"

"I'm recruiting allies. Spreading my network. I've got agents stationed all over the world."

"What agents?"

"Saboteurs. In agriculture. Banking. The automotive and energy industries. And that's just the beginning."

"You're talking about economic sabotage."

"Global revolution, Earl. I'm going to crumble the system."

"Then what?"

"We can begin again and re-build from the ground up. We can live the way we were meant to and do what we were put on this Earth to do."

"Which is?"

"Thrive."

Earl downed his beer. "I have to get going, Murphy. Thanks for the drinks. We should do it again."

"We should." Murphy stood and shook Earl's hand. "Keep this conversation under wraps, will you."

"No problem, Murphy. I hope you'll keep me updated."

"Where are you rushing off to? The night is young. I feel like tying one on."

"I promised my wife I'd be home for dinner. We like cooking together."

"I didn't know you were married, Earl. I'd like to meet her."

"She'll be at the Christmas party." Earl took one last shot of rye and headed for the exit.